THE INVASION OF EUROPE BY THE RUSSIANS HAS BEGUN!

M R   O C H A

Library of Congress Control Number: 2025907444

ISBN
978-1-967804-01-6 (Paperback)
978-1-967804-02-3 (eBook)
978-1-967804-00-9 (Hardcover)

THE
BEARS
AGGRESSION

START

The beginning of the once called end.

Get the driver around to the rear of this building, we are getting the hell out of here.

Yes Sir! Are we going to need all the cars? Or will we be leaving alone?

Just get me my car. The others can play house maids to this bunch of liberal pieces of shit. They soon will find out that this is not what we called for. They heckle back and forth as if they are a garden of chickens in their pen. Who will feed them the scratch in which they feed upon.

Yes Sir! The car rolled up and the Commandant entered as the Ambassadors all stood in the door way. Their hands still holding the glasses filled with Asti Spumonti for the occasion they all thought would be an end to what was truly going to be only the beginning of what should have been a rebuilding from a war that all seen coming, but did nothing to stop. It was their time to what they thought would be a lessen to Russia.

The car sped of as the Commandant talk on the secured phone system. Yes God Damn It!!! I want all nuclear assist to be ready for my order.

No. Does it sound as if I give a rats ass about the Russian Parliament? You take your orders from me and only me, is that understood?

The Commandant hung up the phone as his car raced to the compound. Get our forces ready, I want this ended once and for all.

The car raced through the rain soaked streets as it sped toward the Central Command.

These ass hole will soon find out that I am not the former dead leader of the Once Great Russian Federation. Sending our forces to a country he thought would welcome Russia with open arms. All of those who have died for this old Ukraine play ground was the slide of hand in a card game to occupy the minds of those countries who felt they were smarter then us. A play ground for their assets to be used in war without them stepping one foot into the fight. Not any longer will they sit back and not have the fight right there in their front yards.

The Building Come to Order

The elevator came to a slow stop, and Major Sergi walked out into the dim light of the massive diamond vaults that once housed some of Russia's vast wealth. He showed the soldier his ID and was given the right to enter the restricted area.

As he walked down its halls, he passed the doorways of room after room that had been turned into one of the most secretive places the Russians could ever design. Within every room sat the soldiers, men and woman, of the Great Russian order. The classes were designed to produce the troops of tomorrow, a single working machine. They were being programmed to follow the game to the letter, a game of not just an idea, but of a way of life, a new life to come. Russia was building a living time capsule, one that waited to be opened. Sergi turned and entered his room. Every soldier stood by their seat at attention. He sat his brief case down and told the class to be sealed. Not a word was said as he wrote notes on the plan of the day.

He made a quick check on his monitor of the events happening this day, pulled the screen down behind him, then turned to the class.

LONG BEFORE THE MORNING AFTER, 1946

Europe, in the very early years after WWII, had many changes to deal with. Countries pushing and pulling their way to get the best possible deal that could help them survive these dangerous times. It was the dog eat dog world of the after shock. What a waste of life, and everyone had no love to share with thy neighbor.

Those on the other hand who where spread through out the USSR had thoughts and dreams of their own. But the battle of the fittest was no joke to pass around. If you were not awake you were dead. To survive, you had to become one of them, to look like them, blend in with them. The very way of life that made up the inner circle of the mind of Stalin and his band of murderers. You did for them or died.

But there were a few men, young and very ambitious in the way they viewed their dreams with each other of how it could be. How it should be. They talked in secret and worked on plans to bring their country out of the clouds of darkness, and back to its once greatness. They knew that it was a life time of work that no one could hear of, or know of. They knew the dangers of with each passing day, and as one day passed the other, the closer to the dream they would be.

The plans that they were to set forth were for a new beginning, a new way of life for all of Russia. A new order of men and women that will be the country's life blood again.

It was not going to be easy but they all knew that it could be done. First they had to move past the things that stood in the way of what was to be the culmination their life's dream. Those self-proclaimed leader of the USSR with their bellies full could not help the people of Russia. They were all the back stabbers, the Plight of the peoples will. The land had to put an end to these men, to put the country first before one's personal power. But to get by these men up top would be the hardest climb of all. Though many people who could help were already in place to make changes, there was a need for others to be sent to see that it would take place.

Now the war was over, but millions were gone, and thousands upon thousands were missing from the continent of Europe. Life had come to a stand still, with no hope in sight for the world at the time.

Even so the men that would secretly lead a new Russia found some reason to go on. Many had come home to nothing upon nothing. Home to a world of emptiness that gave way to utter despair. But they knew that life would not be like this forever, and they could make changes in the lives of the others, giving more than what they had in the past.

The great civilization that was once Europe had the chance now to tum from the stench of this devastating war, and their vision of what was to come of Russia was nothing less than the pure will of man.

Even as they begun their plans, new borders were formed as the goods of war were divided and thrown to the victors. How to divide the spoil of war was an endless plight that was older than time, greed was as alive and vibrant now as it was in the times of the Bible's first words.

Right down the middle was a cut so deep it cut families to the bone. Lives were thrown away as if war was not a horrific enough plight to endure. The victors showed off the goods of their catch, and fiercely advertised to the rest of the world the wrongs of the beaten.

"Germany must pay!" was the cry of the now victorious USSR. They must feel the wrath of man that wielded the power of life like some knife through butter. They will know from now until forever passes that the bear had awakened from its hibernation, and its hunger is great. The dark clouds of the USSR stretched far and wide, until they reached deep into the land that was once Russia. A time that no one could ever know was raining down on all that did not do the will of Stalin.

In a small house located in the small town of Kharkov, just south of Moscow, the last of a long line of meetings was coming to a close.

"The years have seen us grow from boys to men in just a short time. We know each other's hearts are pure with the knowledge of what needs to be done.

We must leave here and work hard at each end of the Final picture."

We can do this, we must do this they all replied. "The dreams will come one day, my friends. We will taste the world as we make it from all of this. Let's go and learn, and bring forth the change of our world."

The young Gladimir Klakov brought the meeting to a close.

The room stood up, not a word said by one, as he exited the room and walked down the hall. He could hear his heart beat in his ears. His hands were steady and his steps were ferm.

SUN TZU; THE ART OF WAR

NOTES FOUND IN THE COMMANDANT'S DAIRY.

TO THE VICTORS

Russia did quite well after the Great War, and the spoils that were taken were some the world would never see again. Every natural resource of then Eastern Germany was exploited, the very land sucked dry. It wasn't enough to tum this war prize into a wasteland that was more devastating than Hiroshima's bombing, but to work its life into the ground until all hope, too, was gone. The USSR had everything it had bargained for from the West and then some.

But its greatest wealth was something that the West had somehow turned its back on. The many scientists and specialists were taken from the land of Germany, and were there now to do the job for the New Russian Order. To all these who thought their usefulness had ended, and might suffer the humiliation of a war crime trial in the public courts, their new beginning was now in Russia, and they worked out better than anyone could have thought. They had with them all the knowledge of the Third Reich.

This war prize was not to be taken lightly. These were the minds that held the dreams of Hitler's Pure Arian Race. It was something the US and its legions would not come to understand until many years had passed. Then they would try to build something that they themselves could not fully be prepared for.

At one time the US Military was far too uninterested in what Russia claimed after the war, even though they got their fair share of the German pie. Many American isolationists pleaded to go back to "the way things were" and put an end to the losses that were the result of the fierce fighting over the years, while others sat dazed from surviving yet another war. It was a war that killed even more millions than the first world war which was not even totally over for many of the families that managed to survive it. Though some may have seen it as "doable but mad," no one heeded the words of General Patton to keep on going. He told them about Russia, and that the Russians will come back for them. But no one wanted the many more years of war it would have taken the US to complete it. So they cut their losses and got on with the rebuilding of Europe.

Years had passed and the lines that the United Nation had drawn up for its occupying forces were etched strong and clear. Right down the middle of Germany was the cut. Though it was more than the west could handle, Russia was very pleased. This gave her a place to hide far from the front. The great buffer zone that she could lay waste to. A far enough distance to be able to lick her wounds and do her deeds without the west knee deep into her business, and the dirty business of di information was well on its way.

The first of all came with the Berlin Blockade, something the world could have done without. Berlin was an island city of no real importance to the West, but a symbol of the new freedom that could be had.

Unknown to the West, the blockade was just a front for the Russians. They wanted the US and the other Allies to be preoccupied with the goings on, and the chaos that came with being all alone by themselves so far away from home.

Take away the ability to do much of anything else but show the world, "We can do the will of the free people of Berlin". Or did they really believe that if Russia wanted Berlin, she could have taken her, and the West would have been powerless to do anything?

Oh, how the Russians could play their hand. Keep everyone on their toes as the real war was taking place. The war for time.

The small group of men all agreed as they lifted their glasses in unity. Smiles and plans were exchanged as they could see the difference a few years make. The jobs and positions that they each held was a far cry from where they started, and they had a new power within the bureau, and the chance to move up was within their grasp.

"Who would be the first to put this all behind them? Who would be first to get on with it? To get ready for the change, the real war? This is nothing less than the final war for total dominance of the entire European continent. You all just keep working on the plans, and I will promise you that we will do what no other country on earth have done. The Germans could only hold on to their dream of total control of Europe for a short time. The French had a go of it, but Russia wants it all, forever!"

The laughter and cheers went on into the night. "To Russia!"

The blockade gave the Russians more than a year head start, and before anyone could get wind of what in the hell was going on, it was all under ground and out of sight.

So while the West was knee deep over the questions on Berlin, the planners of the new Russia had something a little more important that needed to be done and the word went out to its people, the survivors of the darkest days of Russian history. The fanfare for the broken lands for the once Russian Motherland fought so bravely for will now go forward. The healing will begin.

The Iron Curten closed up thight, not one could see through. This will be.

THE CALL FOR A NEW BEGINNING

The wagons moved from side to side as they made their way through the ruts in the mud, made by the others who were moving to the gathering place.

A line of tens of thousands of wagon, maybe more, were making their way through the rain to a land that was said to have a place for those who wanted to start over. So many from all over the Russian countryside took that story to heart, and found them elves in line to a new horizon.

"Fredrick, can we make a short stop? I need to go, and all this moving is making it worse to hold it."

"We will stop at that clump of trees. There you can relieve yourself, my love. How are you feeling?"

"I'm all right, just a little wet from the rain coming in."

"I am so sorry that the canopy sprung a leak. I will fix the tarp next time we stop for the night."

"How much more time do you think it will take before we are there?"

"Well, with the rain, it should be another day or even two, plus the horses must top to eat and for a rest. But don't worry, we'll be all right."

"I wonder how many people will show up? Can this really be true? You don't think it is some kind of a joke that is being played? What if we get there and there is nothing going on? Or what if we are too late?"

"Sweetheart, stop worrying, we will get there, and no, I don't think it is a game. Besides, what more can happen to us that already hasn't happened? Just lay back and try to get some rest, I' II take care of you."

Fredrick held onto the reigns and walked along side of the horses. The rain fell lightly, but enough to keep everything wet and cold. He pulled out an apple and cut it in half, then fed it to his horses as they plashed in the mud in the road.

He dreamed about the earlier years as a professor in Stalingrad teaching Engineering at the institute. But the place was leveled to the ground from the terrible fighting that wa5 waged there. He had lost every thing, and so he found himself heading for a new life. A new dream that was just over the horizon. So, through the rain, he walked with his horses to the land of milk and honey.

The wagon pressed on into the night. The rain fell with the passing of time as they all looked into the vast distance head. The more they dreamed of a better life, the more others joined in on the long trail to the new start for them all.

Word was that a great search for those who had more than a good life during the war was going on. A hard and long search for men, and women to take part in the rebuilding of the "Great Russian Empire" was taking place. From far and wide, those who could make the trip left what they had, and followed the calling.

The great search for the right people was a calling for Fredrick; perhaps for him it meant the end to all the madness of war. All over Russia they came to eek a chance for a new future, a chance to get out of what had been for the many thousands upon thousands the end of the world. The war was over and it took a very heavy toll on many of the country's people, "fight and die or run and die". More than 20 million from Russia found that fate, more than any other country.

"We will stop here for the night, my love. The horses need to rest and I promised to stop that leak before it gets too dark."

"Fredrick, could you bring down the water barrel? I want to boil some to wash with. Are you very hungry?"

"I could stand to eat something. Could you cook up that special sausage dish? It is my favorite."

"You're silly, that sausage is the only meat we have, and we have been eating the same thing every night for almost three weeks."

"Well tonight is special. Let us think of ourselves eating out at our most favorite place in St. Petersburg. We will start with a small salad and onion soup. Then we will order up the rabbit with tomato sauce, and a bottle of red wine."

"You can remember all of that while we are way out here? Honey I don't want to wake you, but…"

"No, I am just thinking out loud. It were the times, even right now that I would look at you and just fall in love with you all over again."

She just looked at him and smiled. "You always have the best things to say to me." She placed her hands on his face. "Now, you're not catching a fever are you, talking like that?" as she laughed.

Fredrick just held her close and whispered softly, "Everything will be alright my love, I promise you that everything will be alright." He looked at her as a line of small tears ran down her face. "Here, let me kiss this away." as he placed his lips on her cheek.

"Now, how about that sausage?" Fredrick had a fire going in no time and while he watched his wife go about cooking he grabbed his guitar and played and sang for her as the darkness of the night cairned the sky. He could see all around him the small flickers of light filling the countryside from the campfires of the long line of dreamers and knew that this had to be all true. A new life awaited them in the not-so-distance land.

Morning came with the rain letting up a bit. Fredrick gathered the horses as his wife slept a while longer. He stopped to talk to some passersby, and all in all he was on his way there, too. He teamed up the horses and off they rode, joining the long line that inched its way toward a better place.

They finally arrived at the gathering point and were greeted by the leaders of the camp. The line of wagons were end to end and as far as the eyes could see. But before they were able to enter the camp, they were told that they would all need to have a medical exam at the camp's clinic, to see if they would be a candidate for a new program to get the country back on top. Numbers were handed out as the wagons were lined up just outside the large tents. Those who were the first to arrive at the camp welcomed the new comers with hot soup, and some bread. Soldiers wrote down names, and placed them in large groups.

Their horses and wagons were pulled to a staging area. The horses were let free to run the vast pasture. Belongings that they had brought with them had to be carefully examined for pests. Much that was brought along had to be burnt Many had only the clothing on their backs, and most had no shoes. After some settling in, those who were up to all tJle examinations were told that they were chosen to bear the children of the future.

They were the ones that would make Russia the greatest country on earth. "Do this for Russia", they were told, "and the country will take great care of you for allowing this to happen."

With the new groups moving in and the others going to different check-in points, it all looked very organized. Though they were hurried, not one person, it seemed, was left out.

But like everything, there were always the ones that fell short of having what the doctors called the "right stuff', the ones that didn't measure up. They were not told that they were below the standard that was needed and were filed out to a large group and staging area on the far end of the camp. So, many were placed onto trucks and were being shipped, taken to a place just outside the view of the main camp and far from there they were to never be seen, or heard from again.

The candidates that did measure up were loaded up onto trucks and taken to a beautiful area inside the Ukraine. Every night just before sundown, more and more people from the check in point climbed aboard the trucks and off they drove to a new life. A land of rolling hills, and rich soil. Fresh drinking water and air free from the smell of gasoline. The area was a perfect place to build a new life. There they were all to be given a new beginning, a new chance to start over from what had seemed like, at times, hell.

Fredrick and Darma climbed up into the back of the truck and took a seat near the front. The sides of the canvas covings were rolled up and they looked out over the vast crowd.

"What will happen to our things, Fredrick, will they bring them along later?"

"I don't know, my love." he answered, as the truck drove off into the mist. "We will have time to get more things," he said. "Besides, we have each other, and that is more than I could ever ask for."

Darma just smiled, then took his hand as the truck swayed back and forth from the ruts in the road. They turned around and he placed his arm around his wife."

"Go to sleep, I'll take care of you."

The sound of the many trucks and his warm embrace gave way to the sleep that over took Darma. Fredrick held her tight as he glanced at the shadows of those that filled the truck with them. He wondered, "Where did they all come from and what live did they once live?"

He began to daydream of St. Petersburg and the beautiful little house that they had owned. The flowers that Darma had planted were in full bloom. Songs of the birds that sung rang through the trees. He smiled as he thought of his dog, and how mad Danna would get when he dug up her plants. The classes that he taught at the institute were filled with the wonder of the young men and women of the time, so eager to see what tomorrow would bring. He sat there with a small grin as the good times rolled by with his every thought.

Then the smiles turned to stone on his face and a cold fear ran through him like a knife. He remembered the explosions and the glass that came shattering in on them as they slept. One right after another the balls of fire lit up the night sky. It was all he could do but grab Danna and run.

"Run!" he screamed, "Run!" The world around them crumbed with every crack of the bombs that fell. Screams and cries filled the air as soldiers tried to run up to where the sounds of fighting were taking place. Everything was falling from the sky as he held onto Darma's hand and ran, ran, ran.

He sat there now shivering, remembering the death that he saw. Family, friends, all gone, and for what? His eyes were filled with tears as he held Darma. He kissed her on the head and held her tight, thankful to be alive and going far, far away to a new beginning. He wiped his eyes and soon he was asleep too.

The trucks came to a stop just as morning began to break. The new arrivals were to wait for a representative who was assigned to their group and lead them to the point of entry.

Fredrick stood on the back of the truck and was awe struck about the goings on. He could see buildings going up all over and people every where. He jumped down and reached up to help Darma down.

"If you all will follow me..." one of the soldiers said.

They turned and filed off in a line behind him. They were brought to the in-processing center and were told to be seated for just one moment.

They were greeted by one of the camp's officers and he welcomed them to their new home.

"You are now in a world that is here to take care of you. One that was free from war, and was built on a process that was to be pure."

The officer went on while some personnel handed out food and some hot tea. They were told why they were here. They were told of a new process called genetic planning and it would be they that controlled how far their new life would go.

Not all of those who came to this new life cared about what the reason was. This had to be better than what or where they were before all of this. A life to begin over was better than any offer, or any promise any of them had. The groups then were placed into tents until a more permanent place could be constructed. They were shown where to shower and were given new clothes to wear. They were then temporarily split up, the men and women were given small tasks until they were called upon to move out of the staging area and into the working community.

The leaders of the camp could see, when those that had come from far and wide had arrived, that the time had finally come for the dreams of this great undertaking to be put in the hands of the ones for whom this great task was meant for.

They had to start the work for which they came. So for many, it turned out that it was more than they would have ever dreamed of. It was the start of a new Russian life, one that would have a permanent foothold on this earth. It could have only been destiny.

"Hitler has provided for us, here, the best of the best," the medical director stated, as he moved about the newly built medical complex. Only the very best doctors and specialists of genetic planning had been captured and brought here to plan, and to plot out the lives of so many. And it would be here in the Ukraine, with all that was known and all that is to be learned, that the job of creation was given a perfect place to perform the great task that was at hand.

"We will not fail in our tasks, for we have no adversaries to contend with. It is all right here for us to become what others only dream of."

He led the line of doctors through the construction site, pointing out the different departments of each stage of life's building blocks. He then entered the labs where his guests stood waiting for all to see.

"Gentlemen, I want you to give these people what they need and everything they want."

The German specialists stood in line as if to take a group picture as the director tapped each of them on the shoulder when he passed in front of them. He then turned and spoke in German, "Like the sign said that was hung so carefully over your beloved Dachau: 'Arbite Maches Frie', (your work will set you free); this concept will be your calling card from now on."

The construction of the labs was finally taking shape. Although the German scientists were not there of their own free will, they had great power in deciding what was needed to do the job. Money was made available for everything that was needed. Material thar were asked for came in by truck, in just a matter of days.

"Whoever was in charge of all of this", one scientist thought, "had all the power in the world."

With the labs close to being completed, the first of what would seem to be thousands came in for the first series of tests to see if they could bear the fruits of their labors. Each woman was tagged, with the dates, times, and all their vitals logged. They were placed in different categories, ranging from blood type to the color of their hair to educational back ground, although not everyone could agree that it really made much of a difference. Research was still being gathered and used in every way possible; any and all information that helped to keep track of such a large group of individuals was used.

As the groups of men and women went through many different stages of developmental studies, some German scientists firmly believed in the heredity factor. Much of their research had followed a very simple path with very remarkable results. The theory of acquired characteristics was introduced by the ancient Greeks, and was supported by French biologist Jean Baptiste Lamarck. He had stated that traits acquired by an organism could be passed on to its offspring. The subject that was widely studied was that of the male bloodlines. They charted a line of father-to-son traits many of which were from families of teachers or engineers. A line of higher intellect was needed to advance the Russians' goal for the perfect being.

Some believed with everything that has to do with every human life that you create, "You must have a good environment that surrounds you". As with anything, where you live was also just as important. That was why the lands inside of the Ukraine were used for their purity.

The fresh water and air, along with the uncontaminated soil made it the perfect place to conduct the entire living test.

Still, many more of the scientists went a step further, taking the principles of Gregor Mandel, an Austrian monk, and his remarkable findings. They had studied his "Six principle factors":

- 1st: Segregation and Dominance
- 2nd: Independant Assortment
- 3rd: Linkage and Crossing Over
- 4th: Sex Determination
- 5th: Sex Linkage
- 6th: Interaction of genes

Each group of doctors took one of the ix principles and built their studies around it; each group lending to the others the results of their findings to the tests to be performed later on the men and women of this large complex. Their purpose was to dig deeper into the very heart of what made up man and his inner being, to improve upon it.

Though many scientists world wide dismissed these principles in the early years, many others such as Karl E. Correns, a great biologist who lived and worked in Germany, had republished the findings and had become one of Hitler's most interested subjects. Still, so many more German scientists were working on their own in secret on the subject of genetics during the war, and now were working together in the labs of the colony. The great mix of different minds working for a common goal could only make for a greater possibility to achieve a human of perfect mind, body, and soul. One new life that could be made into thousands. That was the first need of The Russian Order.

The children that would be born in the months and years to come would be nothing short of perfect. The true words of mind, body, and soul, was in itself a winning combination that was remanufactured in the vast human farm of the colony.

While the influx of people began to grow, so was the need for a great construction plan for housing. Lumber and bricks by the truckload were brought in. The job of the military was to over see the equal distribution of material. The vast areas of tents that were the make shift housing for all was no place for the children to live in. So each man and woman were given work plans of the day for the jobs, and the workers pushed forward into the earth to change its face, to tum and make something where nothing stood before.

Each day a voice came over the intercom, saying "What you would build is all yours, a house, a yard, a life. It is so that the children of this vast city can grow and live the dream we now plan. What we must do here is work for our future. We can't go on Living like we have in the past, and once you all realize that this is for the future, there can be no turning back. The work will be harder than you will ever remember, in time something you will never forget. Most of what we ask for as in the work, most of you have never done before. But we will pull together and get the job done."

"This place, this colony, will stand as a monument to life. But let me tell you all something. Here is where you will stay, you can never leave, never trail outside the boundaries of the colony. Your pal is now gone. You have no family but the family you see here before you. All that you will need will be provided, but you must do for the colony to receive. This is the way it will be. The way it must be."

With that having been said, the great task of building the city to house those of the newly formed colony took shape more and more every day, and in no time many houses took the place of the tent that were up all over the place. The jobs were hard and everyone had to do their share.

Food, it seemed, was not a problem. There were scheduled times for eating, and an exercise program to be followed each day. Though the days were long, no one really complained of the work. They could see the up and rising city they were now building. They could see the homes that they would one day live in.

As the rest of the world was rebuilding from the vast destruction of the war, the colony was already rising. The hospital that was needed was completed in the first step of the program.

All the women went through a series of experiments, at different times of the day, as the work went on with the colony. As the specialists found the best formula for success, the final work was planned. The women were all to be artificially inseminated, although they were not discouraged from having sex with their mates while they waited to be seen.

Those who found it possible to get pregnant on their own were given special stimulation to the egg. This was to give a chance for the child to be born in the sex of the doctor's choosing. They would simply manipulate the chromosomes.

Some of the men were to give up their own semen for u e in different women. No one knew that the child that would be raised would not be of his or her own blood. The old cliche claimed that "though all were created equal, there were those who were more equal than others", and the ones who could make it were used to their potential and to the Russian Orders' advantage.

While the women were pregnant, they were placed in rooms during a rest period of the day. Their stomachs were attached with small headphone-type speakers, and the unborn children were read to. They were given minor math and science studies. Different languages were also introduced. It was felt that the children could learn in the wombs of the women, and one could never start soon enough to teach children the things that were needed for a good life.

All the things that were normally taught later in life were introduced right from the start. They were to be programmed, and would know everything that was real. From math to music, there was not a minute wasted on the old ways of schooling a child. There would be no toys, no monsters, or even play animals to be used in the teaching of the children. The real world was on the agenda.

Some mothers did not like the teachings of some of the specialists. "You can't leave out fantasy. Children need to dream, and play games." Those thoughts were crushed in the first lessons of mothering.

"You will do as we ay, the children will be taught as we say. Brain cells do not regenerate, therefore when they are used up to dream about the small shit, then as time goes on it amounts to a lot of shit. We are not here to lose one brain cell to fantasy. The truth, what is real, that is what they will be taught!"

The head specialist in charge of child development had in his hands a toy pig that was found in one of the houses of an expectant mother. He held it up, and then he exploded: "Animals do not talk! How in the hell can an animal teach a child if one moment you play with it, then the next moment you eat it? You tell me?!"

The mothers sat in terror as he talked.

The specialist went on: "The years of teaching children the right and wrong of things are over. There is only the right! There is no wrong. You show an up, naturally there is a down. If you teach a child something, and only that something, he or she will learn that something. There is only one answer, and that is the right answer. There is no wrong answer, because you don't teach him or her the wrong answer. Many problems in the world of children come from those who think they know what children need to be taught, and that they, the children, need to be given a chance to make a mistake. What in the hell for? If you give a child a pencil without an era er, that child doesn't have the means in his or her hands to correct the mistake. An eraser is a device of approval; it promotes the thought of mistakes. Because they see that they can erase the wrong answer. But if you first teach the child that there is only the right answer, he or she will not need the eraser."

The first that were born to the colony were given special treatment, and were used as models to correct any defects in the body or mind. A large program to take care of the growing population of children was developed. Most expectant mothers were in charge of the newly arrived children, and would accompany them to classes to show the proper caring for the young. This would give them first hand experience in raising the children they themselves would have.

Reading and counting numbered equations to the children filled their days. The time passed by fast and without questions. Special foods and exercise, along with all the other needs of life, seemed to have been carefully planned out. The colony was taking shape right before the eye of the founders.

The years passed without incident. Could this be the fate that was in store for the rest of mankind? Or because it was out of the loop of the rest of the world, it couldn't get caught up in the mess. When you plan things down on paper they seem to be perfect. But to let it run its course, and spring up like a well of life, it could only be destiny.

Their lives now were like a fairy tale. For so many years they had lived from day to day, now it was the best of times. The children were all born within the first year of their parents' arrival in the colony. There seemed to be tens of thousands of families living there. All had newborns or a few one to two-year olds. Life seemed to be quite good, and it went on and on, it seemed. All had the means to keep their perfect life going, and the children were the life's blood of the colony. They were more than just "mommy's little boy or girl."

"Sergi, your father will meet you at the clinic after your classes today. Be sure you help him carry your little sister's things back."

"All right, mom, but can Robert spend the night? We both already asked his mom, and she said it would be fine."

"If your father says it is OK…" "Thanks, mom, see you later."

Sergi ran off into the distance as his mom watched him run. She could not believe all the changes their lives have gone through since coming to the colony. She smiled with a joy in her heart and a tear in her eye. She looked to the sky and said, "Thank you." Then went back inside the house.

After some 6 years, there were an even number of boys and girls now making up the colony. Soon there were some 290,000 children born to the families, and all were very proud parents of some of the most intellectual children to be reared. From there they multiplied, and in time the colony grew larger than any one person could have imagined. The lives were good for all, and time went by so fast that everyone forgot why they were brought to this place.

THE STORM OF STORMS

Stop here," the Commander told his driver. He stepped out and had the convoy of trucks stop just outside the view of the city lights. The soldiers all sat quietly in the back of the trucks, awaiting the orders to move. The Commander ordered some of the men to break out the fog machines. While they were taking them off the trucks, other machines were moved and placed in the downwind position and started. The slow clouds of the man-made fog began to move in over the vast site. "Well, Fredrik, you have yourself a good night, it looks like some weather is moving in."

"OK, Peter, I will see you tomorrow."

"I hate the rain," his wife said as she looked over his shoulder. "Why can't it be sunny all the time?"

"You just move back! I thought that I was the sunshine in your life!" Fredrik hugged her and then kissed her on the cheek. "I'll give you some sunshine."

Slowly, those who were still out talking to their neighbors went inside their house, saying their good nights and closing the shutters behind them.

Just outside the city, more and more trucks were arriving. The soldiers waited until all in the town seemed to be asleep. The quad leaders had each soldier's understanding what they were to do. He saw to it that their weapons were checked and loaded, then stood by for orders.

Large groups of soldiers were slowly moving into position as orders were passed out to the platoon leaders. The shuffle of the boots made a sound like a strong breeze was coming in from the distance. Then, in one instant, the attack was sprung with the fury of a storm from the sea.

The soldiers ran along side the trucks as they pulled up in front of the houses. The doors were all kicked in and its residents flushed out into the cold of the very early morning. With the order given, the children were taken, placed in the trucks as their parents were left standing, shivering from the great ordeal taking place. Many of the women were crying and screaming for their babies.

"What in the hell is going on?!" one woman screamed.

She was silenced by the butt of a weapon to her head.

Then the voice came over the intercom. "What we do here is for the children, and for the best of the colony. We have worked hard and long, and have done well for our little ones, because it has always been for our little ones, after all. Your life has never been better, nor will the lives of our children. You have given more than you could have possibly imagined. The future is now set in stone. Your seeds will blossom and take root in a world that truly belongs to them. Your work here is done."

Then, without warning, the soldiers opened fire on the inhabitants of the once great colony. Many parents just froze as bullets cut them in two. Others jumped and dove as rounds bounced on the ground. Falling, and dropping where they stood.

Fredrick grabbed Darma and held her close as their world came crashing down around them. The sweeping gunfire ripped through Darma as it knocked Fredrik down. He tried to pick her up but a second burst tore his arm completely off and threw him to the ground again. He could see her eyes as he pulled himself toward her side. A small line of tears ran down her face as he kissed her cheek and told her that everything will be OK. He lay there as he felt the last breath left his love's mouth. "I love you!" he said as the screams around him went faint, and he was no more.

The slaughter went on from one side of the colony to the next as all fell to the ground. Some of those who tried to run found nothing but the holes that ran their blood out of them.

Everyone and all were killed. The soldiers went through each house to see if anyone was left hiding. The scream were slowly silenced. The cries put away like the dream itself.

The shooting had stopped as men walked over the dead. Many eyes of horror looked skyward with expressions of "Why?" The shouting of the platoon sergeants called for the troops to form up, and then the soldiers themselves loaded up and drove off into the early light. Only the faint roar of the trucks in the distance could be heard. No children's laughter, no mother's call to breakfast. Just the last passing clouds of fog were left behind to swirl through the streets.

Like a plague, all that had grown was swept away. Just as if a great flood or storm engulfed it. The children were carried off to a place that no one heard of before. The town, the colony was destroyed to leave no trace of its past. The families that were killed were buried in mass graves. Tens of thousands of families were taken like the thief in the night had come.

As the last sounds of that night gave way to the first light of a new dawn, the voice once more came over an intercom, as if to offer a last prayer for what had just taken place in the once beautiful colony.

"Good night to you all, for without you there could have not been our tomorrow. Sleep well, good bye."

As quickly as the end came, the new days brought forth the great earth movers that then rolled in over everything. The colony was then turned to dust. Trees, side walks, and playgrounds were wept away into the earth. Everything that once stood was now crushed.

In time no one could even say that there was, or could have been a place like this. It was more like a dream in the mind of a great dreamer. A dreamer of life. But, like all dreams they do come to an end.

The wind made swirl's of dust devils that moved over the now flattened land. Dancing and swaying to their lonely songs. Birds that at one time seemed to fly around the once life filled sight. Like a massive desert it lay open and barren. The birds too left the lands, as only footsteps of worker could be heard coming from far away

In the midst of all the green that surrounded the now vast desert, stood a man, alone and without the feelings that were needed to wonder why. He seemed to look to the past, to all that was there once. To a place oh far away yet, all in all, just a short time to come. The dream seed has been planted in this fertile ground he was now standing on. "Russia will remember in time, but Europe will never forget for all times", he mumbled to himself. He turned and walked into the lifeless land and then vanished like the wind that whistled through them.

With in a few days after his visit to the site, a new construction had started. A fleet of trucks and construction workers began to survey the grounds. Back hoes, dump trucks, bulldozers began to move in on the great site. The hammering joined in with the sounds of grinders and saws. Loads of materials were trucked in. Cement trucks were lined up for miles, and massive cranes were brought to build the great structures.

All time seemed to be consumed. Each day replaced by another and yet another. What was, is no more, and now was the time for rebuilding. Summer gave way to Fall and Winter. Then came another season, and yet another until again a great site stood as the triumph of man.

A sense of urgency fell across the massive site. The excitement was growing just as the first of the great towers were being completed. This would mark one of the greatest undertakings in Soviet history. One that will help her become "the super power of the Communist world", the Commandant said.

The work would go on for years before everything could be put into place. Time and history on every part of the globe turned and twisted in its own true measure. As the race once started o many years before, yet another would start on its own. Like a cold arctic wind it came and would be for decades relentless.

A great parade and fanfare marked the time, as the soldiers' boots pounded out their might. The Prime Minister cut the ribbon and in walked the techs that quickly took their places behind the consoles and instruments of the power plant that would one day be called an "engineering feat".

The newly acquired power of nuclear fusion would be its signature. It would power the vast land before it, and help build the massive power that hurled the USSR into the status of a super power.

The great Chernobyl reactor stood tall and mighty. Its massive cooling towers and the power it produced lit the cities, and powered the industries that stretched out before it. It was the very symbol of the great Soviet Union.

But sometime as the night would come to call, the sounds of faint laughter and far distance cries could still be heard. Some thought it was the laughter of children. It would make the workers search the grounds now and then and wonder what it could have been. As the years passed no one could explain what some could hear. "Maybe it was the rustling leaves that dance around at night, or the cold, cold wind through the trees that had pushed their way upwards over the years, some thought. Or maybe it was the lack of life that surrounded them.

"To plunder a locality, divide up your troops. To expand territory, divide the spoils."

NOTES FOUND IN THE COMMANDANT'S DIARY.

OUR TIME IS AT HAND

So time went on, The Marshall Plan made good its mark as all of Europe rebuilt from the ashes of the war. Businesses grew, new work for all kinds push a once shattered lands into a new and wonderful Europe. Farms to international airports. Towns grew into large cities and a new felling of life was everywhere.

NATO, of the North Atlantic Treaty Organization was the new standard of military cooperation came together so not one force could be one word in Europe's right to defend itself. Many nations signed up, and in time more joined to what they felt was a need to protect it from a Bear called Russia.

Though for time all seemed to be quite. Wars broke out in different places around the world. Its cancer called war was still and answer to those who felt they had to to stop this and that of others wanting all for themselves. Time and time again fights or conflicts broke out, but it was elsewhere, not in Europe. For the new life of not having a war where they lived was an "Oh Well" for those who had to live through it "That's Their Fight. Their Problem". The turning of ones face away from that and to look the other way was the norm of the times.

Yet there was still those who for the one thing about war, was there was the profit side to get arms to one side or another. Lets use our Military Industial Complex to ramp up our sales. To use our weapons in a fight somewhere else and work form there to see them in use by others and judge if what was made and used would be good enough for our War Fighters. So was the new the way of the new normal.

THERE IS THE SANDS OF TIME AT WORK

As new way surpass the old, ways gave way to ways. People had means to take care of one needs and hard work gave way to new fun. Time ran with it and given new chances to see the world and what has become of different lands gave that way to plans for getting a once chance to travel. To how easy now to get away and see the true new world that is being built for all to come and see.

All across Europe, the new means to travel was to fly. None more weeks sitting on a ship to cross waters to distance lands. But to fly and see places only books could show you. So as days made themselves into years. The race to get out and relax was just one thought away. Save up money and let go here. And here and there was getting more easier to get there then anyone could have imagine. So follow the Yellow Brick road was more then just a song, it was there to use.

This too as things go, Russia will one day be right there in the mix of new worlds to see, and it was not too far from being true. But still the mind of Russia, wanting so much be in the world, was still a world of it's own.

"Whenever you want to attack an army, besiege a city, or kill a person, first you must know the identities of their defending Generals, their associates, their visitors, their gatekeepers, and their chamberlains, so have your spies find out".

THE NEW YOUTH OF RUSSIA

Sergi looked the class over and began his roll call. His students were all dressed in gray jumper suites, and their eyes were held straight forward. The class was a 50/50 make up of young men and women, most of them third generation. All were in their fir t year of schooling at the Institute, and Sergi's was the first class of the week.

"Map Reading, people, that is the name of this course, and by the time I am finished with you, you will never want to see another map ever again! I am here to build a map in your mind of a place. A real place, somewhere, but to you it is just a place. You will know everything there is to know about this place, and you will under every circumstance refer to this place as 'The Map'!"

The years have been good in the production of 'The Elite'. Far from any city or village, nestled deep in the Stanovoy Range, the institute was built deep under the permafrost, far from the path of any U2 flyover. The complex was designed to raise the future: The children born of the colony for the New Russian Order. It was here that their parents were brought, they themselves only children at the time, but a very special group of children. No one knew of their existence. They were here to learn and understand only what was the purpose of the goal. Not why or why not. But that it must be. It will be, in the name of Russia!

"From the late 40's and early 50's, this place has been covered in dreams. No one outside these walls even knew that we were alive. The diamond that were once housed here have long been transferred to a vault outside of Moscow. All but a few of those who were once the planners are now gone, and we are the future that will see the dream come true."

"But enough of dreams, we will start on the first series of maps that you will remember like nothing else you could ever know. You will learn what each color of the map means, and you will see how it will all come together, like some 3D image in your mind. You will be able to walk this map in your sleep, even if you lose your sight!"

The classes went on forever it seemed. Each group, each day, every week, they learned their map. Repeatedly, they plotted and charted. In every direction that the map could be entered they learned how and what was there. No member of their group could talk to anyone from another about their certain map. For each map was different, different from any other. This, as with everything there, went on and on. Every detail was examined. Teams were made up to plot different sectors of the map.

"You must understand, people, you are here to do nothing but learn this map! It is as real as you and I. One day you will be asked to control the map. To become a living map. The map will be in your total control!"

Weeks led into months, and the months seemed endless. The maps would take on a shape of their own. Sergi would call for a location of the name of a street. The students would point out the location with adjacent streets that joined them together.

"Good, but what is important about that street?" he would ask.

"It houses several doctors' office there," one would answer.

"Yes," Sergi proclaimed, "but how many, what floor of the building?"

Answers were shouted back to him like musical notes in a melody. Sergi smiled, hook his head and went on to the next subject.

"Part of today's lesson will be outside. You will need to see how the air, rain, and overcast sky may change the way you look at a map... even how the cold or even heat can cloud your judgement. You could walk right past a most important sight in the rain, or the color may look different depending the color of the sky. Shape, design, how far is it to, or from! Everything can and will affect you. If it can, it surely will."

It had seemed not too long ago for us, the first of those who, at the time were only children, arrived here. The trains, and then trucks that were crowded beyond capacity unloaded our future. There were those waiting for us all with warm soup and bread, telling us stories about far away lands where giants lived and people with dreams of their own were willing to kill us all to get what they wanted.

We were sheltered from all the chaos of the rest of the world. Days had been filled with the things that will make us great. The goings on of the rest of the world was not how it would be in the end. So, closely we all listened to the wise ones, and we planned on keeping their dream alive with our own lives.

You are here because it was meant for you to be here. We all have a need to look TO our future as Russians. It i still going on out. Believe in your mind of this great place. We will let them have a go of it for a while longer, but keep this time in your mind. What we learn today will serve you tomorrow!"

WHEN YOU PUT MONEY FIRST

The weather had been beautiful throughout Europe the past few weeks. The skies were filled with everyone going everywhere. Some military leaders were concerned that their flight crews were unable to train properly due to the high traffic in the air. Many squadrons had to fly out of Europe just to get some flying time in. Many of the bombing ranges, like Graffenwier, were closed to bombing runs so the planes had to defer to the open waters outside of Bosnia.

With all progress you will have those who say "this is wrong and that is wrong". The German parliament debated the move of the military outside their own boundaries. The old treaty that was passed saying that no German military aircraft shall fly bombing runs outside their own air pace was revised. Air forces were considered "too dangerous to be flying around while all the new routes were still being learned". The airlines were worried that something might happen one day with a fighter. But you know what happens when money talks.

NATO Supreme Headquarters Allied Powers Europe (SHAPE) had been looking into the problem. Not only have the planes been unable to get enough fly time, but the ADA, or Air Defense Artillery, has had little, if no "live fire" practice. The sky has been dotted with civilian flights back and forth. It was almost like "What was the use of even having an Air Force over Europe if you can't fly?"

There had been many near in-flight accidents involving US based fighters and a passenger liners already. If we were to have an accident and one of these planes go down, and then we would have more than just the press blowing the horn on our presence over here.

The house leader of the German parliament proclaimed at the meeting of the big 12 Economical Countries that it is "too risky to put all those lives in harm's way with the number of military flight that are 'so-called' needed. You are asking us as part of NATO to determine what is more an issue. It is a question of economics verses military training. Both are a necessity, but without the money, there could be no military. So it was forced on NATO to come up with a working model, and move its air forces somewhere out of the newly formed flight paths of this great venture.

England was the only NATO member that really protested moving the air force elsewhere. Said the English Minister of Defense and Foreign Affairs, "We have the farthest to go of all air forces to maintain our defenses. Who will be here to protect the lands of the U.K.?"

Members of NATO each had the floor on this very hot topic.

"Our pilots need real airtime! We can't just sit in a flight simulator and expect to be top guns by mastering the costliest video game in the world!" shouted back the US Commanding General of USAFE. "The air space of all of Europe presents a problem for NATO unlike no other. An adversary could take full advantage of the situation."

The English Prime Minister added, 'The strength of our Forces' is only with a combined force; ground forces can not do it alone."

The bitching back and forth went on forever, with only one real answer to come from it all. The money in the skies was the number one concern from the point of view of those who were up for re-election.

While all the bullshit was going on about air pace, there had been no real live flying on a target since Iraq and Serbia. The great back and forth raid on the Afghanistan's terrorist hide outs, and the Sudan bombing runs were done mostly by the cruise missiles of the US Navy.

No one liked you to fly from, or over their countries. They thought they would be targeted by the terrorists. Damn with the naysayers! Terrorism was as old as the Bible. There wasn't anything new about it, just the way they were deal with.

"So in night battles, you use many fires and drums, in daytime battles you use many banners and flag, so as to manipulate people's ears and eye."

NOTES FOUND IN THE COMMANDANT'S DIARY.

THE FIRST TREES PLANTED

Many years ago, in another location, deep inside the Russian countryside, some of the children were brought for another type of training. These were the children who had an uncanny ability to be in one place and have their minds in another. They were closely monitored and tested for perfect sight. They could pick out things in a mess of confusion, remember everything there was to know, as if having photographic memories. They had wit and zeal, the very ingredients of a true assassin. Segregated from the rest, they had the most freedom of any of the children. They were naturally self-reliant, and their gifts were developed. In addition, they were trained to "blend in their environment", to not attract undue attention to themselves. Independence would take a second eat to the mission.

They were taken away from all that knew them as friends, and were given up as dead, too; but they were paid the most attention to. Special classes were held to really bring out their minds and a world of information was brought forth to drive them well past the simple existence of the rest. They were truly the "elite."

They were taught to be the destroyers of a society. The destroyer of the great democratic process, and they were the ones responsible for its ruin. Trained to kill, not only the ideas of the free world, but also the leaders of that government. The very people that make our laws, the ones that make the world go around.

"You are here today for one purpose, to learn to kill. Your target is an ever-changing one, because man has made it their business to keep things fresh and with a new outlook."

"My name is Captain Andropov Cosline, but you may call me Andy. I've been here forever it seems. I have nothing better to do than to teach you to kill. I have no wife, girlfriend, or any children to think of. My nights are mostly spent alone, and it is because I am alone, the chances of me having children are very unlikely. I have had sex only a few times in my fifty plus years of life. I do not have a birthday anymore, nor do I keep count since my fiftieth birthday. It's because I've been alone, and the lack of sex, that killing is the best thing I can think of."

As I said before, you are here for only one purpose, and that I to learn how to kill. If any of you have a problem with that, then I would invite you to see me after class today."

"You will be given all the best that we have to offer. Everything will be at your dissposal. You will be given the chance to travel, much like those that have been here before you."

"We have been watching you over the years, and you know that the training you received in the past will only help us regain the place that we all have been waiting for. I do not ask for much, I just ask that you give me what I want, and later, I will give you what you need."

"The men and women before you were training for the day of the great redemption, for The Great Russian Order. Their training was driven by the dream of what may well be the last great conquest of Europe by the greatest country on earth."

"Our training started when we were very young, and that had to be so. The fir t of those from the old prominent colony had to be taught to forget. Get us started doing the things that we were bred for. To win, to go out and take what was ours."

"The children were broken up into different groups when we were brought here. Some of us would never see our childhood, nor the children that we grew up with as friends. We thought that we were all by ourselves, and were taught to be self-minded people. To keep on going even if you are the last one in line."

"Like those before you, we are to be like actors and actresses in a play. To Live the roll we are asked to play. Become leaders with a great sense of duty, and compassionate to all that are around us. Be helpful in all our tasks, and be true to the very end."

"In every means we are to act alone, and are trained to live a life of a hermit, even though we may grow up to raise a family ourselves. The classes are of the world, and what makes it tick. How to achieve your best, strive to be better than the rest."

"As you grow older, the training will take on a different flavor. Weapons of many kinds will be introduced to your menu. You will be taught to build bombs of many kinds. To fire all weapons of the world, to be the best in the art of fighting. Every object you see could be made to use as a weapon, and to miss a target is never a question. A fire will be placed into your soul. A fire that can never be extinguished."

Like the map readers, the assassins were trained lo do just what their namesakes meant. Many had been trained in different stages and during different seasons. As the years went by, different means of getting them out of Russia were used. Some were political refugees. Some asked for asylum when sporting events took place outside the confines of Russia But the greatest way for the seeds of death to leave was in the great Soviet Jewish exodus to Israel. With open arms they were welcomed out of the realm of darkness. By train and plane, they arrived in Tel Aviv. Most were coming during the superpower detente. Somewhere between 1972 and 1979 some 130,000 Jews emigrated in that period.

From there they had spread like pores blown into the wind. From Israel they left to all parts of the world to wait. They found jobs, lived right next door to you, and no one even knew what was on their minds. But they have been waiting for the sign, the great sign that will trigger the fall. Many of them were those of the first born to the old colony. They were the only ones who knew of the goings on outside the world they once lived in. They knew that they were the ones that could bring back the great. The power that was truly theirs to hold. The lands that were taken from them so many years ago. So like good little citizens they waited for the sign. The sign of the New Russian Order.

LIKE TIME IN A BOTTLE

The years went by like months for the map readers. Only a few group at a time were let out of the complex on any given day. The landscape in the Stanovoy Range was cold and barren. Small herds of wild horses roamed, unafraid of the presence of man.

"This place is almost like the lesson that must be learned," Sergi said. "Though it my be unfamiliar to you at first, if you take the time to study it, it in tum will be as if you have lived there all your life. You must be unafraid of what will happen. You must not let all the training stop even when you go out into the map. It will all come to you like it is right now. Follow it and you will see the results of your labors."

They all filed inside, and stood by their chairs. It seemed nice to be out of the cold, and back to the confines of the vault.

Sergi called the class to attention, made a right face, and moved out of the room. He walked down the halls of the great vault, passing classroom after classroom. Many of the other instructors met in the hall as Sergi walked up and they all talked about the day's classes.

"Shall we have dinner with the troops, or in the officer's dining?" They all agreed to eat in the officers' mess, and walked to a small room were they could get dressed for dinner. They talked about the progress and the world events, discussed each other's views of the Russian positions in Europe and abroad. They were all pleased with the students and the life that was theirs. There could be no better place in time than the time they all spent together right now. They all agreed as the dinner was finished and the evening came to a close. With all that was needed to do tomorrow they each said their good nights and filed out of the officer's mess.

Sergi turned and walked once more down a long hallway to his quarters, and turned in early from the long day. He lay there on his bed just staring at the wall and remembered those before him.

I was quite young then, he thought to him elf. Where has all the time gone? He grabbed his notebook of different thoughts that he jotted down from time to time. On his wall were poems that over the years he had collected.

Words from Robert Frost were perhaps his favorite. He would read The Road Not Taken, and would dream about the road that his life was on. It was so organized and filled with much to teach and prepare for. He knew what was going to be the outcome, yet imagined another world elsewhere.

His teachers were always tapping him on the head as a little boy, trying to bring him back, out of the clouds.

"You must see the light at the end of the tunnel, Sergi. You will have the time to dream when what is ours is back in our hands."

Some of his own poems draped the walls of room, too. They were a small collection that his favorite instructor liked. Though he was gone many years now, they would remind him of those days. He read aloud some of what he wrote, and finish with his most favorite poem.

THE WALL BETWEEN
By M R Ocha

As I look here through the window
That's in the wall between,
It separates the light from darkness,
The Winter's cold, and Summer's green

On one side the snow is coming down,
Piling higher, and higher.
On the other side it is nice and warm,
Just like a blazing fire.
Yet the window down there, in the wall
Through both sides I have seen,
The separator of light and darkness
Winter's cold, and Summer's green.
Will stay there, just like you, in time,
Until time itself will pass,
But stay there longer for you will find
For time itself will last.
Though many people have seen none
Of sides that I have seen,
For that I am the only one
That sits on the wall between.

A small smile momentarily lit up Sergi's face, then a ho-hum as he fell down on his bed. Tomorrow will soon be here, and another day of classes was on the agenda. He turned off the light, and fell to sleep.

The New Days in the Sun

The world was working out rather well, and the flights were coming and going like the days themselves. The days of reporting the havoc were over, and back to the streets the press went to prowl for the next story.

The planes just kept right on flying, back and forth with seats on the planes filled to capacity. Some of the smaller carriers were offering cuts in airfare. The small price of a good thing got a little ugly when that one got out. Not that the larger carriers weren't making a killing as it was, but again there are reasons why the word BIG stands for something.

In a matter of just a week, the price war was over, and no one mentioned price war again. The small carriers, well, they couldn't cut the price by half like most did. So back to the realization that kept the planes full, and profitable. You've got to love the power.

The changing of the seasons come quickly in Europe, and what little sunny days there are have been filled up with the rainy ones. The rain at times comes down day after day with the color gray everywhere. A lot of people wondered why the travel season to Russia had not started in early spring? Then you could have at least a better chance of a rain free vacation.

But then there were those that didn't care, because some of the best times to travel was in the off season. You can find great bargains if you could put up with the weather, whether you like it or whether you don't. That was just what Russia was thinking. They were enjoying the great influx of the tourist economy. The money was helping boost the economy in a lot of ways, and they wanted to keep right on going with it.

So, not that the cost of a hotel room was a good deal, but a great package deal opened up a mad rush to beat the mad rush. Half off of all three and four star hotels, if you stayed two or more weeks. This included breakfast, and transportation to all the sights. Damn, who said you can't teach on old Bear new tricks?

Not only did the great Bear of Russia have an itchy palm, but you couldn't beat that deal at Kroger's. (That's one of the larger super markets' sayings who are located in the northern U.S.)

The passing of time is like everything else. It is time that really takes it time, and the world filled that spot with all the wonders and worries humans could take.

So much of the world has gone crazy over time. Small wars were fought, infighting was always on going so much that no one could see what was going on right in front of them. It was too much for too many to keep up with and the time of all things do catch up with all things.

The wars split up the old Yugoslavia, the fighting between groups did not matter, the Governments of the world would not have this so close to a free Europe. Right there in its back yard the fighting, the killing could spill over and creep into its naburs countries fast as those wanting to get away from the fighting over run borders of others. Trying to feed the millions is an out of pocket cost many countries did not want.

Then once more the USA, the so called worlds police ramps up and takes sides. Give arms take arms let some fight stop others from getting into the fight. Many people died and the war creator went to jail. The modern word was changing and making an outcome that best reflects their so called values.

Years come and years go. Then the WTC, (World Trade Cnt) New York City. Planes ram the the Twin Towers and down they fall. "OH NO YOU DIDN'T"! This time America was caught with it pants down and the intel failed to see the punch in the USA mouth left her busted and bleeding, with many folks from around the world took their last leap off this rock called earth.

As a world stood shocked, fingers were pointed and then all hell broke lose. The famous "Those who knocked these Towers Down, Will hear All of Us soon! Words for the US President rang out and the US War machine fired up on all levels and the walls throughout an old world and a land of Iraq came came crashing down with what was a Big Gun Fight to a Knife show. Bombs and Big Money came raining down like nothing else.

The US thumped their chest and men in tall hats proclaimed "You want some, come and Get Some! And the USA put that boot up there ass cause it's the American Way.

Still else where time moved on. While America fought for the right to kill, other countries such as China and Russia sat back and watched. Watch and learn from the self proclaimed Masters of the world, until what a country of change took a step and got dog shit on its foot instead.

The first Black President shook the tree of life and broke the hell out of many branches and its fruit laid wasted on the ground. Change is one thing, but change for the few over the change of the many was and still is hard for all to see. Yet China and Russia sat back and learned. America came to a hault as the worlds leader in everything. And had dropped it pants and had the wrong Greek effect leaving to this day not even a good cream could make feel better.

Yet China and Russia sat and wondered WTF?

A new President came roaring in and tried to make things right to many but not too all. Because he said thing that others didn't like he was shot down at every turn. Even his on party wanted the good ol days where the elite had everything to do with it and the watchers got WTF?

Still China and Russia became stronger. America again took a turn for the worse. No one in their right mind could think what was happening in America was the right thing to do. Yet those who have made sure the have not's had no say in the WTF. Millions over ran the border, A virus killed so many world wide, or maybe a jab had some things to do with it. All in all those who wanted to run the world were happy that so many died and the first steps to population control worked better then a war could have done in less time.

Then China and Russia made a move. China went all out in Tiawon and Russia invaded Ukraine thinking that's what the people their wanted.

And again the USA threw money and equipment into the wars as they let others fight it out. Hundreds of thousands of people died as fight back and forth brought America so close to the fight the outcry had to come out. Billions upon billions of dollars flowed into Ukraine. So much that no one could keep count. Ha, it was even thru war to money skimmers were ready with their slid of hand.

The Ukraine Gov, along with the US were just picking up the cash of war. Millions of dollars here, more there. All while the ones who bore the fight died or waited to die was the clashes of giants for the game of war.

Russia sent hundreds of thousands of men to their death. The bodies of the young, the old the imprisoned were forced to the drum beat of the mad man, the once head of the KGB, and not a true leader but a dreamer of the past Russian Motherland. Distroy the Ukraine at all cost. Make her suffer. Its people will learn not to fuck with Russia. Kill. Kill, kill them all. Crumble the buildings, make waist of the land. How dare they defy what we know is what is ours.

And those who do not fight wars with hand and fist pumped in the money and the tools of war were made to order. One could almost hear the clapping of hands as more contract were signed, and the money dealt out to those who make the machines of war. The true War Pigs of the human race.

So with what had happened in the years leading to the madness of war, a melding of the mind brought slowly an ease to conflicts and cooler mind started to ease the damage.

Then again China and Russia still sat back and watched. "Look Here" some thing shiny. Well in what was already going on, the more to come was not the world as one seen it. And in the end of a beginning, "STUPID FUCKED THE RETARD OUT OF EVERYONE!

"So it is said that when you know yourself and others, victory is not in danger; when you know the sky and earth, victory is inexhaustible."

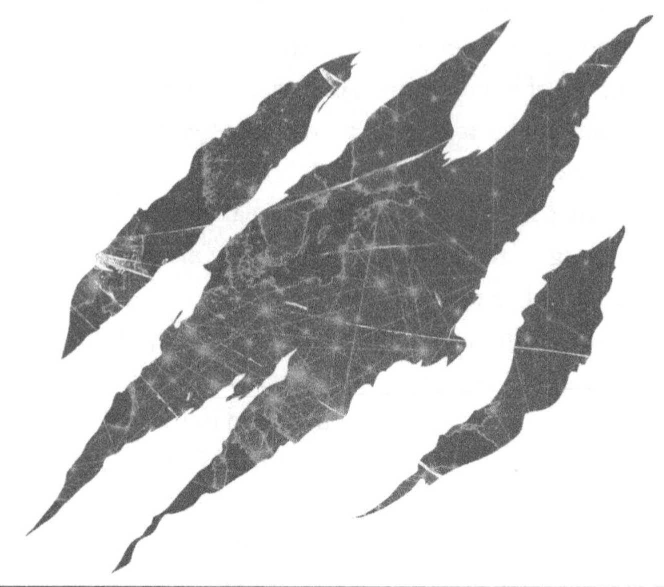

THE WORD IS GIVEN

"Sir, the weather reports for Tuesday are calling for rain and fog for most of the western European continent. England, Ireland, and Scotland were having afternoon rain for much of the week up to Friday. France, Germany and the rest have a low moving slowly through that will cause rain to be off and on with patches of den e fog during the nighttime hours.

This pattern will be increasing as a larger low moves in from off the cost of Portugal and Spain."

"How does it look in Italy, and Sicily?"

"Sir, Lower Italy, to include Naples has partly sunny skies with a chance of afternoon rain showers. Sicily will be experiencing high winds until tomorrow with a low causing thunderstorms off and on until Wednesday, with that front from Spain moving in close to Friday, with another low heading into the weekend."

"Well, people, we can't wait until a better front comes our way. We must begin to prepare to move."

"Sir, is the word given?" "Yes, the word is given!"

While information was pouring in from the map readers as they returned from their locations, others were on their way to complete the tasks set forth. AJI the years of planning were coming together to make the 3-D picture come true. Street names were checked. Location of everything were noted. Doctors, Bankers, Teachers, Police Officers, Firemen, Professors, The Mayor and his cabinet, all those that made up the infrastructure of the society. Everything that had something to do with the way life went on, was logged.

It was time to give those who have the task of putting down the makers of the map a call. We need to give all the Mayors, and their cabinets, and all of those who help run the governments a visit. We need to put them in their rightful place: 6 feet under.

"The troops are ready; aircraft are standing by, Sir!"

"Very good, Lt. Kloft, do you have your report ready for us about the southern communication situation?"

"Yes, Sir, I do."

"OK, you may present it to the staff m five minutes."

"Very well, Sir."

The Commandant entered the plans and projects room and the room was called to order.

"As you were, people. We have plans readied for the southern European Theater. Lt. Kloft, the floor is yours."

"Thank you, Sir. U.S. Naval Air Station Sigonella, Sicily, Italy is in the very best interest of the New Russian order. Naples also had our attention when it came to putting a close to communications. NAS Sigonella consists of two separate bases. You have the NAS I site that houses all the base support such as shopping centers and others store that are in control by the US Navy forces. Housing and all services that take care of the military member and their families are in place there. It is the only US base on the Island.

NAS II is controlled by the Italians, but the US Navy has the largest of the 2 military concentration of the NATO nations. All support for military operations are there, from aircraft maintenance to mail delivery. It is known as the Hub of the Med. Meaning that it covers all operations throughout the entire Mediterranean Theater. This is the busiest air station in Europe with an average of some 1,000,000 passengers passing through the terminal. It is something that needs to be put in its place.

The US Naval Computer and Telecommunications Station, NAVCOMTELSTA Sigonella is the southern-most comm link that services one hell of a lot of customers from commercial, to the President of the United States. Not to say that they are only one of ' three in the world lo have GBS, Global Broadcasting System. It is the system designed to assist the war fighter. The station itself houses the entire comm link of southern Europe.

It is in our better interest that NAS SIGONELLA SICILY be drawn down, if you understand my meaning, Sir?"

The Commandant just sat looking at the reports as one of his adviser stood up and reported.

"Sir, our recruitment of local nationals has been very successful. Most have been laid off from their jobs at the base because of new contracts."

"The mass rallies seen here from the local news paper taking place outside the base have been like fishing in a frozen sea food section; they were just laying there for us to pick what we wanted."

"Most hated the US and were fed up with the American presence there. Our men joined in on some of the protesting. Brought some food to some of the guys, worked the crowd. They met a few people that seemed very upset at the way the US is doing their business. They were contacted, offered a bit of change, it was rather simple."

"I will tell you Sir, there is nothing like an Italian when it comes to selling out an old friend. The Italians thought that if you worked for the US, you worked for them forever. They feel cheated."

"That's good to know, what other news do we have about our target?"

"Down range communications for acquired targeting can be made by cell phone. Maps of the airfield and of COMSTA are plotted down to a 5-digit grid. With most of our contacts already knowing the air station, we have all primary targets and all secondary targets within range of our 82mm mortars. It is just a matter of when you need us to tum off the lights."

"As you can see by the aerial view of the air station, we will hit the targets marked from a series of bamboo growth across the street from the air station."

"No one really patrols the sector near the COMSTA, or the airfield. We will be able to take the field as well, if need be. Just a show of their unwillingness, or shall we say, the inability to defend the base. An early morning knock down in the bad weather will be our best bet."

"Who's unwillingness are you talking about? The American?"

"No Sir, the Italians. Though the base flies a NATO flag, and the Americans operate most of its facilities, the base is an Italian base."

"Yet they are the most uncaring, lazy-minded soldiers you can find anywhere. All you have to do to get on the base is offer one a cigarette, and what more can I say?"

"Also, you go and tart firing, their gun will hit the ground faster than those seen in Iraq when the Coalition Forces started going in there."

"Though I do not wish to have the bad taste in my mouth for knocking out the US facility, it is all or nothing. The Naples site and the US Army site in Camp Darby are in your plans to be shut down also?"

"Yes, Sir. We have it all under our control. The three stations will go down simultaneously. It is going to be one hell of a show."

"Well, the weather reports are beginning to work in our favor; troop readiness is a go. We need to keep a watch on the time, and be ready to act with little or no notice. The three sites must be hit no earlier than 30 minutes prior to total control of all objectives."

"We are ready Sir"!

"Those who use arms well cultivate the Way and keep the rules. Thus they can govern in such a way as to prevail over the corrupt."

NOTES FOUND IN THE COMMANDANT'S DIARY.

THE COMING OF AGE

"People, you must not let the distortion of what you see before you be your reality, but feel the total isolation of true reality. It isn't a matter of needing to hit the target, but rather of seeing no other reality than eliminating the target. You don't walk up and say 'hello'. It is more like you walk up and say 'good bye'."

"Now, see the target as one target, Mikal. You remind me of one of my former students, Roberto. Like you, he had to learn to feel an end. When you do, just like him, it will feel like no other. Like the blinking of your eye, it is on to another. You must feel the weight of your purpose in your mind. It may at times seem very heavy, but when you know how to deal with the weight, you can move it."

"We have what is ours. What you see right before you is ours. The world is ours! Like the target right in front of you is ours! Feel the weight of your weapon. Feel the closeness to your face. It has a smell and feel of a fine hand sculptured wood."

"Smooth, like no other feeling. This is all done, not by chance, but with the will to see more than the light at the end of the tunnel."

"People, you have all done well today. I want you to study the briefs I have given to you tonight. Your final hand gun lessons will start tomorrow at 1300 hrs. I expect to see you all in seminar later after dinner. Out briefings of your travel orders will be this week. Bank accounts and job placements will be taken care of in your place in the Map."

"It has been more than just a privilege serving with you here. I hope that you will remember all that I have tried to instill into you. You hold the future of all that we have worked for. You have done well. May you be safe on your travels."

"It will be one day, the night before our calling. So you must always be ready for that time. Keep your head about your self, and love every moment you can while you are here on earth, until the very end. You are dismissed."

Years before the Time Of Right Now:

THE RECORD FOUND IN THE COMMANDANT'S DIARY.

While years had passed with many of the earth's own problems helping its up and downs piling up, the whole world could see the changes in the distance. The wars locked the world in a fight against the Communists.

Korea, and later Vietnam, would be a staging ground for those countries to uS e, to see whose machines of war, working their deadly purpose, were the best. The sale of arms to those with nothing more than one's need to kill for the fact of killing was good business.

Everyday, and every year the winds of change molded the world. It was happening faster than it wanted it to, and in places where no one ever thought it could happen. Yet with all that was going on, the leader of the New Russian order kept good tabs on the world itself.

Uprisings in the Czech Republic in the 60' were crushed, and still the New Russian Order kept time, and its people under the gun. War was what the world seemed to be about, and it could never get enough of it.

First the French in the late 40's and 50's, then the US in the early 60's and 70's, and once more China invaded Vietnam in the late 70's and were pushed back. Kadafe got bombed badly by the U.S. in the 80's and he remains quiet. Then Russia had its chance with Afghanistan, all to no avail. Then one more great "hurrah" came from the West in Iraq. So many more would die from this disease called War before the end of this century.

The Russian order knew the years would change the face of the world. They worked for their time to come and trained for the awaking of the Bear from the north. Many things had to be endured, and the bad taste of what was to come had to be taken with more than just a grain of salt.

They knew that they were powerless to stop the governments from dissolving the USSR, and returning each country to its former self.

They could not call for a halt of the new partnership for peace talk that were taking place all over. But more than that, they could not directly stop those who wanted to know what was going on in those counties that were under their control all those years, yet something had to be done before this could take place.

"Carl, have you been keeping the track records of number 4?"
"Yeah, sure."
"Who do you have down there near the reactors?" "Pauly and Osker."
"OK, bring power level down and et for restart number 4."

"Damn, another night of these stupid ass experiment! Who gives a fuck what happens? You and me don't get paid any more for them."

"Shit, what are you talking about? We haven't gotten paid for this period and it looks like it is going to be another month before we even get the money from the other 4 months."

"Whose bag is that over there, it doesn't belong there."

"It looks like Carl's, just leave it alone. You know how he gets when someone even look at something of his wrong."

"Yeah, he's a dick head. Mr. Big shot, now that he is in the main control room."

"It doesn't matter where he is. He doesn't get paid like we don't get paid. It's just a bunch of horse shit. You get up to come to work to say you have a job. It's what they have you doing. A job, that's all."

"Just look at this place, it's broken every where you look. The floor is cracked. The showers don't work."

'They work, they just don't want you using the water. They haven't even paid the water bill in months."

"You know, what was the use of even going to the University and getting a degree? All we've been doing lately is mopping the fucking floors."

"It's just like everything going on, cuts here, cuts there. Cut the water so you don't use the toilet, so they even cut out the shit breaks, man what a life."

"Hey, hello?"

"What are you doing down here?" Thup! Thup!

Within a split second two shots entered and then exited Pauly's head. Shit, nice shot.

"Get your hands up. Come on, don't look at him, he is no longer with us."

"Get the keys, just leave the body." "What are you guys doing down here?"

"Come on, we need to get this over with and the hell out of here."

"No, no, I want to answer the nice gentleman. You see, we are down here to kill you!"

Thup! Thup!

"Why did you have to say that? Just put the poor bastards out of their hard life. Shit, could you imagine, mopping floors at this shit hole? Now let's get the he]) out of here."

"Wait just a minute, I need to do one more thing. OK, switching off the reactor protection system. That should do it, now let's get out of here!"

BEEP, BEEP, BEEP!

"What in the hell is that? Number 4 reactor is off the scale! The panel is showing a rise in core temper ature!"

"You asshole, get someone down there to restart it and get it back up to the normal reaction levels!"

"We already have people down there doing the best they can, Sir!"

"Get the Director on the phone!!"

"What in the hell do you want me to tell him? That the damn reactor is not doing what we planned for?"

KABOOM!!!

Oh my God, what in the hell was that?"

"She just blew the roof right off the damn place!"

"What about the workers? Get those people out of there!"

"Jesus Christ, help us!"

"SIR! SIR, WE'RE LOSING HER!!!"

A WORLD AWAKING

"This is CNN Headline news. The worst nuclear mishap has taken place at the Chernobyl Nuclear Power Plant in the Ukraine just last night on Apr. 26, 1986 around 1:23 am."

"Reports are sketchy right now, but sources have confirmed that at least one of the four main reactors has had a core melt down and is on fire."

"The U.S., along with many of the world's experts on nuclear power, and many medical personnel are standing by if needed."

"We go now live to a checkpoint just outside the city of Chernobyl. Our people are standing by with a report."

"At approximately 1:20 am the No. 4 reactor was undergoing a routine test when within minutes, it all seemed to go terribly wrong."

"People are being bussed out of the region at an alarming rate. Soldiers and emergency personnel are flooding in from all over to try to fight the fires that are now out of control."

"A radioactive cloud is now being tracked, and the radioactivity is more than 100 times that of Hiroshima. Please stay tuned to the latest developments, here, on CNN."

The world could only watch as a radioactive cloud drifted over parts of the Ukraine, Poland, and seemed to drift towards Western Europe.

The fires claimed many lives, as well did the massive radiation. The once great reactor crackled with the sound of Geiger counters, and the surrounding community was evacuated.

Workers were only allowed in a few minutes at a time to shovel the debris left from the massive explosion. Soon a great containment wall had to be constructed to enclose the now destroyed reactor. A towering mass of material, lead, concrete and steel, larger then the plant itself surrounded it on four sides and capped off on top. Like the great Chernobyl reactor, it stands as one of the greatest engineering feats of man.

Now still many years later, the life is still missing from the area. No birds, or even the occasional stray dog can be found. The last of the reactors are down, with plans to keep at least one still operating off and on. Small work crews try to clean up what is still the worst disaster in nuclear history. It may be more than ten thousand years, perhaps, until life can reenter the area.

Knock, knock, knock.

"Come in. Oh yes, come in, come in!"

"Sir, Captain Tometzski reporting, Sir."

"Stand at ease, gentlemen."

"Though the resolve of some must be the plight of others, I want to thank you all involved for a job well done. Quite a mess, I could imagine. Any losses?"

"Yes, Sir, the three men answered."

"That won't be a problem?"

"No, Sir, they will be unable to identify anyone for at least a hundred years. They are completely burnt, and too close to the main reactor for anyone to get close enough to even examine the bodies."

"Well, is that all?"

"Yes, Sir."

"All right, I will see you all in the morning. I am going to need a full report from you on the operation by C.0.B. tomorrow. You people have yourselves a good night and congratulations on a job well done."

"Yes, Sir!"

Commandant Kalkov sat in his chair and took a long sip from his cup of tea. "A little insurance policy," he thought, "to keep the archaeologists', and anthropologists' noses out of our business."

"It is not the time for you all to know," he mumbled to himself as he picked up a book, and sat back in his chair.

The Commandant smiled as he read a book told about a US president who let one head think for the other. Right under Mr Clinton's nose ones entered America. Planned a great attack on her, never seen since Pearl Harbor. Great building fell, it's people ran like Henny Penny, "The Shy is Falling"! The stories that make us run from all that is good sometimes don't seem like they could ever happen but they do. And what we had believe is thought as good is now dirtied because some little girl could not hold what she had in her mouth, and the small spill destroyed the greatest office on earth. If time is the only thing that takes its time, then the wind of change needs to blow a little harder than she did.

THE CLASS OF CLASS REUNIONS

"Where is my damn blue shirt? Shit, I can never find anything."
Ring! Ring!

"Hello? Oh, hi honey, do you know where my blue shirt is, you know the one with the straight collar. Top drawer of the big dresser? OK, wait a minute. Thanks, I have it."

"I know that you wish you could have been home to see me off, but your work needs you there, I know, I know. It's not like I haven't gone away before. I will call you from the airport. You tell the boys to be good, and I expect them to help you around the house, OK? Talk to you later, I love you, 'bye."

What was that damn number to the taxi? Oh, here it is.

"Good morning, yes, could I please have a taxi sent to 9476 Holland Rd? Where will I need to be going? To Detroit Metro Airport. OK, thank you, 'bye."

Bob reopened the Western Union letter and reread the thing through once more. He smiled as he folded it up and placed it in the briefcase that sat on the edge of the bed.

So the class reunion is finally here. He walked into his den and sat down in his oversized lazy boy chair. Looking around the room at the different deer heads he had mounted on the walls, he thought back in time about all of them. There was his son's first 7 point buck. Bob smiled when he looked over to see his own 12 point. Now that was a beautiful animal.

He stood up and walked over to the gun case he himself had built. He had a good collection of rifles. He loved his Browning 306 and his 7mm. "Boy, sure wish I could take them with me."

He returned to his bedroom and grabbed the briefcase and his two bags and his coat, then went outside to wait for the taxi, closing, then locking the door behind him. He glanced up and down the neighborhood and nodded his head. "Life was good", he thought to himself.

He turned to take a good look at his own house; the roses were all bagged for the colder weather. Winter was one of the best times, he thought. The leaves were gone from the trees, and the smell in the air of the changing time only stood as a reminder of how fast things come and go. Should have shoveled the bit of snow, he thought to himself. Oh, let the boys do it; they like to ride on the snow master, anyway.

The taxi stopped in front of his house, and Bob grabbed his things and put them in the trunk of the cab.

"Could you wait a moment? I have to check to see if the garage is locked."

"Sure", the driver said as he turned the meter on. "I'll just be a moment."

He ran and opened the fence to the back yard, kicked the basketball off the driveway and grabbed the door handle to the garage. Yeah, it's locked. Good, he thought to himself, and then he turned and walked to the cab, closing the gate behind him for the last time.

He grabbed the handle to the back door of the cab, and jumped in.

"Could you please take me to the airport?" "Yes, Sir."

The cab drove off and Bob watched his house and then hi neighbor' house, then his block vanish in the distance. He sat back, picked up a newspaper that was on the seat next to him and began to read it.

"Sure is a lot of shit going on already in this new century. Everything's new. Cuba has a new leader. Now who would have ever thought that? I thought that the Castro brother and their eilk would live forever."

"Yeah, I know what you mean. Now you have this new government down there, looking for help from us. Businessmen flying down there in hordes. Maybe I should buy some stock in some hotel business or something."

"Well, I don't know if that would be a good idea, with the way things are going today. Things could be different by tomorrow."

The twenty minutes it took to get to the Detroit Metro Airport from Highland Park was faster than normal. They had finally finished the intersection at Telegraph Road and Eureka in Taylor. It had been closed for a year because of some underground tunnel work.

Bob looked at the White Castle Hamburger joint from the back seat of the cab as it raced by, and wished that he could have one last "gut buster". But he knew that it was probably better to get to the airport first.

"Excuse me, driver, could you stop at the Denny's across from the airport, I would like to get something to eat first. They never really feed you on the morning flights."

"Not a problem, Sir."

The cab stopped out in front, and Bob paid the fare and then grabbed the bags from the trunk. There was a shuttle bus that left from in front of Denny's every thirty minutes, so he thought he could eat and catch the ride over to the terminal. So, he marched himself into Denny's to fill up.

Bob has stopped in many a morning on his way to here and there. Becky, the head waitress, was working the morning shift there at the restaurant for some fifteen years, and she could see him corning from the parking lot, and through the doors.

"Hey, Becky, how ya doing?"

"Bob, you shit for brain, what will it be this morning?"

"Come on, gal, you know what I like. It's been the same thing every time I come into the joint, why do you ask me that each time?"

Just then, a small and very young gentleman came up from behind and spoke softly into her ear.

"Excuse me, Becky, may I have a word with you?" "Oh shit, the new guy wants a word with me. Why do they always put the new guys with me?" She turned and followed the young manager into the back. "Becky, I don't think 'shit head' is a good phrase to say to the customer when they walk in to this restaurant. The rest of the customers need not to hear that type of language coming from our employees. Now, if you don't mind, that man at table three needs more coffee."

"Thank you, Ken, for correcting me on my manner. Dumb fuck, backwards-ass little bastard. Your mother should have swallowed you instead, but no, she let you grow up to be."

"What's the matter Beck? You letting junior get under that skin of yours? I know that those younger guys like the older women, but damn!"

"Oh, hut up, and eat your food. Where are you heading this time, Mr. POS?"

"Oh, it's my class reunion, back in Germany." "You never said you were from Germany."

"No, I didn't, but I went to high school there. It's been a long time since I've seen the place. I'm sure a lot has changed."

"What is it, your twenty fifth?"

"Yeah, right, I wish. It's my thirty fifth and it's been a long time coming. Why, do I look that young?"

"No, but you look like you could use a compliment."

Talk about who's the POS."

"Come on now, Bob, it's because it looks like nothing else was helping. Is that the only reason you're going?"

"No, I also have a little business to take care of over there."

"Well, you know I was lying about your looks, Bob, you look great and I would have never guessed your age."

"Come on, Beck, if you just wanted to get into my pants all you had to do is say so, all this last minute brown nosing is too late for the beef cake. Oh shit, I've got to get going. Thanks, Becky." and he gave her a kis on the cheek as he pulled out the money for the breakfast.

"You take care of yourself, and junior, too. Don't be too hard on him."

Becky stood with her jaw open. "You never told me that, come on we can do it in the walk-in fridge," Becky said as she pulled on his arm.

Bob smiled and told her to be good, and he ran out the door to catch the bus. Bob got out just in time to catch the shuttle over to the terminal. It stopped in front of the Delta Airlines terminal for his baggage check-in. Walking around Detroit Metro brought back a long line of memories. Too many to put a finger on just one, though.

"So, I am on my way back", he thought to himself. "Man have the years gone by fast! I thought I would be dead before I would be called to do this. Sometimes I wish I were", then pondered "Was this all really worth it?"

He stopped for just a moment, then this cold chill came over him. "Damn right, it' worth it, get your head on straight, Bob. The time has come!"

As he stood, he remembered the voice, one that came to him from the past.

"You will have a great sense of duty, and the compassion to do what it is needed to get the job done when it is time. Follow your head, not your heart. For your heart will lie to you every time it gets the chance."

He wandered around for a moment, then strolled up to the ticket counter and pulled out his tickets.

"Here you go, miss." "Bob Goldwin?" "Yes, ma'am."

"Will that be a window or an aisle seat?"

"A window, if you don't mind. I love seeing the Great Lakes below."

"Not a problem, Sir. So you will be on flight 51 1 out of Detroit, your seat is 14 A, this is a flight to New York's Kennedy Int. Airport with connecting flight to Brussels, Belgium leaving New York at 1630 hrs. Thank you for flying Delta. Remember that you must be sure to check in your baggage on the international flight first, after arriving at New York."

Bob walked away and sat his stuff at the flight lounge bar.

"May I have an MGD?" "Right away, Sir."

"Could you watch this for one moment. I need to make a phone call."

"Courtesy phones are at the end of the bar if you need to place a call in the area, Sir."

"Thank you, very much."

I know I have the number memorized, now, what it is? Bob pushed in the numbers on the phone, and waited for the tone.

"Hi, can I please speak to Connie? Yes, I will hold. Hi, honey, I am waiting to get on the plane and I thought I would call and tell you just how much I love you. Yeah, yeah, I am sweet like rhubarb. I don't have much time, so I will call you when I arrive at the hotel. OK, you be good. Love ya, 'bye."

"Flight 511 to New York now boarding at gate 21." He downed the MGD as he grabbed what was not checked in, tossed a five dollar bill on the bar and headed down the long hallway to the gate.

"Good morning Sir, may 1 see your boarding pass?"

Bob handed it over to the flight attendant.

"Yes, Sir, your seat number is 14a, that will be over here on the right side of the plane. If you will be sure to place your carry on bag in the overhead and be seated, we will be taking off shortly."

Bob placed his things in the above rack and had a seat. The plane then backed away from the gate, and began to taxi down for take off. Within minutes the plane was off, and air bound. He could see 1-94 pass below as the plane rose higher into the sky. Detroit came into view, and he could see the new Tiger stadium, the Lion's new place. He loved the Detroit teams, and he really loved Detroit, it had come a long way to be a great city, not to say America wa a great place to call his second home.

The plane turned right, and the Detroit River, Windsor, Canada, then lake Erie was below. He followed the coastline and looked at the distant borders of Ohio and Canada. The lakes weren't frozen yet, but he knew that the real cold was just around the corner. Bob then found himself kind of staring out the window not really looking at anything. So much time had gone by. Michigan was so beautiful this time of year. He just found himself floating above it all.

"Would you like some coffee, Sir?" "Oh please, that would be great."

Damn, I've got to get my head out of my ass. Get with the program, Bob, the time is now. Quit your day dreaming.

The flight attendant brought back a cup, and Bob thanked her. He just sat there sipping it, sometimes looking down, watching the clouds pass under the silver wings of the plane.

Every now and then Bob would dream of the fishing trips he took his boys on all throughout the Great Lakes. The wonder he would see in the faces of his kids when they would catch a fish. Ice fishing was maybe one of the most enjoyable times that he could spend with his boys. They would be sitting in the ice shanty all nice and warm, just waiting for a pike to jump on the baitfish, and boy, when it did. The kid almost jumped out of their clothes.

Bob smiled in a way only a father could smile when it came to the thought of how much love he had shared with his kids. He knew nothing could ever take that feeling away, although he may never see his boys again. Bob stared out the window, and looked into the distance for a land that he once knew as a boy, and the true love for the country that was driving him back to claim it once again for Russia. He knew that his family would not understand, and leaving them was one of the hardest things in his life that he had ever done. The plane turned left and up into the clouds of that rainy day.

The crowd was really into the match with the third game of the World Cup finals being held in St. Petersburg, Russia, even though the colder weather had set in for the evening.

France had defeated the Russians in the earlier round but was defeated by England later on. This meant that the games had to return to St. Petersburg for a rematch of the tourney favorites. The fight to be the best in the world of soccer only meant that you had to be the best to be#1.

Playing in Russia in the cold was tough for any team, and what was tougher was winning away in a not too friendly stadium. But then again, the visiting French didn't care where the damn game was being held. The games would eventually have to go back to France, or at least that was what the French were thinking.

The rain was coming down over much of Europe and it started to rain down hard at the stadium. The cold weather made for a sleet type of rain, but that made no difference the French or the Russians; it was wintertime. You have to get used to the weather in Europe if you stay there long enough. The games must go on.

"Sir, the reports are in on the final Map Readers' assessment of on-going missions."

"Good, make sure that everyone receives copies of the updated info. We need everyone at the point of debarkation to be fully advised on the current changes, if any."

The Major came in and started to fill the Commandant in about critical information.

"Things are really filling in, Sir, and there is a ton of info that needs crypto, in order for the special operations people to receive it. We must have them come here to hand carry all information, with 'for their eyes only' confirmation notice on them."

"Very well, Major; have them placed for the earliest in-briefing. Be sure that all Company Commanders know about the briefing, please. I hope the weather holds up. Damn, I do love the rain o." Commandant Kalkov turned away from the window, and sat his glass of tea down on the table.

"It is a good feeling to be back from the confines of the business," he said aloud. "I find myself, these past days, increasingly pulled away from what I truly love. Though I know that there is a world out there, and in order to understand it, one needs to know what the world is thinking. One must take a long look at what makes it tick. What makes sense in the midst of all the confusion?"

You know Major Kizir, there has been one thing that has been ever so present in my mind about all of this."

"No, Sir, what is that?"

"You must keep things at its utmost simplistic value. Trust the people that you have put in charge of the things that you need to have a control of. To keep out of sight, and out of mind, the things which are the key tools in order to get the job done, until the time is right."

"Never micro-manage your people to where they feel that their own judgement is not that of your own. Because it was you who put them in that position in the first place to do the job that you needed to get done."

"Be prepared to do everything, or don't do anything. A great General of the US, to wit I am honored to have one of his books, personally autographed. Retired General and former Chairman of the US Joint Chiefs of Staff, Colin Powell showed me that."

"Use overwhelming force in every operation you plan, or the undertaking that you do will surely have a different outcome. An outcome that may not be in your favor."

"Very good advice, Sir."

"Remind everyone that the staff call meeting will take place this evening at 2130 hrs. I am excited to hear the reports on where we stand for the operation."

"Yes, Sir, right away, Sir!"

The fog in Germany has caused some of the delays in some of the flight, coming and going. The tourists were just lying around the airports from Nuburg, Munchen, Frankfurt, and Stuttgart. But then again, it was Germany, the weather here had its own idea of how it could make your plans change without notice. So all you have to do is grab yourself a liter of beer, find someone to bullshit with and you'll be fine.

There are always delays in Europe while traveling in the later part of the year. But who cares when you've been busting your ass the whole year long. "Rain never stopped anyone from having a bloody good time", one English man said. "Just keep hitting those pints. You won't give a shit about the rain either."

The Commandant who loved to read about his enimies leaders placed a book maker on the page where he could return at some later date. His eyes seemed to smile as he checked his watch and nodded at the last words he had just read. The Commandant smerked as he read a page told about a US president who let one head think for the other. Right under Mr Clinton's nose the killers all made their plan and set forth its glory when all was said and done. They entered America. Planned a great attack on her, never seen since Pearl Harbor. Great building fell, it's people ran like Henny Penny, "The Shy is Falling"! The stories that make us run from all that is good sometimes don't seem like they could ever happen but they do. And what we had believed and thought of it as good is now dirtied because some little girl could not hold what she had in her mouth, and the small spill destroyed the greatest office on earth. If time is the only thing that takes its time, then the wind of change needs to blow a little harder than she did.

The alarm was sounding all through the massive complex.

"THIS IS NOT A DRILL! THIS IS NOT A DRILL! All units report to your staging area. All units report to your staging areas."

The large auditoriums throughout the complex were filled in just a matter of a few moments. Their large screens di played the message from the Commandant.

"As you all know by now, the time for us to conduct the operations that we have been training for these many plus years is finally upon us. We are going to use the bad and worsening weather to move you all to a forward staging area near the supply points were you will receive all of your final gear. There, you will be joined by others and be matched up for unit size detachment Then you will proceed to your rendezvou points. We must go now in anticipation of the large weather front that is forecast in the coming days."

"Most of you have seen the maps, in which you will be returning to. You are to control, and by all means, hold the map until such a time that you are told differently. Most of your comrades are already over at the maps waiting for you. They will return to each airport in their prospective map, to receive supplies that you will be bring to them."

"Your timely manner will be needed to get the weapons and other devices off the air craft swiftly, for there will be others following you in just moments. Some of you will be meeting with those who are coming from afar, and have other jobs to do. You will assist them in every way possible."

"It is our time to take back what is rightfully Russia's. This is the last turning point in our history of being the greatest country on earth. We were here well before Columbus sailed to that other land. We will be here well after all else is gone. So, good luck to us all. I am sure that you will do the job needed to get us back as the true leader of this world, and the next."

The special operations people were waiting for their in-briefings, when the Commandant walked up to the podium.

"I want to start by telling you all, just how proud I am of you. You are the future of this great day. And your mission is the tightest kept and most important secret of this entire project."

The Commandant came from behind the podium, and stepped down from the platform. He walked in and out of the men and women that sat with complete stillness, eyes forward. He went on with his speech a he held up a map of Europe in his hands.

"You are going to a place that others have gone to map out, and hold for you. A place that has a date with time and history."

He moved back up to the podium and rested his elbows on it.

"Upon your arrival, you are going to have to separate yourself from all others."

You must not talk to or listen to those outside your group. You must take what is yours and move out quickly, set up and wait for the time to act.

You must be alert and keep your head clear.

When all your comrades have done what is necessary for our mission, they will be found. They will be surrounded and may become in danger of losing their ground."

"This is where you all come into play. You are the answer to the plague that may surround you. But understand, there are those who will learn about your efforts, and will try to trick you into topping all that you have trained for. They will look for you, they will hear of your might, and they will try to challenge you."

"When they find out about you, they will come for you like nothing you have ever known. A force that will make the thunder in the sky as silent as a single raindrop that falls in the ocean. From every position that seems possible to take, they will come for you. They know what you are about, and they have the means to stop you from your mission. But you can not fail. You have to defend all that is coming for you; from deep down in ide you mu t fight it. The beast that makes you feel the need for revenge for the life of Russia. Trust yourself, and those of your team; only your training will see you through. I cannot be there with you, though I will be there with all my heart for you."

The Commandant stared, and looked outward through the window pelted by the rain that was being hurled against it. Then he looked back at his troops.

"You must hold on to your beliefs. Don't sway from your mission, and if all other means somehow fail, and you are cut off from those that you are there to protect, then believe that they are lost, don't hesitate to act, don't look for answers, you will know it is what needs to be done. If this time comes: Execute, Execute, Execute!!!"

"That is all, stand by for your individual m briefings."

As the trucks began to pull up just outside, the troops climbed on board, and took a seat. The weather was very rainy with the mix of some snow as the winds blew its fury from the north. The canvas tops cracked like a whip from the blowing winds that rushed through and into each soldier's soul like a knife.

The drive to the railhead was a long and cold one. The very early morning did not help matters much for those still sleepy headed. But now was the time to get things together. Cold or hot, sleepy or not.

Back at the complex, there were still more of the troops that were filtering out to get on their way to the trucks. A small group of the special operations soldiers were sitting in a lone room awaiting their OIC to give them their in-brief.

Major Sergi entered the room and told the soldiers to keep their seats. As he opened a letter jacket, he pulled out orders for the up coming operation.

"You all know the time is now for u to act. We will be leaving here shortly by helicopter to our destination. There we will be flying to the map indicated here in the in-briefing."

"Our mission is one that will demonstrate our resolve in all of this. We come to a point in time that we can no longer let what is ours be taken by those who have no right to it."

"Our job is simple. We will move upon arrival to a location just outside the map. There we will set up operations, then take care of business there, then go and wait for word to act."

"I cannot tell you the importance of this operation. I will need your help to get this job done. With all that will be going on, ours is the one that will stand out of the chaos, and it will bring dignity to the battlefield."

"Gather up your things, and let's get going."

The weather kept a lot of the late year's vacationers in the hotels throughout Russia. Many hotels offered live entertainment nightly, and it made for a very pleasant evening for those who had time on their hands.

Others waded out into the rain and still took in the sights that this beautiful country had to offer. Some just liked to stop into the small pubs that the town's people visited each night.

To sit and hear the stories, trying to understand what half of them were saying was the fun part. But just being yourself, from a different place was all you needed to have a great time. Not that the vodka wasn't helping at all.

A Return to One's Past

"Ladies and gentleman, we are beginning to make our final approach into New York. On behalf of the crew and Delta airlines, I would like to say that it has been a pleasure. If you have connecting flights with us, plea e stop by one of our representatives."

The plane touched down, and Bob filed his way to the baggage claim area. Then it was off to the KLM counter for the check-in to Brussels, Belgium.

"Good afternoon, Mr. Goldwin, will that be smoking or non-smoking?"

"Non smoking, please, and could I have a window seat if possible?"

"That is not a problem, can you lift 50 pounds? If so, would you mind sitting near an emergency exit? It offer a little more room for your feet."

"What, are you saying I have big feet?"

"Excuse me, Sir? Oh, no, Sir, I am not simply..." "No, that will be fine, I'm sorry for the bad humor. The seat will be fine, really." "Sir, may I see your passport?"

"Yes, of course, just a minute." Bob reached inside his brief case and pulled it out.

"Mr. Goldwin, you're from Israel?"

"No, I emigrated there from Russia, a very long time ago."

"OK Sir, you'll be on flight 1423 from New York to Brussels, Belgium. Your bags have been checked in all the way to Brussels. I want to thank you for flying KLM Air lines."

Bob placed his boarding pass in his brief case along with his passport. He turned and walked away from the counter.

"I've got a little time to burn before flying; sure could use a cold one. I can just taste those beers over there in Belgium! Oh, it's going to be good!"

He sat down at one of the many bars that dot themselves all over the terminal. The barmaid, a very attractive young lady, he thought to himself, came right over as soon as he hit the stool.

"Hi, my name is Sandy, and I'll be serving you today, can I get you anything?"

"Yes, Sandy, could you get me an MGD?" "Sure thing, coming right up."

Bob was checking out the bar, slowly glancing about the room when he came to a pair of staring eyes from across the lobby.

Bob's stomach felt empty, and his throat dry. "My God, is it…?"

A small smile followed with a nod. Bob's face lit up along with his own smiling eyes.

"Here you go, Sir."

Bob turned around.

"If I can get you anything else, please let me know."

She smiled, and took her tongue and slowly glided it across her teeth just touching her top lip.

Bob almost spit his beer all over the counter as she laughed and showed off her beautiful smile.

His head was filled with thoughts as she walked away, then turned to look back at him. He could see that he knew it, too.

Just then he heard a voice came up from behind and asked, "Is this seat taken?"

Bob turned to see an older but once familiar face drop down in the stool next to him.

"Timothy, how in the hell are you?"

Bob reached out his hand to embrace his. "How many years has it been?"

"Thirty plus, I think."

"My God, you look great, where's your gray hair? I always thought you would get gray hair," Bob said jokingly.

"Well, I thought you would be one of those old hippie types, but look at you. Doing well, it looks like."

Bob smiled, then called the barmaid over. "Can I buy you a beer?"

Tim made a small nod.

"Miss, could you please get my friend here an MGD, is that good for you?"

"Right away, Sir."

"My God! If I were only born at a different time, that is one beautiful woman!"

"I can see you haven't changed, Bob. You were always the one with the good eye for beautiful things."

"Yeah, too bad the years are not too easy on them. But I can say that my day was surely one in the sun."

They sat there for a couple of hours, downing a few, and reminiscing about the lives that each was living. Then the time came for them to part ways.

"Attention all passengers, Air France flight 554 is now open for boarding, please have your tickets handy. Thank You."

"That would be me!" Tim said.

"Well, here we are." Tim grabbed Bobs' hand, "Take care of yourself. Maybe we will see each other one day soon."

Bob smiled and replied, "That would be great." Then Tim turned and walked away through the crowd. Just then, Bob heard his plane being called, too.

Bob turned around, downed his beer then stood up.

The young bar maid came up and asked, "Is there something else I can get you?"

She put her elbows on the counter in front of him and smiled.

Bob smiled back, reached into his pocket and pulled out a good tip. He put it in her hand, said "Thank you, very much." grabbed his things and walked away.

He thought to himself, "You cannot tell me that there isn't a God in heaven. I thank you so much, Lord."

RECON: NAS SIGONELLA, SICILY

"Yo, Giueseppi, come sta? Hey Keith, you speak pretty good Italian."

"Really? You should wait until I drink one or two liters of vino, then I can speak perfect Siciliano." Everyone laughed.

"Where in the hell did you find this piece of hit of truck?"

"Hey, don't knock it. It belongs to my grandfather. It sure beats the hell out of walking."

"Are you sure this will be able to pick up what we need, and get us to the job? My people have lot of things that we have ordered. I need to get there and back."

"No problem, now just sit back and I will give you a first hand look at the whole shebang."

The drive took them right past the base. The single strand fence was not guarded. The huge satellite dish of COMSTA AS Sigonella, Sicily was lit up in the night. The rain was really coming down, and made for a very eerie sight.

"The rest of the base was split into two parts. First was the Italian side. Only a few run down buildings marked where they claimed their part of the base. This is the one and only entry to the base from the outside that is guarded by the Italians." They looked out the window as they passed the gate heading for the American sector.

"Here comes the American side. It was well lit and very built up. Beautiful buildings, a big ball field, a sports bar. Shit, the US really knows how to build a base."

"But the base is ours, it's Italian. The Americans are here because we let them stay. They are a bunch of shit. They think they are God's gift to the world. We just like the money they spend here. Other than that, Fuck em!"

"Up ahead is the main gate to the US air base. Only at two points did they have any type of sentry. You see, when it is time for us to act, all they can do is shit their pants."

The guys laughed as they turned on to the main road away from Naval Air Station Sigonella. "Boy, oh boy, are they going to take a beating! HA, ha, ha, ha…"

They drove back to the TLA (Temporary Lodging Apartments) in the city of Motta San Anastasia, just 20 minutes from NAS II Giueseppi and Pipo grabbed a bottle of some homemade wine.

"Hey Keith? Lets see how good that Sicilian can really get."

"Now you are talking boys, come on in." "Hey Jack, you remember these guys? " "You, boys, come in, sit down."

"Hey Jack, what the hell? You should have been out tonight with us."

"Well, I don't like the rain all that much." "Oh, afraid you are going to melt?"

"Why don't you blow me, now what do we have going on?"

"Well, we made a dry run at the joint, and it looks clear."

"Yea Jack, we will get you right were you need to be." Pipo rolled out a map of the entire base. "You guys can have this to study compliments of the PAO, public affairs office. Those assholes over there think they are so cool. I mean their Lieutenant is this fat pudgy bastard who thinks he knows it all. Fuck him!"

"Well, that's good news. ow I will show you guys the good news." Jack pulled out a backpack from under his bed; he unzipped it and opened the bag before the eyes of his newly found friends.

"My God, Jack!" they sat down on the floor with their jaws opened.

"$ 20,000 each, plus expenses. The rest after the deed is done to make the total of $50,000 each. Do you have your people in place on base to direct the shelling?"

"Shit Jack", Pipo said, "if I have to carry the damn things by hand, they will hit the target."

"So, we have ourselves a deal?"

"A great deal, and then a great deal more." They lifted their glasses high, all laughing way into the night.

The guys partied until early morning. Then they packed up all their things and left Keith and Jack at the TLA. "Do you think it was a good idea to give them the money before the job was done?"

"Oh, but of course. Trust is a very important thing you must establish. Without it you are nowhere.

"But are you sure that they know how to keep their mouths shut about all of this? What if they just keep the money and run?"

"Relax, young man. You are talking about guys that are out of work, no money for their families. That won't hold them over for shit if they know that there is additional money to be made. They see we mean business, so the money has done the talking."

"By the way, after this is all over, who is going to give a shit about any money anyway? Let's get some sleep, it looks like it is going to be a very long weekend. I just hope that Mario and his people are doing just as well in Naples."

"Good Lord, man, could you have gotten a bigger boat? Shit, they will see us coming for thirty clicks'."

"Don't worry my friend, the night will hide us from anyone who could be in the least bit interested."

"I surly hope so. Besides, you need to haul over, say, some kind of ordinance? What were you thinking you were going to need, a rowboat?"

"Listen here, fuck face: you are getting paid to do something here. I didn't ask you for anything but to do this job for me. If you have anything to say, it should be thanking me for making your life better than the shit milker that you are!"

"My, my aren't we sensitive! You need to learn to loosen up a bit. We must work together, so let's put aside the bad feelings and get what we need done, done. OK?"

"You' re right, I am just a little bit pissed off at this weather. I've never been one with good sea legs. I would hate to get seasick on the night in question.

"Don't worry, I have some good smoke to ease the feeling. Plus I have a good stereo on board, tunes and some smoke; you'll be feeling all right."

"I sure hope so, it is very important to get this done. I should also tell you, if we do this thing right, there will be more than a shit load of money in it for both of us. All right!"

Nino stood up to the controls and began to throttle up. Mario joined him as the boat sped through the water.

"As you can see, your target is a point out on this island. The NCTAMS MED site was twice the size as the one down there in Sicily. Both of equal importance that made them need to have them put out of a job."

"I know a good spot that we can put to shore that will be more than adequate for your 82's. Since the only access is by boat we will not have too much response from the local shit herders. I will be able to get you in and out and back at the beach-side disco before it is on the late news."

"That sounds good to me. Now let's get this thing under way. The time is very near." Nino turned out to sea and both the guys headed to the main land and Naples.

The Eye of the Storm

The second front was heading into Portugal and Spain. The heavier rain was forecasted for England, France, and the Netherlands. We are to expect a forecast of mixed rain and some snow for parts of Finland, Sweden, and Poland. Italy and the Balkans were going to have high winds, with late afternoon thundershowers. Sicily was to receive rain showers for the remaining of the week. The weather couldn't be more perfect.

"Much of the troop from the first leg have reached the airfield and airports that were standing by with the equipment to be loaded on, Sir. That is the way we need to have all this operation to work, standing by and ready."

The rain was coming down in buckets, only like it could be in Sigonella. Commander Earhart was the CDO or (the Command Duty Officer) making his rounds at COMSTA. The air was entirely too cold for him inside of the building, but the computers needed to be kept at the same temperature, cold to insure that they would not overheat.

He poked his head outside for just a moment. "Good lord, the angels are surely dropping their load this night. It is going to be a very wet winter this year, I can just see it."

Sicily was very wet in winter, but for the most part, it was very welcomed. The hot summers that climbed into the hundreds for weeks on end could only have you wish for wetter weather.

The Commander stepped outside to watch the rain come down in the lights of the parking lot. The sound was kind of comforting, and he always said it would keep the shit heads in. Because there are only two things that melt in the rain: sugar and shit, and there wasn't a damn thing about being here that was sweet.

The quarterdeck watch was talking to him through the monitor on the wall.

"Hey Sir, go get yourself wet, then when you come back inside you'll freeze into a pop sickle."

"You better be good. You are not in a very good position to be talking shit. I'll have your ass out here looking for cigarette butts in just about a minute."

"But I don't smoke, Sir." "But I don't care, sailor." "Sorry, Sir."

"I knew you would see it my way."

Some P3's were coming in from their night runs. He thought to himself, "what a shitty night for flying." But here at SIG, you ran 24-7 in the subwatch campaign.

"Well, enough bull shitting around. Let me get back to SATCOM." He opened the door to the outside of the station, and begun to make his way back to the rear of the building.

THE LONG ROAD HOME

Bob sat down by the window; late afternoon flights to Europe were lined up on the taxiway eight or nine deep, with more getting ready. Bob was watching one of the British Airway's AB 350 DB getting ready to fly. "Boy I always wanted to fly in one of those. I think it would have been fun."

"Sir, are you interested in having some kind of snack before dinner?"

"Well, what do you offer?"

"We have a great shrimp salad with crackers, or roast beef, ham, cheese, on small wheat bread."

"The shrimp sounds good, thank you." "It will be right up."

Just then a young woman looked back from her seat in front of Bob's.

"I ordered a cheese and wine plate for after dinner, would you like to join me later?"

Bob almost choked as she climbed into the seat next to him and began to talk.

"I was kind of hoping that you were going on the same flight that I was."

He looked at her and said, "Why is that?"

"Well, I am a person who believes in saying what is on their mind when there is something that I want. I was watching you at the airport in New York, and I saw that you were all by yourself, so I made my move."

"No kidding," Bob said. "Is there something that you want?"

She just looked at him and smiled

The flight was getting ready to go so the young lady jumped back up in her seat and fastened her seat belt.

Bob had a grin on from ear to ear. He poked his head through the seats and said, "You didn't tell me your name."

"Well, you didn't say if you would have the wine and cheese with me later."

"I would love to share that with you later."

"Ok, my name is Stella, and you are?"

"Well, you didn't say what you wanted yet."

She laughed and said, "Oooh, you're bad!"

Bob sat back and looked out the window. OMG he thought, so young, so beautiful. She is absolutly stunning. The picture of her burnt deep into his mind. Perfectly straight, thick, long red hair. Eyes that cut right thru me. He thought of her, daydreaming of her long nails. Beautiful hands. Just her looks said "Woman", not some little girl. Her smile was something that told me I want this woman. He could smell her, sweet, so close. I need a damn drink he whispered to himself.

Hang on Bob she said to him from the seat in front of his. We're going to have a great ride together. The plane surged forward and off it flew into the night sky.

OMG he thought, OMG!

A Beginning Without End

The helicopter was not even down for a minute before Sergi and his men had loaded all the gear that they would need for their mission. He ordered everyone on board and turned to see the figure of the Commandant standing under the light in the doorway. Sergi saluted, then turned and entered the chopper. With the swirling wind and rain the chopper took off into the storm.

"Pay attention people, we will be making one stop before heading out for the plane at the airfield. We must pick up our device first, then we well be on our way. We have all trained for this. It must be like clockwork upon arrival at the map site. People will be standing by to help us et out for our point. There we will wait until it is time to act."

The chopper banked left then rose into the eye of the storm.

The last troops were gone from the main complex.

The Commandant had called for his Chief of Staff and Commanding Officers to stay behind to get the last briefing on the final deployment.

They all stood at attention when the Commandant walked in. He made his way around the room stopping to congratulate his commanders for all the hard work over the years.

"We have now started to merge on the dreams of those before us. For so many years we have seen great progress in our ability to make ourselves better as soldiers and as leaders. Our efforts have been nothing short of the will it takes to create a world. We have done that."

"Right now, some 565,000 troops are now on their way to the maps. Already more then 410,000 are there, waiting for the arrival of the other 13,000 from the rest of the world to take their place in the maps. Many of them have already arrived and have received their orders."

"As we speak the ones that will knock down all communications are in place and the orders to act have been given, on Friday morning beginning at 0200 hrs our time, the clock will be up and running. We must go now and take our place in all of this. I will be flying to Moscow to announce to the President and his advisers of the up coming plans that have been set into motion. It may be somewhat hard for them to swallow at first, but our people have been in office from the start of our great undertaking."

"The next step will be one that the rest of the world will have lit1le to do but stare off into the space of time. Though we may have the great advantage of surprise, we also possess the best weapon of all."

As the great wave of rain from the storm began to move into Eastern Europe, flight delays were just what the Russian order needed to let things catch up with the rest of the works.

JUST THREE WEEKS EARLIER

Just weeks before in the midst of all the great thing that have taken place over a long and drawn out process, the world took time to look at itself.

The applause was long and loud with champagne flowing and glasses clanging. The night's Chairperson walked up to the podium.

"I would like to welcome all of you here tonight to the first European Business Man of the Year Awards ceremony of this new millenium, being held here at the beautiful new Hyatt Regency Hotel here in the great city of Berlin, FRG. We all have many people in mind who have made great contributions, and have made their mark, bringing about the true beginning of the New Europe."

"The old saying that goes, 'We have no where else left to go' was put to the test when the dreams of Europe became a reality. Many came forth with ideas of what we as Europeans stand for. It stands for greatness; it stands now as one. United from East to West, from ocean to ocean. Truly the center of commerce, culture, and humanity.

Our skies are once again filled with the coming and going of our peoples. Within a month we will be having the holidays at home. For many of us it will be in a different country, for most of us it will be the first time. Life is good with the unemployment of Europe at an all time low. More jobs are being filled, people are working hard. Many new businesses have started. These times are truly the best of times. So, without further ado, may I introduce the President of the European Community, the Honorable Johan Burg man."

The audience stood as the European National Anthem was played, and His Honor took center stage at the podium.

"Since the beginning, Russia had the ball rolling and their planes flying. They helped start the beginning of this great exchange of culture and economics. It was truly the hard work of those who had the insight of the transportation industry along with engineering to come up with the truly singular best means to get us all together as one people."

"The air industry was built to launch such a great venture. Tonight we would like to honor one man and his great vision of the future of Europe. May I please have your attention, for it is my great honor to introduce the European Business Man of the Year. From Rosneft Industries, Mr. Gladimir Klakov!"

The entire auditorium rose to their feet. The cheers were loud and hard as was the rain falling outside in the streets. "Gladimir!" was being slowly chanted and began to get loader as he made his way to the stage. Everyone was stopping him and shaking the hand of the great architect of this new millenium. He finally made his way to the podium, and with a few waves of his hands he slowly silenced the crowd.

Well, who would have thought? You who are on the committee that selects such an honor must come from the Old Russian school of secrecy!" The crowd broke out with laughter. "Because I like to believe that I hold myself as being one who knows the outcome of many things. But you all have done a great job of hiding this wonderful prize from me. I cannot say to you what an honor it is to receive this. We all at Aeroflot have worked hard to bring everyone closer together. We refurbished an old friend, a great transport plane, the An-124 Condor, refitted with the latest in comfort and technology to help transport the masses coming together."

Gladimir spoke of the old Europe and the hard times that everyone went through. "Almost from the ashes we pulled ourselves up and began anew. Who is to say what was truly lost with all the millions of people that had died during the last I 00 years? How many Ein Leins or Mozarts could have come from the masse? We can never begin lo imagine the bloodline that were vanquished in the past millenium?" The crowd was silent and many had their heads hung low as he spoke.

"We are on the road to a new way of life. We can no longer live as the little continent that holds the Majority of the Eco 28, and still lag behind the United States and Japan when it comes to Gross National Product.

China too has grown in ways no one could think was possible. So like China not too long ago. Some leaders of our nations wanted to show the world through its military might that we can force peoples to be what we wanted them to be. A hush fell over the guest.

May I say now, it was the "Mad Men" of times gone by. Like Russia's move on Ukraine. Where again the world seemed to stop and hold their breath. China and Tiawan. To what ends? Then with thoughts of a so called "One World Government. They set to carve up the planet knowing that we had no fear of "Outside Events" that could invade us from other worlds. The fear of that notion is not a real possibility. They, the Loonies of the so called "Davos". Have all but faded away. The playing of Gods over all of us are over. Population control because of what? "Their Own Greed"! Gladimir's voice began to sound enraged. They Dressed up as if they were fucking characters from "Star Track". You'll have Nothing and be Happy! What a crock of shit!

We will no longer be just Europe. Here we are together, East and West.. Things have changed. We are not second fiddle in the music of this world. Europe will be the center of which all others rotate around!"

The crowd rose to their feet and cheered the newly appointed European Man of the Year.

The night went on for some time, with introductions of everyone who felt it necessary to shake this man's hand. Gladimir was relieved to be able to call it a night. His early morning flight would be something to look forward to, getting him back to head the forces' movement to their targets. He entered his car and drove off to the airport.

The city of Berlin was lit up and full of life. It seemed funny to him to be driving around Germany when just over a half of a century ago it was barren and in ruins. Now the big brother was so much better off than his own country of Russia. His own anger began to emerge, thinking of all the time that was lost, and people that were killed in order that those who sat in the Kremlin could have the very best of life. His car sped up as it approached the airfield and his crew that awaited him. The short walk to the plane gave him one last look at the power to be.

"There was nothing standing here when our troops captured the city at the end of WW II," he told the Major. "It was all gone and no one was left standing." The Commandant turned and entered the plane as the engines began to roar to life.

The plane flew skyward as the ground passed under the watchful eyes of the Commandant. Into the clouds they flew, and almost immediately they blocked out the lights of the countryside below. Only through a small break in the clouds could he see any signs of life. The Commandant grabbed his briefcase and walked into the control room of the plane.

The stars began to show through as the plane climbed and turned to the south east en route to Russia. He sat down next to the pilot and asked if he could take the controls for awhile.

A pilot himself, it was the big bombers that he loved. "Oh, the Blinder-A was my bird of choice back in the early days. I would love to fly to the target ranges and drop what we carried, then fly back over to see what had been done to the target."

"Did I ever tell you that story, Major Kizir?"

"Yes, Sir, but your stories are always great to listen to."

"This one time I remembered seeing the big bombers The B-52 of the US when I was on our monitoring ships out in the Sea of Japan during the US's war with Vietnam. They would fly in, wave after wave, into Nam and return almost untouched. The sound that they made as they tried to get altitude from their take off filled the sky with an endless thunder. They were a beautiful sight."

"It was a shame that we helped to bring them down. When the B-52's started their bombing runs into the North, we taught the North not to fire into the wave of jets that were approaching their targets. They would fly at different altitudes and routes, and were accompanied by many different aircraft that would jam the radar signal as different waves came in. That would be very hard to track and adjust. But as they dropped their loads they would climb and turn towards home, always taking the same line of retreat back to their air bases. We had the North fire into those retreat lanes and have the missiles go up in front of the oncoming jets. It is not a pretty sight to see one of those magnificent birds come down in a ball of flames."

The Commandant returned the controls to the Major.

"Major?"

"Yes, Sir?"

"Could you get us home, I have some work I must look over before we get back. Besides, I'm a little tired after all that show and tell."

"Yes, Sir," the Major said as he placed his head set on. "We will be back in six hours, Sir. You even have time to take a small nap."

The Commandant returned to his seat in the back and stared out the window for just a moment. The blackness of the sky gave way to very little light from down below. "There were many a night," he thought to himself, "that the darkness covered up all that one could see." He stared at the faint outline of his own face on the plane's window, then turned, placed his papers aside and though. This old man that I have become well lead all here from this day forward, till no longer breath is taken into my body. He pondered that thought then fell asleep.

THE MATTER AT HAND

The flight leveled off as the Capt came over the speakers.

The night is coming thru your windows. I have taken the fasten your seat belts off. You may move around the cabin. Our flight attendants will be serving you drinks and our night time dinner. Please let me say Thank You for flying with us. The fight should take several hours. Weather here is clear night skys.

Stella got up and came to sit with Bob. So do you know what you want to have first she asked? Bob just tried not to stare so hard and he made himself blink.

Oh I would like to start with the Rein wine and the cheese and crackers. And you?

Hmmmm, a white wine drinker. We could have several things in common I feel.

Oh yeah, and what may those be. She called the flight attendant over and whispered her order to her. The attendant smiled as she looked at Bob with big eyes. Right away Miss. Bob just smiled and let Stella do what she seems to be most comfortable with.

Time went by and small take gave way to laughter. Both Bob and Stella seemed to be having just a great time, and yes time flew by.

Bob had a little buzz going by the time they both finished the second bottle of wine.

"My God, Stella, you have gotten me a bit drunk. It has been a very enjoyable evening."

"Well, I'm glad you opened up a bit." she said as she poured the last of the bottle into Bob's glass.

"Well," Bob said, "I am not accustomed to having young women hit on me."

"Is that so?" Stella said. "People get so uncomfortable when someone looks good to them, and they don't say, like, 'hey you look great to me!'" They seem to get their panties all up in a bunch about it. I found out that you must say what you've got to say. Don't worry about the other person's hang-ups."

"You sure did that, all right!" Bob replied. Would you like a cup of tea before I say 'lights out'?"

"Oh, you're tired?" Stella asked, bottom lip out in a mock pout.

"Well, we could get a little shut-eye before we land in Brussels."

"OK, I see what you mean. First the tea, then a nap. Do you mind if I stay here next to you for that nap?"

Bob smiled and said "You are more than welcome."

They both sipped their tea, grabbed the pillows and a blankets and Stella gave Bob a small kiss on his cheek, placed her head on his chest just under Bobs arm that wrapped a blanket over them and held her close. Soon she fell asleep. Bob shut the blind and soon was asleep holding her.

A QUICK REVIEW

"Everyone has arrived here, Sir. The troops have received their gear and are now in the hangers resting."

"Good, is the rain still coming in?"

"Yes, Sir, the bigger storm off Portugal has come ashore. Heavier rains will not reach inland until late Friday night over most of the European continent."

"The Commandant will like that a lot."

"Yes, Sir, we are ready to get this job done." "Very good, Captain. Carry on."

BACK AT THE COMPLEX

The Commandant grabbed his pointer and began to explain what was going on. He lead officers sat straight and focused. They knew it was time.

"What you will see in the next two days is the planning of those who have been before you. Of course some of the means to get the dream from there to here had to change with the times. If you all look at the screen in front of you, and also the map of Europe in the middle of the table. Major Kizir, will you do us the honor?"

"Right away, Sir." The table lit up into a 3-D like hologram, with indicator lights flashing throughout the map.

"You will notice the areas that are in red. Those are the maps that we currently hold, by that I mean that we already have a large number of troops there standing by for the order. Of the 167 locations that we had listed, only a very few do we feel were not a point of interest when this all would climax, nor make any difference in the mission. We did not need to have our troops spread out too thin. Many of the targeted areas that have little or no support are in the field of influence. They are ours though we are not in possession of them."

In alphabetical order, Commandant Klakov showed which part of the maps were under their influence.

Austria:	3 of the 4 targets influenced
Belgium:	2 of the 4 targets influenced
Denmark:	2 of the 4 targets influenced
Finland:	7 of the 22 targets influenced
France:	15 of the 18 targets influenced
Germany:	16 of the 19 targets influenced
Greece:	1 of the 1 targets influenced
Ireland:	3 of the 4 targets influenced
Italy, and Sicily:	10 of the 15 targets influenced
Luxembourg:	1 of the 1 targets influenced
Malta:	1 of the 2 targets influenced
Netherlands:	5 of the 8 targets influenced
Norway:	1 of the 1 targets influenced
Poland:	2 of the 2 targets influenced

Portugal:	4 of the 6 targets influenced
Spain:	18 of the 27 targets influenced
Sweden:	1 of the 2 targets influenced
Turkey:	6 of the 12 targets influenced
United Kingdom:	2 of the 18 targets influenced

"Our people are in position, and awaiting the reinforcements that are currently underway. Countries such as Croatia, Czech Republic, Estonia, Lithuania, Macedonia, Switzerland and those of the former USSR need not be targeted. Our objectives are those governments that have been operating and are part of the Eco 24. We feel that by the end of the operation, many governments will fall because of unwillingness to act."

"Complete and total control of Europe is ours, and by the time anyone can see what is going on, well, need I say more? Now, gentlemen, I mu t be on my way to Moscow to brief the President and his staff. Good luck to us all, and do not let this time pass you by.

COMING HOME TO BELGIUM

The plane came to a stop, and the catwalk slowly made its way to the door. People were already standing to get their things out of the overhead compartments. Bob was waiting until some of the people got out of the way.

Stella stood up and moved to grab her over head things. Bob sat and watch her move and then she grabbed her hair brush and ran it through her beautiful long hair. Bob said aloud. I would love to brush your hair. Stella looked down at him and said, Really? I'd love a man to brush my hair. Bob answered, Truely? You know I am not just any man. I am a man among men.

Stella gave out a giggle and grabbed the pillow and softly hit him with it.

"Come on, aren't you going to get off?"

Bobs mind almost let out words come out of his mouth. But some slipped out anyways. Get off he answered? One could only hope.

The look she gave back at him was priceless. Her smile was an OMG moment.

Well, the flight was so good I thought I just might stay. He added.

"Stop your BS-ing and come on. Where are you staying? I am down town at the Best Western."

Bob looked reluctant to say, then said that he was staying here at the Airport Sheraton.

"Well, aren't we the well-to-do one?" Stella said with her nose in the air.

''There is nothing I can do about it. My business is here near the airport; it is best that I stay here."

Stella looked at him for a moment, "Then are you going to give me a chance to see you sometime while you are here?"

"Stella, I told you that I was married, and I have a very good chance of not having much time to do anything while I am here."

She stuck out her lip and said, "But A: I don't care about the first answer. I don't want to marry you. I just want to see you. And B: All work and no play can make Bob a very dull boy."

Bob was just about to answer when Stella said, "Hey, why don't we just see where the cards fall. If it is to be it is to be."

Bob said, "We'll see." He moved over and kissed her on the cheek. "I had a great time, you be good. I will be seeing you.

Stella smiled and turned as they both walked down the ilse. Theb Bob got close behind her and whispered. But if, "I were ever to get the chance to go down on you. You may never see my face again"!

Stella turned and looked at him. Her face truned a bright red and her eyes got so big. Her mouth was just opened enough to exhail. She turned and made her way off the plane. Bob just smiled and followed. They both worked their way over to the baggage claim area without saying much.

Stella was still speechless as Bob retrieved his bags. Stella looked at him as Bob asked. Do you see your bags? She smiled and pointed, and Bob pulled them off for her. He signaled for a porter and placed her bags on the cart, leaned over and kissed her tenderly on her lips, smiled and squeezed her hand. Bob smiled, turned away and took the door near by and crossed the street to the hotel. He looked back to see Stella enter a cab and they drove off. Damn he said as he thought. Turned back and seen the hotel right in front of him. "Now that is what I am talking about: jump off the plane and you're in the hotel."

The Brussels Airport Sheridan Hotel was beautiful. Everything you need in a hotel and a lot more. Bob walked up to the counter to check in. No sooner did he say his name and, "Oh yes, Mr. Goldwin, your suite is ready for you. Porter, please assist Mr. Goldwin up to his Suite."

Right away, this way, Sir."

The porter grabbed Bob's bags and they entered the glass elevator.

"Boy, this is beautiful."

"Your first time to Brussels, Sir?

"No, I've been here before, but not at this hotel. That is what I meant was beautiful."

"Well, thank you, Sir." The elevator stopped on the top floor and they got out in the lobby of his room.

"Here is your access key to your room. Only you can enter with it."

"Well, what do I do when someone wishes to come and see me?"

"Oh, they just ring the bell from inside. The camera will let you see who it is. Then just push this button and there you are."

Bob thanked the young man for all his help. "Everything you need is right there on the bar. For room service dial I. I will be your personal aid." "Wow! Thanks again!" and Bob gave him a 50 bill for all his help. He left the room and the elevator door closed.

"Well, well, well, this is nice!" Bob went to the window and looked out into the gray sky. Rain was running down the glass and it made it a little hard to see very far, but Bob was sure that it would have been beautiful.

He was just about to settle in when the bell to the elevator rung. "What in the hell"? Bob looked into the monitor to see a woman in a raincoat holding an umbrella.

"Yes, can I help you?" Bob said.

"I just love the rain, can you come out and play?" Bob took a step back and shook his head. "Already?" he thought as he pushed the button and the door opened slowly.

There stood this young woman in a yellow rain coat and she jumped right into Bob's room, the door closing behind her.

Well, how are you doing? I'm Beth." And she held out her hand.

"I'm well, thank you." Bob took her hand into his. "Boy, oh boy, do you ever have a nice room. I'm here with a few friends that I left down at the bar in the lobby. I saw you come in, so I thought that I would come on up to see you."

"Beth, you have me at a little bit of a disadvantage."

"No, I don't." She threw off her coat and turned around.

"You are Robert Goldwin, 64 years old. You presently live in Highland Park, Michigan. You are married to Donna Goldwin, maiden name Retherford. Two sons, Jerry, and Ken. You work as a heavy tool and die rep. for Chrysler Corp. You immigrated to Israel from Russia in 1972. There you left to the U.S. in 1975. You like to drink beer and hunt deer, and you are not a bad looking man, if I can say that. Welcome to the map. Now I have you at a disadvantage."

Bob smiled, "Well, would you like a drink?" He moved around to the back of the bar.

"Sure." and she and jumped up onto one of the bar stools. "A bloody Mary would be great."

Bob said "Coming right up. How long have you been here?"

She looked at him, "This time?" "Oh, you've been here before?"

"Many of us have been back and forth three or four times now. This is a hell of a big map."

"So, are you finding time to have some fun?"

"Oh yes, it is fun to find all you could possibly know about a place that you are going to call home. Do you have a laptop with you?"

Bob said, "One moment." and went and pulled it out of his brief case. Beth walked over to her coat and pulled out a disk.

"Here you go, I need you to study this. Right now I need to get back down to the others. We have some night planning to do. I will return here to take you out for lunch, say 11:30 tomorrow morning? We have so much to show you. Try to get some rest."

Beth got up and downed her drink. "Thanks much!" then turned and left down the elevator. Bob just stood there a moment behind the bar, stirring the small pitcher of bloody Mary. He picked up the disk, placed it into the laptop, and sat down on a stool and drank down all that was in his glass.

FRIDAY, MOSCOW

The limo pulled up to the plane moments after it came to a halt. Major Kizir pulled off the head set and entered the rear of the plane.

"Sir, do you have everything you need?"

"Yes, Major? You have been my aid for some twenty two years now. I am not a man that shows his inner feelings very much."

The Major stood there, a small, knowing grin showed he was aware of the fact.

"I just wanted you to know that I have always thought of you as one of the most professional officers in my command."

"Well, thank you, Sir. It is a pleasure assisting you."

"Shall we go, Major?"

Commandant Klakov got up and stood for a short time in the door of the plane. He watched the rain blow across the tarmac. Some of the puddles were illuminated and reflected the light from one of the hangers that lay open for his plane. He thought to himself. "It's coming, like the thief in the night." He climbed down the steps and entered the limo. Major Kizir had the bags put into the trunk, then he got into the front seat of the vehicle.

"I need to go to the home of the Prime Minister." "Right away, Sir." and the driver sped off into the darkness.

FRIDAY, SICILY

"Are you about finished with that damn shower, Jack? I need to jump in there myself." Jack came out with a towel wrapped around his head.

"What in the hell are you looking like, Mohammed?"

"Do you know how to say 'blow me'?"

"Shit, I thought you were going to stay in there the entire day."

"Well, unlike you, Keith, some of us know how to take a shower."

"You can stop the damn cry baby story even before you start it. We'll be getting the shower all night long, starting tonight."

"When is Giueseppi coming over?"

"He called when you were in the bathroom all that time. He had said around 7 o'clock, but that is a few minutes away, and I wanted to shower."

"Now who's doing the crying, Keith? You just said we would be getting a shower all night long."

"Fuck you, you little bitch!"

"You're going to have to shower first because you stink. Fuck you."

The doorbell rang, and then a knock. Jack looked out the peek hole.

"Hey, Keith, it's Giueseppi, hurry up!"

Jack opened the door, "Hey boys how are you doing this morning?"

"Bonjourno, Jack." they said as they came in. "Are you all ready for the day?"

"Hell yes, Jack, things are going to be good. Where's Keith, is he going with us today?"

"Yea, he's just washing his nasty ass."

"I'll give you 'nasty ass'!" Keith said as he exited the bathroom.

"Hope that was a cold shower, because it's cold and wet as hell out, and tonight don't look any better."

"Not a problem. Unlike Jack, here, I am not going to melt like that piece of shit. You used up all the hot water!"

"Do you guys always talk to each other that way?" "Oh yea," Jack said. "We are best friends. You all ready to go?" Everyone grabbed their things and headed out into the rain.

FRIDAY, MOSCOW

After several times knocking at the door, the butler finally answered it.

"Yes, may I help you?"

"I'm Major Kizir, and this is the Commandant. We need to speak with the Prime Minister."

"Well, his Excellency had a birthday party last night and got to bed very late."

"I don't give a shit if last night was his birthday; you just get him up and tell him Commandant Klakov said so."

"Right away, Sir!" The butler turned and walked away.

"Shit, now you can see how some people spend their time. I'll give him a birthday that he will never forget!"

Knock, knock, knock. "Yes, what is it?"

"Commandant Klakov is here to see you, Sir." "What time is it?"

"Early morning, Sir. He told me to get your ass out of bed. Those are hi words, Sir."

"OK, tell him to meet me in the study, I'll be right down. Sweetheart, I am sorry. I have a visitor. You stay in bed. I'll have something sent up to you, OK?"

He kissed his wife on the cheek and got out of bed. "The Prime Minister said to make yourself at home in the study. Would you like something this morning?"

"Yes, could you bring some black tea please?" "Yes, Sir, right away, Sir."

"The man lives very nice. Did you know that this was the winter home of the tzar Fredrick the Great? That was a time in our history when we should have had it all."

"Sir, the Prime Minister."

"Gladimir, good to see you!" The Prime Minister grabbed and kissed him. "It has been a long time.'

"Yes, Sir, it has. You remember my aid, Major Kizir?"

"Oh yes, of course, how are you doing?" "Very well, Sir."

"Come, Gladimir, let's sit. Do you need anything to eat or drink?"

"We had ordered some tea; it should be here momentarily."

"Yes, here it is now. You do drink it black don't you? That's if my memory serves me."

"Yes, I do, Sir."

"You have been flying most of the night, right? You must be hungry. Yoz, please prepare a breakfast for us."

"Yes, Sir, at this very moment." The butler turned and left the room.

"Please, Gladimir, what is it that I can help you with?" The Prime Minister motioned for the both of them to draw closer to his desk.

The Commandant stood up, and walked over to the door of the study and closed them. "Sir, we have started."

The Prime Minister dropped his own cup of tea. "Oh, shit!" he whispered as he sat back into his chair. Major Kizir went to pick up the mess.

"No, that is all right, Major, you can just leave it." The Prime Minister got up, and walked around the room, then returned to his desk and sat down.

"When did it Stan?"

"We decided to go with it three days ago with this large weather front coming in off the Atlantic. Tonight we move against the maps. We have everyone in place; it is now up to you to call for a special meeting of the Parliament. But not everyone needs to be there. The President, his advisors, and the military Chiefs of Staff. This has to be done a fast as possible with as little ruckus as possible. A lot is still needed to be done before the night i over in the west."

The Prime Minister looked hard into the eyes of the Commandant. They looked gray, as gray as the weather that has been around forever it seems.

"Can I ask you a question, Commandant?" Gladimir looked up.

"What do you think about all of this?"

"Sir, their pants are so far down, some may even have them off. The time is now!"

A smile came over the Prime Minister' face.

"You always had a way with words, Gladimir. Come, let us have a toast." They stood by the fireplace as the Prime Minister retrieved a bottle from a hidden cabinet, grabbed some glasses, and poured them a small shot of vodka.

The Prime Minister stood there with the bottle in his hands, and a dream like look took over his expression.

"This bottle I have here, was found by myself some forty years ago when I was an aid to Brezhnev. I stumbled across it while cleaning the bookshelf. It was in a small hidden keep just behind some books. I never told him what I had found. Brezhnev, that ass hole, would have drunken it without care for who or what it was."

They all looked at the small glasses that they held in their hands as the Prime Minister went on with the story.

The bottle had the original wrapping paper around it, with a small card that was embossed with gold lettering. It was a gift from the King of Bavaria, King Ludwig 11, to the tzar, Alexander 11. "I have only drunken from it once before. That was when the news that the US President had been shot came out, back in '63. JFK's picture was being draped everywhere throughout Moscow. Everyone loved him, even though he was the USSR's nemesis! Even so, I felt rather sad that a country could do that to their own President. What balls it would have taken to give that order!"

The Commandant stood and stared out into space, as if to recall the time.

"Just as King Ludwig's country did to him. They found the King dead, face down in the water in one of his beautiful lakes. Some said it was suicide, but others knew it was murder."

"Just as there will be those of us that will really know what this time is really about. It is nothing short of the rebirth of our nation after a long death!" the Commandant said.

They raised their glasses and downed the shot.

"We are no different." the Commandant murmured as he placed his glass down. All three men just stood there contemplating the impact history has had thoughout time.

"Our countrymen did away with a tzar and his entire family, without a care in the world!" the Commandant roared into the dead space around him, created by the silence that only accompanies men in deep thought.

"What we have done to our own people over the years? Our own poor people that make up our blood line for centuries! It was bad enough what other had done, but when one kills his own!" The Major and the Prime Minister looked at the Commandant.

"I know, I gave such an order many years ago that started all of this." The Commandant turned and picked up his glass and threw it into the fireplace.

The Prime Minister just listened as the words of passion came flowing out of the Commandant.

"Those that I have readied now for all of this, where is their past? It has been eating away at me like a cancer."

He turned and shouted. "You know, you were there when this all started! All of this that we are working for now was taken away from us so many years ago. But unlike those who made the decisions for our lives, we will to take back what was ours in this new beginning, we do this for our people! Not for the push-me-pull-you of power since the tzars' end. For us, the Russian people!"

They all just stared in space, as the Prime Minister grabbed another glass and poured another round.

"TO RUSSIA!!"

"To Russia!" they all said. Then they drank down their shot and turned to throw the glasses in to the fireplace.

"Wait here, I need to get dressed, then we will get started." The Prime Minister left the room with the Commandant and the Major still standing.

"Our people will see this through, Major. Our blood, our land, all that is Russia will see this as a new beginning. No one will deny the right of our people again."

The butler called to tell the two men that breakfast was ready, as the Prime Minister returned and motioned for them to come and have something to eat. The Commandant picked up the bottle of vodka, and looked at it very hard.

"A king to a king. They are gone because of other's ignorance. What a waste of history." He sat it back down and they ate the only good meal they would have time for in the next few weeks.

"You must get those seats off that plane, people! We need the room for the equipment to be put on them. Sergeant, what is the status of the other planes?"

"Sir, we are presently loading forty-seven AN-124 Condors. Reports from all remaining deployment areas say that things are on schedule. Mo t of the remaining troops are almost here for loading, ready for deployment. Special Ops people have already taken off for their assignments."

"Very good, Sergeant, keep me posted.

SICILY

"Hey boys, here we are! Time to earn some of that money we are paying you." Keith said, as he followed Jack who was turning off the road into a small parking lot, and came to a stop.

"Not a problem, Keith, this is going to be fun."

"Here!" Jack grabbed up and then tossed some garbage that had been piling up in his car from all the shitty fastfood places throughout Catania that he had visited the past few weeks into the front seat of Keith's truck, which landed on everyone. Smiling, he ran around the front.

"Just wait one moment!" Jack said, as he came up the passenger side window. "I need to make sure that our people know it's us, and not to blow our heads off before it's time."

"Damn good idea! This money does no one any good if we are all dead!" Keith said with a smile as he looked around at the others.

Jack motioned that it was OK to pull the truck in back. "We need to load this shit up and get the hell out of here, so hurry up!"

Jack popped his head outside of the garage for one moment "You guys take a break. I need to see if everything is here." He went back inside as the others started to smoke.

Jack walked around a large table as the others started to bring bows out from under a tarp. "All right, boys, what do you have for me?"

"Well, there are:

4 82 mm mortars, complete

30 HE 82mm rounds (High Explosive)

10 PD Fuses (Point Detonating)

20 Timed Fuses

6x AK-47 rifles

3000 rounds 7.62mm"

"That should be the ticket. How are things on your end?"

"Well, we have it all wrapped up. It is just a matter of time, and this place is ours. Shit, we watched the movie <u>PATTON</u> last night, and they had one hell of a time getting this place under their control back then. Shit, we'll do it in just a day. Ha, ha, ha!"

"Yea, but this place is too primitive for my u e. There is no need to stay in the Stone Age. Just because everyone here knows how to use a cellular phone, the people think they really have it made.

"Do you know what the definition of a WOP is?"

"An Italian?"

"No, a turd hitting the water. Get it? WOP."

"Oh, get the fuck out of here! You guys, good luck with the mission."

"It's all in the bag. See you around."

Jack poked his head out again, and then opened the doors.

"OK, drive that truck back here." Just as they came around the back, the guys inside left through the front of the place.

"Sure hope they do the job right. I hate having to use other people outside my own group.

"Yea, but Jack and Keith are the right guys for the job. Come on, let's get back to the airport."

They loaded everything onto the truck and drove off to the holding area.

Jack had been out looking over different places with Giueseppi earlier. They needed a place to hide the truck until it was time for them lo unload for the night.

It was just a half klick from the target, a great place with a garage big enough to house the truck and then some. The old run-down farmhouse was used by the geep herders and their animals in the summertime that graze the fields surrounding NAS Sigonella. The truck pulled in and came to a stop. Everyone got out as the car that Keith was driving pulled in behind the truck.

"Damn, this place stinks, what is this, shit floors?"

"Well, considering that geep stay here, yes."

"Fuck all this business. I'm so hungry, I could eat a frozen dog. I'm going to go get us something to eat. Anyone want to come with me?" Keith asked. "Pipo said that he knew of a great place to get some paninies made. This place makes a great sandwich; we'll get everyone something."

"All right, let's go." They both left, and Jack went around back to see the items they had just picked up. He grabbed an AK-47 and begun to place rounds into the clip. Giueseppi was watching when Jack lifted his head.

"First things first, you have to have the firepower on hand to stop those who need stopping. This should do the trick don't you agree?"

Giueseppi just smiled.

BELGUIM

Bob looked up; he turned over off the bed.

What is that sound?" Ringgggg. "What the hell? Oh, shit!" He looked around, damn near forgot that he was at the hotel already.

"Just a moment!" Ringgggggg. "I said that I'll be there in just a moment! Yes, who is it?"

"It's Beth. We've come to take you out for lunch."

"Oh, hey, I forgot! Why don't you all come on in and just let me hit the shower, OK?" He buzzed them in and ran to the bath. "I'll be right out, make yourself at home!" The girls piled into the suite and took of their coats.

"Thanks!" Beth said, "We're going to hit your bar if you don't mind. Our room doesn't have one."

"That's fine, could you make me a drink with some ice in it?"

"Anything special?"

"No, but make it a good one, if you know what I mean."

"Coming right up! Could you get me some ice, Kim?"

"You shouldn't make it too strong, he has a job to do here."

"That's OK, you wait until you meet him. My God, is he good looking!"

"But he's almost sixty + something!"

"That doesn't mean anything. It only means that he has what it takes to get the job done right."

"Who's got what it takes to get the job right?" Bob was standing there with a towel wrapped around him and his wet graying hair hanging down into eyes.

Kim jumped and threw the ice into the air.

"Bob, how long were you standing there?" cried Beth.

"Oh, long enough. Is my drink ready? I sure hope it's strong, I've got a job to do, you know!"

Kim stood with her mouth open as she looked at Bob's body. "My God, are you ever built! I mean, sorry if you thought that I meant. "

She put her hand over her mouth and turned away, looking at the other girl with wide eyes.

"Don't worry about it, Kim. That's your name right? Hi, I'm Robert Goldwin, but you can call me Bob."

"Well, Bob, here is your drink." Beth handed it to him, smiling. "The ice has been somewhat 'shaken'."

"Thanks, so who do we have here?"

"Well, you know Kim. This is Barb, and Dana. We have come to take you out for lunch. ls there anywhere you would like to go first?"

"Yea, there is this great little restaurant down town that I would like to take you all to. Lunch is on me."

"All right, lunch is on Bob", Kim said. "Let's get our things together and go."

"Are you going to give me a minute to get dressed or do you think this is good enough?"

"Do I need to call us a cab, Beth, or do you have a rental car?"

"We have a car. Do you want to drive or just look?"

"I'll look, for right now, but I do know my way around alright."

"Good, because after lunch we need to get you a car and do all the things we need to do before tonight's action."

"Tonight?" Bob said, "Shit, that is really fast. Do you have everything I need?"

"Not a problem, everything you need and more." They all filed into the elevator for the ride down and went out to get in the car.

Moscow

The Prime Minister sat down at the table and was ready to go. The Commandant sat down at the table, grabbed his tea, and took a long sip from it.

"Do you all have something special that you would like to eat?" the Prime Minister asked. "I have a great cook that can fix you up anything that you may like."

"No, this will be fine." the Commandant said, as he bit into a buttered bagel. "I don't like to go on the attack with a full stomach." They all just sat there a moment making small talk about the time that has passed since the time that everyone had seen each other last.

"Well then, let's get this thing underway." The men got up from the table and left the room. Their walk from the warm house to the outside gave way to a fine mist of rain that was being blown around by the morning's breeze. They hurried down the steps and got into the car that was waiting for them out in the front of the building.

The Commandant turned and looked back at the building that was trying to take shape out of the mist and fog. He thought, "How many times did the tzar walk out of this house, and look back at a time that would be forever changed in the moments just ahead?" The Commandant shook his head and turned to enter the car.

"You know, it was snowing here just a few days ago."

"Really?" the Commandant answered. "That means that it's going to be a long and cold winter."

The Prime Minister went on, "Well, the weather is cold because of the fact that it is something that effects us physically."

The Commandant broke in with, "A heart that is cold effects us emotionally and mentally. We must approach this matter with a heart of ice. Not that it could be seen on the surface, but that it is so deep inside us the soul becomes solid. Unbreakable in it's will, and unthinkable in its doing. Do we have time to have a walk around the square?"

"Why, yes, of course!" the Prime Minister said. "Then after a walk we can stop to pick up something for lunch to take with us. Unlike you, I am always better with a full stomach."

"Do you know a place that is secret enough? I don't want to be seen out too long before the news is released."

"Oh yes, I know just the spot. Driver take us to it."

After the walk and the lunch to go, the car sped toward the great Hall of the People. As it pulled in front of the building, the Commandant placed his hand on the shoulder of his Prime Minister. They walked together as one.

"Sir, we must do this with every fiber that make us men; everything that makes us Russian!" With that being said, they got out of the car and walked up the stairs of the Great Hall.

"BAD WEATHER YOU SAY? WAIT 5 MINUTES."

Not to say that the weather was shitty, but it was. The people were still having the time of their lives. So were the ones that catered to those that craved the opera, or the theatre. From Paris to London. From Berlin to Madrid. The nightlife was popping like the fire works each and every night at Euro Disney, come rain or shine.

All that rain meant that the snow was really falling on the mountains all over Europe. The Alp were covered like never before. All the new skiing throughout the newly wedded continent was great. The lopes in Russia that were opened to the West for the first time were really the hot spot for those who wanted something new to conquer.

Skiing was something relatively new to the mountains of lower Russia. The Tien Shan mountains that bordered Afghanistan and China housed Communism Peak, a 24,590-ft. monster that could only be reached by helicopter. The all day affair was booked solid for the thrill seekers. Everywhere and anywhere the peaks had snow, there were the people with boards and ski underfoot, downward bound.

JUST PLUG HIM IN

Bob and the girls finally arrived at the restaurant right in the middle of downtown Brussels. The Mirror-O-Mine was right on the best comer of the Kings Garden Court. A magnificent garden place in the heart of Brussels that once a year would be decorated with thousands upon thou ands of flowering plants that formed a picture, when seen from above. The fantastic buildings that surrounded the square took days just to see every little design carved in stone. To see this left no doubt in one's mind why the new European Capital was placed here.

"Well, ladies, shall we?"

"Are we not going inside?"

"What is the matter, are you ladies made of that special substance that melts in the rain?"

"Well, I'm sweet," said Kim, "so you can guess what I am made of."

"Well, all the shit you talk no one has to guess."

"Come on, girls, let's have a nice day. Do you all drink beer? They have a dark beer here that will almost put hair on your chest."

The girls looked over at him as they took a seat.

"What can I say, other than 'this is where I want to live.'"

They all got themselves a liter of beer and shared each other's meal. They talked about the afternoon in the rain, then packed up and headed to the appointed area.

"First, we need to get you a rental car." Bob turned into a car lot, parked and then jumped out with a spring in his step. "What can you afford, Bob?"

He smiled as they walked over to the money cars.

"Anything you like, ladies?"

"Oh, you have to get the new Mercedes 600 LES! That is all you, Bob!"

"Yea, you would blend right in to the scene."

"Mercedes it is," and Bob dropped down the heavy card and in no time it was "Bamm!", as the girls said.

Bob took Kim with him in his car and followed Beth to the point. There they went inside this rented show room that they had booked from their first visit. A screen opened as the lights were dimmed for the show.

Bob sat with his eyes glued to the screen, and a head set was placed on him. He sat there as if he was in a trance.

"You are one of eight individuals here to strike the infrastructure of the map. Twenty-four targets plus secondary targets are for you. This sector of the map shows you where locations, buildings, what floor if any, and different routes. Along with categorized times, and events of targets from this day to the next. Cars and other vehicles have been highlighted, if used by each target. The who, where, what, when, and why has been worked out for you. Study this map segment. This is your sector; you must complete NLT 0200 Saturday morning."

He viewed the map and the routes to and from each target. Times were noted. He was then plugged in for the targets. Pictures of each primary and secondary targets were viewed, memorized. He sat there as if his eyes were eating the visions before him.

"Any family members or friends near the target need to be neutralized." Bob just shook his head as the description of his mission was laid out in front of him.

"After completion of your mission, you are to join the rest of the contingency at the port of control."

The lights came on and Bob stood up. He removed the headset and let them drop to the floor. He just stared off into space for the longest moment.

Kim said, "Should we do something?"

Beth answered, "No, just let him be. He will be all right."

Bob then turned and looked at the girls.

"Wow, Bob, are you OK?" Beth asked. He just looked and then wiped his face with his hand. He hook his head as he walked over by table that the girls had prepared for him.

"This should be more than you will ever need for the mission." He took a fast look at all the weaponry and selected some, and placed other items aside that he did not need. The girls grabbed all the weapons that Bob inspected and loaded them up into cases for him to take.

"Here is a cell phone." Beth added. "It has auto-dial and auto-memory. You are on an open-air line. Not that anyone monitors this frequency. You should use this only in extreme measures. From now on you are on your own. From here on out, we must go our separate ways. We will be everywhere, just in case. Good luck Bob. We will see you again." The girls looked at him and each gave him a kiss on the cheek.

He looked around the room at each of the girls. His tight-lipped expression said it all. They gave him a smile, then they all left the building. Bob walked alone to his car, got in and drove off.

"Use humility to make them haughty. Tire them by fight. Cause division among them. Attack when they are unprepared, make your move when they do not expect it."

FOUND IN THE COMMANDANT'S DAIRY

FRIDAY, MOSCOW

The Commandant entered the large auditorium and moved high, way down to the floor. Many of the members that had been called to this special meeting were already talking to one another. Some committee members were already seated, along with the Chairman that had arrived moments before. The rest slowly made their way to their seats when the Prime Minister approached the podium.

"Members, council of this great institution, we have been called here today, this great day for a closed session of our Parliament. We live now in a time that has taken shape very fast. Governments throughout Europe have worked hard to bring this great continent together. We ourselves have done what no one person or one party from past years has done for this mighty country. The time, money, and in many cases, lives it took to get where we are now is immeasurable. This was not done by chance, it was continually pushed; no matter how bitter it was at times or how hard it was to swallow one's pride. We all can take heed that what has been done here in this short time is not the final product. It must for all involved be just the beginning of what will be the final chapter of this great union of East and West."

The Prime Minister then turned around and added, "Here we have a man, so caught up with the welfare of our country, that he has catapulted us up from the breadline to the head of the line. His was the vision to bring the East and West together. His was the will of time, and the truth of what is the great name of Russia, and what it will stand for tomorrow. May I please present to you, Commandant Gladimir Klakov!"

The great Hall of the People broke out with the loud sound of thunderous applause. He stood up and it seemed that the sound only got louder. For a moment he looked around, then raised his hand to motion the crowd to silence.

"Russia has been great for many things. Over the countless years she has been forever Russia. For a thousand years Mother Russia has been just that. 'A Mother to us in our needs, our pain, and our triumphs'. Yet for almost 100 years we laid waste to our own land. We killed our own people, and still we live with a Mother that has always loved us. How in the world could anyone in the past see that what had been done to her children was for the good of Russia?"

"Many of you here today had only a small taste of the imposed stagnation. Who were we to say what was to come after the death of our great tzar? That these years of the 'one for all and all for one', were the best of time? Oh yes, my older friends, those of you who sit here today know it deeply in your hearts the troubles that we ourselves had made to this great nation of people. Yet what was there to be aid? We grabbed the rail of this ride and held on with all our might, hoping everyday that when we awoke from it, we could consider it just a bad dream."

The auditorium was as quiet as it had ever been. The members sat looking at the Commandant with bewildered eyes as his words rang out throughout the hall.

"Some even had the hardness of the soul, so many years ago, to rename her The USSR. What arrogance, what tyranny? Can you believe that?" He hit the podium with a great strike of his fist, that made everyone jump out of their seats.

"They renamed something that is MY LAND, OUR LAND! Yet in the end she stood there with open arms. She has welcomed us home from wars, she has cried for al) her children! There were those who charge us from the outside. For a thousand years we repelled them! They came so many times and we stood our ground.

But of all the wars that we have fought, none were more destructive to Russia than our own hatred of our own people! The fear of our government was passed on to its own people. We said, 'it was history that we feared!' But yet, it was those from outside of Russia that we feared! 'Those that surrounded us'. Our own paranoia kept us shaking deep inside, like the cold of our Siberia. What the men who controlled everything said, we did, because of the fear of being lost like so many under their rule. But here at this time in history it is 'None of the above'. But it was we who did the most to destroy Mother Russia than all those countries combined."

He then stood in silence, and wiped his head with a handkerchief. "We will never be hurt from those who fear us, nor will we hurt ourselves, ever, ever again."

The crowd for the first time applauded as he shook his head up and down.

"No one has a right over us. They are below the intricate being that makes Russia one-of-a-kind. We have hidden from all others the things that no one needs to know. That business is Russia's alone. No other country on earth has kept the secrets that are Russia's alone. We stand here on this earth a great mass in the midst of all the chaos that is the rest of the world."

"Today, my fellow members of this great country, of this great land, of this great love for that what we know is Russia, I will give you a new beginning!"

There are things now that I must tell you. Not Just those who are here today but all of Russia. The North, the South, the East and West. The things that we and we alone have made for you. The gifts of the Mother Land that are yours, The Russian People.

As things were beginning so many years ago. Plans laid out out. Projects set in motion. The time after the great war where we took the power and closed a land. Many of those who were on the other side after the war, made their plans as well as well have too. Yet ours were not seen, not talked about, not even yet dreamed year at a time, and He stood and looked out at the members that at there in silence, he turned and looked over at the Prime Minister and the President of Russia. He took a drink of water.

We made plans, vast plans and nknew as far back as our first Nuclear Test "Operation First Lightning". Every was there who was anyone. But some of us knew right then and there. This was an answer to the Americans Nuclear Program.

Test after test we watched. We grew as a force. Then came RDS-37, 22 NOV 1955. Our first Hydrogen Bomb. We build thousands, more then anyone could. We had plans. For the thought of air flight came later Rockets, Missiles. We built ICBM's. Planned usage were to hit target in the US, and later others who built their own as time came a rolling.

The Iron Curtain kept this all to ourselves. Some spied for America, some spied for us. The game was played hard and with real outcome.

But as Amer and the rest were trying to do what they could to save their people. "Duck and Cover" was the laughable setting that was for sure to do one thing. It would "COVER" all America. Their Cities, their towns, their people and everything they thought was safe. They gathered around the dinner table and told their children that "We, The United States of America was the one true Super Power of the world. Have no fear, we will all be just fine.

"CAN YOU ALL NOT SEE????" Up to these final days they walk around in the clouds. Face down still looking into their cell phones. Their People don't even know what the hell they are. Man? Woman? Boy? Girl? I will tell you what they will soon be. "ALL DEAD!"

We, Yes We, have taken out time and planned. Under our vast land we planned for the day when it is Light Out! I am here to tell you right under your feet. Thousands upon thousands on mile streching form all our major cities, towns. A vast sub-trainian world that runs into the massive permafrost regions of Siberia. We have it all. From fresh water to food to housing. All under ground waiting for this very time.

We are a land mass of 57+% larger the that of the USA. We have every thing to provide for Russia. But most important, We have our people, OUR PEOPLE! That is what we have been doing, Planning, waiting. And NOW!!!!!!!!

The trains are waiting at their stations.

Waiting? Waiting for what? The Commandant looked for the one who questioned him. He looked and then pointed him out. Soldiers rushed and pulled him out of the meeting and through the doors.

The members rustled about as the room was called to order.

"At this very moment, we stand on the threshold of a new beginning. We reclaim all that, which, over the years we have lost what truly belongs to us, the Russian people." He stood there for a moment, just looking out, passing over the members that sat looking for the answer of the moment. "At this moment, Russian troops have…"

SICILY

When Keith returned from the food run, he asked everyone, "What do you want, shredded pork with onions and cheese, or shredded lamb with onion and cheese? Oh, I'll have the lamb," Keith. aid, and handed Jack the pork sandwich.

"Why in the hell did you ask me what I wanted if you are going to give me what you didn't want in the first place?"

"Oh, bite me, you are never satisfied! Look, it is only a sandwich. ow what is going on with that?" Keith looked over at the AK-47.

"I thought that I would hook you and me up. By the way, we are going to need them later. Do you have anything for them?" Jack nodded to the Italians.

"Yea, sure, maybe the sweat off my balls! What do you want me to give them, they already have a shit load of money."

"Hey, come on. Are you letting this smell get to that so-called brain of yours?"

"Look, Jack, I'm only asking you things that I need to know, shit!"

"You guys are always talking shit to one another. How do you know if one is mad or not?"

"Look, didn't I say that we are best friends? Do you have a best friend? Do you not talk shit to your best friend? Eat your damn sandwich, fuck. Why do I have to go through the million questions?"

"Easy Jack, what the fuck? All we have to do is relax and the time will pass."

"Did you bring us something to drink?"

"I've got these Moretti beers; they didn't have anything bigger."

"As long as it helps these nasty motherfuckers (Jack holds up this mess that was earlier a sandwich) go down, I don't care what size they are."

"Are we about ready to go down range?"

Jack sat back and said, "In just a moment. Can we eat first?"

"Not a problem, but I think we need to go set up before it gets too dark, and we start running into each other."

"Come over here for a moment, Keith." Jack had a little place set up in the back of the barn with the map that Giueseppi gave them earlier.

"Look, I will take up the position here in the bamboo by the aqua duct. I have all of this plotted. Now, you are here. This will maximize our range to where we can inflict the most damage. Now, let me finish my food here, and we will go and set up, OK?"

Keith seemed satisfied with that arrangement, and sat down by the front of the barn, looking for anything that would come up the driveway.

RUSSIAN SPECIAL OPERATIONS

"Load up!" Sergi said, and the team reached down and grabbed their gear. "I want all of you near the back of the plane. Keep your back to the rest of the crew. We have a few things to go over before we reach our landing area. Everyone ready?" Each of them checked their watches. "It is now 16:35, mark! We will be leaving here in exactly twenty-two minute. I want you all to get your heads into this. We must act fast we only have a few minutes after we land. Things should be in place for us as we get there. Be prepared to move, and move quickly." The team looked each other over and shook their heads in approval.

NAPLES, ITALY

"Mario, my good friend! I see you have some more people with you this time."

"Yea, I told you that we must pick up a few things, you dumb-ass half-breed. What did you want me to do, carry all of this by myself?"

"Were you beat as a child? Because I think you needed your ass beat, and then maybe you wouldn't be such a prick."

"I like being a prick, if you don't mind, now give me a hand with this."

"Why, is it heavy?"

"What in the world are you asking a stupid ass question for? Of course it is heavy, now help me."

"You know this is going to cost you extra. I've got a bad back, and the doc told me not to lift things that weigh more than my dick."

"You better get your ass over here and help me with this, or I'm going to put that over sized dick of yours up your ass!"

"Now that is the man I love, good to have you back where you belong."

"Don't mind that dip-shit, if it wasn't for that boat of his I would have had him shot the first day."

"Is this all that you are going to need? Here, take this 9mm along. Maybe you can still shoot the dumb bastard."

"Thanks. You guys take care."

"We will see each other again. Good luck."

"Oh, your friends are not coming with us?"

"No, I don't need anyone."

"You don't need little ol' me?"

"You've been smoking some shit, haven't you?"

"You could say that; I have some more for you if you get sick tonight."

"Thanks, but if it makes you look that dumb, then I could imagine what it would do to me."

"Not a smoker, I see. No matter. When this is all over, you and I can go take a little smoke break and watch the fire show from off shore.

BELGIUM

Bob parked the car in the under ground garage, and took the elevator up to his room. He turned on the TV and clicked over to the weather channel for the updates of the night's weather. Yep, it's going to be one wet pisser. He went behind the bar to see just what he had to work with. The girls sure did make a mess.

"OK, I've got this and a little of that, now I need some ice. Oh, there it is in the fridge door. Now I wonder if this room is taken in this next life. Would have to change a few things around but I could make it livable."

Bob went over the floppy disk one more time. He had it all set up in his mind, who he would visit first. Just then the bell rang. "Damn, this place is busier than the train station. He got up to answer it. He looked into the monitor and said, "Shit, it's Stella."

He pushed the elevator to open, and there stood Stella. This sweet little thing.

"Hi, I thought since you were home that I would drop by for a few minutes."

"My God!" he thought to himself.

"Come in!" he said as she stepped out of the elevator. Her high heels, beautiful legs. Everything about her seemed perfect.

"Are you busy?" she asked as she took her coat off.

Bob had to hold his jaw in place as she turned around.

"What do you think? I just got it from this cute little place down town."

"You look good enough to eat." Bob slapped his hand in front of his mouth, and turned around and walked to the bar. "Would you like something?"

She gave him a sweet smile."Well, I kind of like that first thing you said. He held his glass so hard he thought it was going to break in his hand.

MOSCOW

The Commandant paused for a moment. "Our troops have started their move on Western Europe." The assembly took in a big breath as they started to talk to each other.

"What do you mean our troops are moving? To where, and for what reason?"

At that moment Major Kizir signaled, and some soldiers stepped in and sealed the door.

"What I am saying here, is for you all to sit your asses down, and don't move it again until I tell you to!"

The Commandant became outraged. "It was you, not all of you but most of you that put us in the third class seat. You expected us to make do with the scraps off your table. You did not see the troops return from the harsh fighting with Germany after the Great War? You were not there when those who did not know that they could not retreat to regroup, that they were killed by ones like you. OUR OWN MEN KILLED! Because they were cold, hungry, barely had shoes on there feet. OUR OWN MEN! You here now and talk with one another about 'what do I mean?' WHAT IN THE HELL DO YOU MEAN?!"

The Prime Minister put his hand on the Commandant's shoulder. "We, and I mean many of us after the war, had a dream of this day. The time and hard work it took to get here from there. The waiting for those of you to get off your ass and do something for this country. We tried to bring about change, and many of those courageous people died at the hands of our own government."

He began to pound the podium and point outward to the crowd. "Stand and show yourselves! The ones that work for Russia! Show yourselves! Not the self-centered individuals of a government that only a few of the so-called elite were a part of, and so, caused our people to suffer. They worked their fingers to the bone, OUR OWN PEOPLE! And for what, to say we are a 'Super Power'? You don't know the meaning of 'Super Power'! Stand up, I said, it is all right. You have done it and I will show you."

Members looked back and forth at each other, then one stood and put his jacket down and stood at attention. Then another, and still more began to stand tall. Heads moved back and forth as they watched the men and women who worked so hard on a dream in total secret. The ones who knew that there was nothing left to be done but send Russia into the next stage; the New Age, the New Order.

The Russian President got up and looked around. He turned to the Prime Minister. He looked into the eyes of a great dreamer, and knew that what was happening was the turning point of a country. A birth of a land that needed to be woken up from a bad dream. Russia used to be called "the sleeping Bear", but she sleeps no more!

The Commandant turned and spoke: "Mr. President." then looked back to the assembly. "What we have done here is for the future. What you don't see here is the hard work it took to get here. You don't see what we have created over time. Major Kizir, could you please show this great gathering of people what we have done, and what we are doing at this very moment?"

A large screen appeared from behind the curtain that covered the wall behind those who were seated in the Ministry's place.

"I will take questions from you as we go along. But it should be perfectly clear what is taking place here."

"At this very moment, we are having our guests, who are visiting our beautiful country, detained for a period until we get word from the advancing troops of our victory. The state's police are standing by to move in on all individuals not of Russian descent. This must first take place with the announcement of many cancelled flights. We know that there are many reporters from the We t that are vacationing here, that have access to the West by phone. It has to be a timed matter, so that by the time our troops are in position, it will be a clean sweep."

"Now, let me give you all here a minute to catch up with what we are doing, and how it came around. Could all of you please come closer to the front and fill the chairs that are empty? I need you to see the screen clearly."

The Commandant walked over to the large screen and began his discussion on the matters at hand.

"Many years ago, even before some of you were born, there were a small number of us that came to an under standing that, as a country, Russia could not go on with the way others wanted her to do. We had in our possession those who were from Hitler's own war machine. Scientists that had the ability to create life, different from the one you and I possess. Life that took on a greatness of knowledge. A programmed life that could get us back on top. Was it wrong to conceive life, pre-made to answer to the calling of a better way? They are Russian through and through, and are the answer to those that had us take a second seat to the world."

"It would be a lifetime before we thought that we could finally use what we created. A lifetime to get the chance to really live the life that was to be 'Russian'."

"I can't take all the credit for this. Many of us died before they could see the dream come true. But it was those of us that were left, we knew that it had to be done."

The Commandant then signaled to Major Kizir. A screen of the European continent showed up. All the cities of Europe were highlighted.

"This, my friends, is the way we are going to look tomorrow. The boundaries that you had lived with all your lives will change. From the Atlantic to the Pacific, from the North Sea to the Mediterranean. This is the New Russian Order!"

Many just sat back in their chairs and stared. The Commandant continued, "Don't tell me that you haven't dreamed of this once in your life. We are well on the way to completing this. In just a matter of a few hours we will control the whole continent! No one will know until the morning comes, and they will see a New World looking at them. Many countries will welcome the change. Their parties will finally have the chance to get what they really wanted. So you see, I don't need to tell you all what will be tomorrow. You can see it here for yourself."

As the meeting went on, the Commandant spoke of the plans. He even had dinner brought in for the members. Some of the foreign press began to gather outside of the great hall, wondering what the closed session was about. Major Kizir passed word to the Commandant about the press.

"How many people are there?"

"About fifteen reporters were hanging around just outside the main corridor."

"Let them in, but I want no cameras and no cell phones; they can take notes."

"Yes, Sir." The Major went and brought in the reporters.

"You all, come on down here so that you can get the best position on the story." They came hauling ass to the front of the assembly.

"Here, sit here. What I will allow you to do is takes notes. Your cameras will be returned to you after this is all over."

One of the reporters raised her hand.

"Commandant, after what is over?"

"The invasion of Europe, what else?"

They all broke out in laughter. "The invasion of Europe! Come on, Commandant, what's the story?"

Just then two soldiers ran up behind the reporters.

"As I said, Europe is now the property of Russia and you get the breaking news to report it to all the people of Europe and the world."

They turned around and saw the armed soldiers, then looked up at the Commandant as he walked over to the large screen.

"Some planes have landed by now and the soldiers are distributing equipment to the map readers that are already in country. We have issued flight delays corning into our country for the time being in order for our troops to be air born. At that time flights will be allowed to enter Russia. You see people, our troops have been in all the positions you see here flashing on the screen for several months now."

One reporter raised his hand and asked "How? How did you get them over there?"

"Come on, now!" the Commandant said jokingly. "You all reported it as if it was the story of the century. 'The Russians are coming! The Russians are coming!' As if you were the modern day Paul Revere."

"You know, this is one hell of a Trojan Horse story if you look at it. But instead of the old wooden cliche, we used the more modern method. 'Air traffic control, This is Russia, take us to your leaders!'" The Commandant started laughing aloud. Then the laughter turned to anger.

"We have every European country under our influence, and do you know what? The best is yet to come.

SICILY, FRIDAY

"OK Keith, are you ready for the lights to go out here?"

Keith raised the small radio and answered the call.

"One more moment, Jack, I have to get this thing sighted in on a distant object to be set. Are we in contact with Mari io to call in fire?"

"Yea, I have him on the other line. The planes should be landing soon. We are to give them twenty mikes before hand, then down she goes. Mario called me and told me that he has made it to shore. Damn, he had an easy target. No one to worry about in this rain. Everyone is in hiding. It goes to show you how much shit is just walking around."

"OK, Jack, I will go on your signal. Hang tight.

BELGIUM

Bob took just a moment to set Stella on the straight and narrow.

"Could I have you wait here for me? I must go out for a few hours or maybe less. But I sure would like it if you could wait here for me." He walked up to her and placed a kiss on her that seemed endless. She just stood there dazed, if you don't mind.

"Can I do a little eating of my own?" She pushed him over to the bed and slowly dropped down.

"Wait a moment!" as he grabbed her up. "I'll be right back, I promise. Then we can do what ever you want."

"What ever I want?"

"Here, make a list of what you would like for a late dinner, then when I get back we'll have a candle lit evening, OK?" He gave her another kiss. "You wait right here for me." He entered the elevator and turned around. She stood there smiling. As the doors closed he thought to him self, "Oh, my God!"

He went to the garage and got into the car. As he drove off he reached over to the case next to him and opened it. This beautiful Walter P-5 9mm with the new WP 1.7 Silent muzzle adapter sat right here gleaming. He smiled and said, "Yep, that will do the trick."

The short drive in the rain made him dream of the last time he was in Brussels. He was here about twenty years ago and kind of fell into a little bit of the same thing with an older woman. Her French accent drove him crazy. He just smiled thinking about it all.

He arrived to his first appointment and slowly drove by and parked just across the street. He loved the way Europeans lived. There was very little violent crime anywhere. People can walk the streets at night without the worry of someone pulling out a gun and killing them. (Well, until tonight). It was clean, orderly, and compliant. Stores closed by 8 O'clock in the evening. Nice little pubs with their stained glass windows were everywhere. Life was peaceful. So to get the chance to get the job done and back to Lori was going to be quick and painless, at least for him.

He turned off the car and assembled his piece, stepped out of the car and reached in back for his umbrella. He opened it then closed the door and pushed the auto lock on his key set. If you don't lock you car over here you might get a ticket if a police officer comes by and they found it open. "Damn, I'm so compliant, but I don't need any tickets!" and laughed as he walked toward the house.

The rain was coming down hard. It was the kind of rain that came up from the ground and got you wet that way. He turned up the sidewalk to the front door, took a big breath and rang the bell.

The door opened and a woman asked, "Is there something that I could help you with?"

"Why yes, I have an appointment with the Chief of Police tonight, is he at home?"

"Why, yes he is, but he didn't mention an appointment. Honey, you have a visitor tonight."

The Chief came out from behind the curtain that separated the kitchen and the hallway.

"Yes, can I help you?"

Bob looked up, and in an instant the vision in his mind of the target flashed.

"Sir, I have this for you."

Bob pulled out the 9mm and two shots were off.

The rounds entered and exited the head of the Chief of Police. He fell instantly backward and pulled down the curtains in his fall. His wife stood there for a second, just staring.

"Oh, Hello!" Bob aimed and shot once into her face before she even had a chance to react. It blew the back of her head off and she dropped to the floor.

He stood there for a moment with his lips pressed tightly together.

"Goodnight!" he said, and he closed the door and looked up into the rain, He then placed the gun back into his coat and returned to the car. He sat back and started it. Turning the radio on, he took a cassette out of his pocket. "Oh yea, Black Sabbath's Heaven and Hell. Now that was rock and roll!" He turned it up and drove off to the next target.

FRIDAY

Well, the first planes began to arrive from Russia.

"Flight 314 you are to tum right to heading 443, your altitude should come down to 13000 feet. ow tum left to 306. You are to head to runway 17A." The plane put its landing gears down as it made its last decent into Paris's Orly International Airport. The Pilot looked over at his Copilot, "Flaps down one third."

The rain made it a bit hard to see the runway but the plane touched down and reversed its engines to slow the aircraft down. It turned to the taxi way as a "Follow Me" vehicle drove up in front of the plane. It guided it to the parkway and then sped off.

The ground crew then signaled for the plane to turn left into its resting place.

As the plane came to a stop, the ground guide blinked for a moment then wiped the water from his face. He just stood there as the huge nose of the plane began to open. "What in the hell?" He stepped up to get a better look.

The rain was pouring down, and the light from inside began to illuminate the ground around it. Just then soldiers began to run off, and out of the front of the plane. The ground guide just stood there as one of the men walked up to him.

"What in the hell is that?" They both turned around and looked at the two rocket launchers that started up and begun to drive off the plane.

"Those, Sir, are the SA-8 Geckos."

"What are they doing here? I thought that this was a commercial flight."

The soldier turned to the man and said, "Well your thinking is all wrong!"

"My thinking is what?"

The soldier stepped back and said "Buzzzzzz, All Wrong!" He pulled out his pistol and shot him in the head.

"Come on, people, we need to get this aircraft out of here. There are several more flights that will use this zone to unload their gear."

"I want everyone rounded up and the downstairs secured, now move it!"

Up in the lobby of the airport many of the map readers were just landing around, having drinks or just bull-shitting as they gathered in force. They returned to get the supplies and assist those who would be bring in the armaments to seize the airports and the maps as a whole.

"Hey guys, come over here!" Some of the map readers moved over to the windows. "Look, it is the first plane, we need to get with the squad leader of that flight, and tell them that we are ready up here."

"Damn good timing. Shit, we do better than Air France for on-time flights! Ok, let's go."

All over Europe the same thing was taking place. Troops were entering there target maps one right after another. As soon as one plane landed, in came another. Machines, trucks, and some small tracks were removed from the aircraft. They took up positions close to the air terminal.

As they finished up with the plane, the airport police pulled up to one to them to see what all the commotion was about.

"Hey, what's going on?"

"We were on patrol and had a small problem with an engine."

"Is there anything we can do?"

"Yea!" Just then one of the soldiers yelled from the other side of the car. The police turned to look.

"Why don't you all die!"

"What?" Their eyes saw the AK-47 pointing at them and they tried to duck.

Just then, a small blast of gunfire came from one of the soldiers.

"Shit! Did you have to use o much ammo?"

"You wanted them dead didn't you?

"Ok, ok. Get this car out of here".

MOSCOW

"Sir," Major Kizir leaned over to the Commandant. "We are in, twenty-three airport positions have reported in and the planes are clear to go."

"Very good, very good!" the Commandant smiled. He turned to the assembly and said, "In two hour, we will have some 872,000 troops throughout almost every major city of Europe. Things are looking as good as we could have hoped for. Now we will get an old friend into the show."

SICILY

"Do you have duty again tonight, Sir?"

"Yea, I just pulled it the other night and here I am, again! We need more officers in this place; duty three times a month is a bit too much."

"No shit, Sir, one time here after hours is more than enough. Do you think this rain will ever stop, Sir?"

"Hey, don't knock it, you just wait until summer comes. You will wish for the rain. Is everything up here OK?"

"Yes, Sir, I just wish there was a TV to watch."

"Well, you have those screens to look at."

"But there's nothing on those screens, Sir."

"Well, that is a good thing, don't you think? I am going to make my rounds here. I'll call you from back in SATCOM. Maybe if you are good, I'll go get a pizza."

'That sounds good to me, Sir."

Ok, I'll be right back." Commander Earhart started to walk through the building of NCTS.

"I need to get something on, this damn place is cold!" The Commander went to retrieve his jacket out of his office, then continued back to SATCOM.

The hook up with Marisio was good as he called in from just outside the COMSTA complex.

"Jack said everything is Ok, you just tell me where the first round hits." He looked over at Giueseppi, "Are you ready?" He just shook his head. "Well, here we go!"

Jack held the round, "1, 2, 3…" BANG! "It's off, and now, 4, 5, 6, 7…" BOOM!

The night lit up like it was day light.

How was that?" Giueseppi asked over the cell phone.

"You have to come over eighteen meters left."

"Ok, adjust a bit here, ready!"

1, 2, 3, BANG! 4, 5, 6, 7, BOOM!

You've hit it! You've hit it!" Giueseppi yelled.

"Good, now just sit back and observe."

The Commander was walking down the hall when the first round hit.

BAMB!

It knocked him half way back to the front. He lay there, stunned from the blast. As he sat up and brushed the dust and rocks from his head, the ringing in is ears made it hard to even think. He looked up to see the rain coming in where the roof to Tech Control once was.

"What in the hell?" He tried to get up when the second round hit.

KABOOM!

The whole back of the building began to move in his direction. The mortar round tore through the roof of SATCOM as those who were left standing from the first blast tried in vain to get out of the building. The blast ripped the walls right off the steel frames as a fireball as bright as the sun lit up the site. The quarterdeck watch just stood there looking through the inspection window as all the dust and smoke filled the entrance corridor. The Commander pulled himself up and screamed for him to call security.

"Did you see that, Guesippi?" The big 39-B heavy ground terminal went up in a ball of fire. "That damn dish just disintegrated! Now we do a little 'walking the dog.' Keep your eye on that GBS dish." Giueseppi stood up in the bamboo and pushed it aside for a better look. "Barn, crack!" and just that fast, it was gone.

"Shit, Jack, that was a great shot! Those mother fuckers are going to be pissed off in Washington. This shit is too easy."

Jack turned the quadrant knob on the mortar.

"Have your friend get me on the airfield. I have a bit deconstruction work to do."

Giueseppi started to speak in Italian on the cell phone to his man on base when Keith called in.

"What in the hell is going on? When do I get to get into this?"

"Give me nine more rounds, then you get Pipo to have his guy call fire for you. Just stand by. Do you see any action on base from where you are?"

Keith said, "Just a few people, some are on the road that leads to the Sports Bar."

"Nothing else? How about the firehouse?"

"I can't see that far, but I don't see any lights from the truck yet."

Jack said, "You see? They have all those fucking lazy Italians working the night shift. This is perfect!"

Jack just started to let them fly. The airfield was beginning to look like Swiss cheese with some deep ass holes in it.

"Now, Giueseppi, I will give our friends at the NAVY EOD (Explosive Ordinance Detachment) something to play with later." Jack quickly grabbed the box.

"Here, help me put these timed fuses on a few rounds." They tightened them up, and Jack said, "Now let them bury themselves into the wet ground around the airfield. In a few hours while the EOD are out looking over the damage: 'Happy Birthday!'"

Jack plopped the rounds down and his bit was over.

"Ok, Keith, it's all yours."

"Pipo, have your friend plot this."

1, 2, 3, Bang! 4, 5, 6, BOOM! Concrete shot up in the air as the fireball lit things up.

"Come right forty meters and you should hit the hanger. There are three planes and two helicopters there. Cut loose and walk the damn things!"

Keith was dropping the rounds down the tube when Pipo said, "Stop, Stop!"

"What are you talking about 'stop'?" Keith blasted back.

"My friend said that you are getting too close to Burger King! He loves Burger King!"

"Oh, tell him to kiss my ass!"

"He said walk it right one hundred meters."

"What in the hell for?"

"The Public Affairs Office is there, along with Human Resource Office. The fat little bastard LT. of the PAO who works there thinks he is so cool. He was always taking pictures of us striking. He's nothing but a pudgy little bastard. And HRO never gets you the right job unless you are ready to do what they want, if you know what I mean!"

"Yea, that kind if shit is all over. How far is it from this?"

1, 2, 3, BANG! 4, 5, 6, BOOM!

"Nice hit, just let the shit fly and let's get the hell out of this place."

"Here," Keith said. "Do you want to drop a few?"

"Can I?"

"Sure you can."

Keith called Jack and said that he was winding things up.

"I'll be down there in about ten minutes. Out here." Pipo dropped another round, turned and said, "This is great!"

Keith pointed the rifle at him and said, "Glad that you are having o much fun." Keith pulled the trigger. He damn neared emptied the clip into Pipo. The first blast of fire just about tore him in half. "Pipo, you stay here, I've got to go. Thanks for all your help." Keith started back to Jack's location.

"Hey, Giueseppi, get your ass over here! We need to get the hell out here!"

"Hey, Jack, what are we going to do with the mortars?" Giueseppi asked.

"Well, I thought that we would stick it up your ass!" Jack turned and cut loose with the AK-47. Giueseppi came apart as the rounds hit. He fell into the bamboo that surrounded him.

Jack looked at the barrel as the rain made the sound like butter on a hot griddle. "Damn, I can't wait for the rain to stop!"

Just then Keith came running up. "Oh, shit what a mess!"

"Don't tell me that you think Pipo looks any better!"

"Yes he does, there is the top and the bottom. He doesn't even look like this mess."

"Oh, stop it, and let's get out of here. Just leave everything."

They jumped into the truck and headed to the airport to meet up with the incoming troops.

NAPLES, ITALY

"Damn, Mario, you really know how to put those rounds on target. Boy, that place is on fire. I bet you can see that blaze from the mainland."

"Do you think so?" Mario put the night vision goggles up to his eyes. "Yea, it's a good fire, all right. I always loved building a good fire. When I was a little boy, oh what the fuck!" Mario pulled out the 9mm and blasted off a quick six round into his poor friend Nina's chest. He fell back and hit his head on a big rock.

"Damn, Nino, you have to be careful where you lay your head these days." Nina's eyes were wide open, just looking up at Mario.

"Now, what are you looking at? I know I need to relax. Well, my friend, as soon as I get off this rock I will." Mario made his way back to the boat, climbed aboard, and started it. " Wow, where did you hide that smoke?" He pushed the throttle forward, and off into the rainy seas he went.

SPECIAL OPS IN BORDEAUX, FRANCE

"Come on, come on, get that shit off-loaded and over here!" Sergi backed the truck over to the back of the An-124 Condor, and his men unloaded the gear into the back of the truck.

"We have to get out of here!" Sergi ordered.

Just then they heard some small arms fire.

Sergi said that it was bound to happen. Everyone loaded up and they moved out. A firefight between the Russian soldiers and some security police was breaking out as Sergi and his team raced for their objective just outside the airport.

The fighting was short and furious, and several policemen were dead in a flash.

"Be prepared for more action!" the unit Commander shouted.

"You men get that pair of ASU-57's out to point. Make sure that your fields of fire are covered. Get those people suited and geared up!" Many of the map readers were all ready and had been waiting for the show. They helped with the off loading and waited for the next flight to arrive.

THE RUSSIAN BEAR'S SHADOW

"Of the 1,670 flights that were underway, only seventeen have yet to land, Sir. We are moving out over the maps. Some small firefights have broken out in several locations, but they were met with a heavy response from our troops. The Special Ops people have all arrived. They have moved out to their locations and are standing by."

The Commandant thanked the Major, then he walked over to the large screen.

"You see that we have here a large area that is blank. I cannot tell you about this area yet. But what I can say is that our friends from across the water will shit the whole nest when that time comes into play."

The city police entered the Moscow Hilton with guns drawn. The police Lieutenant walked up to the main desk and asked them to cut all outside lines, then call all guests, and tell them to leave their hotel rooms, and come down to the lobby.

"Tell them that there was something wrong with the gas heating." Then he turned to the main lobby.

"You wait at the door and search everyone that comes in." He got on the radio and called in that all was under control.

Throughout all the forward bases in Russia, the main alarm was sounded. Orders were coming in over flash traffic. The Officer on duty was decoding the messages as fast as they were coming in.

"Commander! What is going on here?"

"We have received a message from Command Central Forces West."

"Here, let me see." The base Commandant grabbed the message from the Officer of the Watch. "Jesus, it's happening!"

"What's happening, Sir?"

"The invasion! Get everyone assembled and ready to move to the Forward Deployment Area!

The Commandant's Briefing

"You will have noted by now that all of our ground and air forces have been deployed, and are beginning to move to their forward deployment areas. The massing of our troops will not be seen so well by Landstat 6 but we have known of the US's ability to pick up infrared movement from their Twilight orbiter. This is of no consequence to us because we have knocked down their ability to transmit messages from their Naval Computer and Telecommunications Station down in Sicily. The NCTAMS MED facility in Naples is also down, as well as the Army's facility at Camp Darby in Northern Italy.""All they know is that some terrorist gang has attacked their facilities, and we are massing on the borders. They have no other indication. Because of the actions taken in these steps, we have a giant advantage. Soon the President of the United States will be calling the President of Russia. But by the time that all his advisors here have called from the Consulate to our State's Office, only a small but most productive part of this grand show will left to do.

Doing Up the Town

Bob was sipping on his tea when the Head of the Belgium Reform Party came into the study. Bob stood up as he held out is hand.

"Mr. Goldwin, I am sorry for making you wait."

"No, Sir, 1 am sorry for calling on you at this hour, but I need to talk to you about a financial contribution, that I would like to give to your party."

"Well, well, it is never too late in the evening when we have money to talk about."

"Good, I was hoping you would say that. I was wondering if your party takes shares in mineral deposits instead of cash?"

"Well, it depends on the type of mineral and how much. What type of mineral are we talking about?"

"The mineral deposit will be lead," then Bob pulled out his 9mm, "and it will be two rounds."

Thump, thump, the body dropped immediately. Bob picked up his cup of tea and walked to the kitchen.

"Excuse me!" Bob called.

The butler looked over to Bob and said, "May I help you?"

"Yes, this cup is empty can you take this please?" The man moved to take it from him.

"But this," Bob pulled the gun, "this is not empty." He fired off the remaining rounds into the kitchen help. Blood was splattered everywhere. He popped out the clip and replaced it.

"You all need to keep this place a little cleaner." He turned and walked out of the apartment. He passed a couple kissing on the stairs on his way out. He smiled at them and thought of Lori as he headed to his car.

Bob started to drive off as three unmarked police cars went flying by. He knew that things have started and he had little time to worry about the others. He started out to his last target of the night.

His trip took him past the airport, and that is when he saw all the rescue trucks and police car out on the inlet leading to the runways. "Shit," he thought to himself, "this is going to be a mess by the time morning comes around." He turned right on a street away from all the commotion.

As he turned onto the street leading to his last target, there were two unmarked cars out in front. He pulled over and got out of his car fast. A he started to walk up to the house he could barely make out one of the men standing in the door. "Shit, it was the Chief Justice standing there!" He was putting on a coal and there were five other men with him. He kissed his wife and tarted down the sidewalk.

Bob hurried back to his car, and pulled out a large case from the trunk. He placed it on the hood and opened it.

"Oh yea, a good answer to any situation."

Bob started talking to himself, quoting his weapons trainer, almost like a chant, as he assembled the Dragunov SVD sniper rifle.

"7.62mm long rimmed ammo, with type 54R, 3.1 1g propellants. With the PSO-1 sight and loaded mag-azine, its weight comes to 9.95 lbs. Its length is 48 ¼ in. without the bayonet. I don't think that is needed at this moment. Muzzle velocity is a 2,275 ft./sec. Effective combat range will be 800m."

Bob dropped down by the side of the car. He sighted in on the target closest to him to see if optics were visible. Then he grabbed two RGD-5 hand grenades.

"Now we pull the pins, and with a little toss here and one over here 3, 2, 1..." Boom, Boom!

The two unmarked cars were heading skyward in flames. One of the men grabbed the Chief Justice and threw him to the ground.

Bob picked up the rifle and said, "That's what I thought you would do with him. Thanks for the target."

Bob popped off a round. The man fell into the arms of His Honor.

"Nice catch, now who will catch..." off went another round. It entered the neck of the Chief Justice and ripped the head clean off. Bob finished the sentence with "...you?" The other men were trying to take cover when Bob open fire on the front door of the house. He did not know who was looking out of it but it no longer looked human.

His car then took two hits.

"Shit!" he said, "My insurance will not cover that!" He went around back and watch two men trying to run for the cover of the house. Bob sighted in and picked off the lead man. As he fired, the man fell to the ground and reached for what was left of his right leg. The other man stopped to help him up when Bob took out his back with a second shot that went right through his chest. He dropped like a deer during hunting season.

"That's what you get for trying to be a hero." Bob aimed and popped off one more round. It stopped the man who was in search of his leg.

Bob dropped the rifle in the back of the car and ran to the other side of the street. He pulled out the 9mm and was holding the gun when he walked up to the last two men. They looked like they were trying to get the Chief Justice to some cover.

"Now, now boys, you have been watching too much TV. The man you are fucking with…" Bob shot off a round into one of the men and he slumped over, "… is dead! Can you see that now?"

The last cop stood up.

"Well, do you know the difference between him," Bob pointed to the man on the ground, "and you?" He then pointed back to the cop.

The man just looked blank. Just then a round tore through the right cheek and out the side of his head. It spun the man around as he hit the ground.

He didn't have to fall very far. Bob reached into his coat for a handkerchief. He pulled it out and wiped the rain from his face. Then he blew his nose and returned the handkerchief to his pocket.

"Now, I wish you all a good night!" and he turned around and walked back to his car.

The Bear has Landed

The last of the planes were coming in as the police outside the airport were blocking off the traffic. The planes were flying right over head on their way to land, and the authorities didn't even know what was on the planes. They touched down and the last of the troops and equipment were off-loaded. The airports were completely in the hands of the Russians.

Information was flooding in now on what was going on. News crews were franticly working to get the story on the air.

"This is a News Flash from CNBC in Paris. We have been receiving reports that many airports throughout France has fallen captive 10 some unknown forces. Authorities have yet to receive any answers to what seems to be a large-scale effort to encapsulate our airports here in Paris, as well as those all over Europe. Please stand by this station for further information about this major news event."

"This is Der Nochreiten, throughout all of Europe, many of their major airports were in the hands or under the control of what seem to be Russian troop! The Russian forces have seized control of the airports of Frankfurt, Nuremberg, Stuttgart, and München air ports. German police have surrounded the areas and have not allowed anyone in or out. Some small fighting has been reported near Frankfurt. Please stay tuned to this station for further reports."

As the troops took up positions in and around the perimeter of the airport, other troops had the people rounded up in the airports and taken to large hangers for holding. Many of them didn't understand what was going on. Many of them haven't even seen there own military yet those of the Russian Army. Very little protest was given as they were moved to the holding areas.

Throughout the early morning hours the Russians sat up defensive positions and stood fast for information on the others throughout Europe.

EARLY SATURDAY, SICILY

Captain Makeo, the Commanding Officer of the US side was just arriving at the US Naval Air Station Sigonella as the sun was an hour or two from coming up. The rain had tapered off a little, but more was forecasted for later that afternoon.

"Get my ass down to COMSTA!" He told his driver, "Drive down to NCTS so I can see for myself the damage." Just as they were entering the Italian side of the base, the Italian police, along with am1y soldiers, were guarding the road to the sire. The Captain got out and asked for the base Commandant, who was already down at NCTS.

"Sir you cannot enter until our superior officer takes you there."

"Shit man, those are my people down there!"

"I am sorry but I do have my orders."

Captain Makeo was pissed, "What kind of horse shit is that? You get your CO down here, NOW!"

He got back into the car. "Turn this thing around and let's go see the flight line."

"Right away, Sir." The car sped back to the US side of the base.

He could see the mess even before he got there.

"What in the hell is going on around here?" Two P3 Orions, and three AH0-53 Black Stallion helicopters lay in waste on the flight line. EOD was out searching the area for any unexploded rounds, as the CO walked up and everyone turned to salute.

"What do we have here, Master Chief?"

"Well, Sir, you can see that we have five aircraft down, two hangers destroyed, and from what we can see, the runway took one hell of a beating. It's out of commission. Over on this side we have the PAO, and HRO offices destroyed. Why those two buildings were targeted we have yet come up with a reason."

"Do we have any injuries?"

"Well, Sir, other than your minor cuts and bruise from people working the night shift it was not that bad here. But NCTS took it real bad. I can't tell you how many were killed. They were the main targets, it seems. The Caribinari are now searching the outside of the base for any evidence. EOD thinks it came from 82mm mortars."

"What? How in the hell could we be hit by something like that? Can we assume that a possible terrorist group is responsible?"

"Yes, Sir, but we will know more when everything is looked at. That is the best I can do for you, Sir, sorry."

"Thank you, Master Chief, I am going to try to get down to COMSTA. You can call my car if you need me."

"Yes, Sir!" then the CO walked back to his car.

The Captain got back in and said, "Let's head over to NCTS." The rain started coming down a little harder and it made for an eerie sight to see those aircraf1 still burning in the rain. As they pulled up to the checkpoint, they were stopped once again by the Italians. The Captain got back out and walked up to the sentry.

"You go down there and get that Commandant of yours, and tell him that I want him here, NOW!"

The soldier said, "Right away, Sir!" then got into a jeep and drove down to the site.

Not even five minutes passed and the Commandant came riding up. They each got out and met each other.

"Enzo, what is the problem with me coming down there to see my people?"

"Come with me." The Commandant reached out his hand to Captain Makeo. "I am sorry but you can understand that I need to be careful. I would say 'good morning', but it is not. We took a great amount of damage. Not everything is in yet. All we have down here is our bomb squad and some of your EOD."

The site came into view and it was wasted. The rain had stopped some of the fire, but it was still burning.

"Until your guys tell me that the place is clear, I can't even bring in an ambulance. EOD have already found one timed fuse 82mm round. That makes me suspect that there are more just waiting for us to get complacent and head down here like the Calvary."

The Captain looked at the Base Commandant and agreed. They both got out of the car as it came to a stop. Shit was burning everywhere. The whole building was a total loss. Both satellite dishes were down and out of business. Some of the bodies were lying over by the bus stop. The Captain ran towards the bodies and was met by Commander Earhart as he got up from the curb.

He tried to salute but his arms were badly burnt from the fires. The Captain held out his arms and tried to comfort him.

"Frank, are you OK?"

"Sir, I don't know what I am. What happened, Sir?"

"The Captain said, "Come with me to the car."

"All due respect, Sir, I have to stay with my people." Frank looked down at three bodies that were covered with gray blankets.

"Those were just kids, Sir. I can't say how many more there are, because EOD won't let anyone back there. But I have nine more missing."

Commander Earhart broke down and cried. "Why can't we get my people out of the rain, Sir? They don't need to be lying in the rain. These were good kids! They did their jobs, Sir and didn't run. They just did their jobs, Sir. I was just talking to some of them moments before all this shit came crumbling down on top of us."

Captain Makeo asked Frank if he was going to be all right. He nodded his head, and went back to sit down with his kids. He tried to keep the blankets straight on them.

The Captain turned and looked at some EOD guys running from the blown runway.

"Fire in the hole!"

One of the Petty Officers ran up to the CO and said, "There must be at least seven unexploded rounds out there, Sir. We have one up and lying on its side. It had some kind of Arabic writing, along with what looked like Russian. What do you think, Sir, terrorists?"

"Maybe, but it sure was Russia who make's the 82mm."

"That beast kicked the shit out of this place, Sir. Has anyone found the mortars yet? I hope that they don't come back for a little more action."

Just then the Italian Commandant came running over.

"I just got a call from my Commanding Officer in Naples. He said that your Rear Admiral Spencer was flying in from his boat just south of Agrigento. He should be here in fifteen minutes."

Just then, Boom! One of the unexploded rounds was detonated by EOD. Shit was thrown into the air two-hundred feet or more.

The Captain commented that, "It looks like we are going to have a long weekend."

Both men got into the car, and the CO rolled down his window as they rode up on Frank.

"You take it easy, Commander."

"I will, Sir. I just want my kids out of there."

"I know." the CO said, and the car sped off to the US side of Sigonella.

BELGIUM

Bob parked the car and got out. He looked at the two holes in it. He said, "Shit, that is a bitch. I was getting to love this car. I can't drive it around looking like it came out of, what do the American's like to say, 'Beirut'." He locked the car doors and walked over to the elevator and entered it.

Stella was glued to the TV when the elevator opened and Bob walked in. She looked over at the time and said, "You told me just a few hours."

Bob just stood there with a tired look on his face.

"That don't matter. Did you hear of all the shit that is going on?"

Bob's eyes got big and said not a thing.

She got up and gave him a fast kiss then grabbed his hand and pulled him to the TV.

"Look at this shit!"

Bob sat down, and Lori said that someone has taken over the Brussels Airport.

'That was what was holding me up. I must have been outside the area for more than two hours, or I would have been here with you."

"You tried to get here to me?"

Bob smiled a small smile. He said, "Wait here for a second." He went to the elevator and opened it. He reached inside and pulled out a rose. He turned and walked up to Stella and said "Sorry for being late. I know I said that we'd have a good dinner."

"That is OK, I sent for a late sandwich. Where did you get this at this time of the morning?"

"Well, I stopped by the kitchen to see if it was too early to have breakfast sent up here. The cook kind of looked at the clock on the wall. I pulled out a $100.00 and slipped it to him. He almost shit! He started pulling out the whole kitchen asking me what I would like to have. He grabbed this vase of flowers, so I picked one and said that we would call down."

Stella walked up to Bob and put her arms around his neck. She looked into his eyes and said, "You are so sweet." She kissed him slowly and then said, "You just wait!

MOSCOW

Most of the members of the assembly were taking turns sleeping in the chamber's rest room adjoining the Great Hall. The Commandant himself took a few winks with orders to be woken up if anything important developed. The Major entered the room and slowly woke up the Prime Minister.

"Sir, you have a call, along with the President."

"Where is the President?"

"He is already out on the phone."

The Commandant got up, got dressed and came out to join them.

"How do you feel, Sir?"

"Pretty good, Major. Did you get some rest?"

"Yes, Sir, I did, I have made arrangements for breakfast to be delivered here."

"Very good, Major, I'm sure that our guests are a bit hungry."

The food was brought in and placed on the long front tables that lined the front of the hall. Last night's platters were taken out as the food was being brought past the line of hungry guests. People got up and started serving themselves. It looked pretty good, but most just stopped for the coffee first.

"Do you need a cup of tea, Sir?"

"Why, that would be great, Major. You have been priceless to me during this time."

"Sir, it is an honor to serve with you."

The giant screen was fully lit with the sites that had come under Russian occupation. The Commandant was speaking to some of his Commanders via satellite. He conveyed his pride that he had for them, and that they will be rewarded for their great accomplishments. They all signed off and he returned to the breakfast area.

"We had just launched the new generation of military communication satellites, last year, that will give us uninterrupted communications worldwide without breaking bands that belonged to the NATO worldwide net." He showed the Prime Minister on the monitor a picture of what he called the "edge over the West".

"The launch of the Molniya Alfa 5 COMSAT gave us an almost covert communications satellite that could be maneuvered without outside tracking. We climb into the driver's chair and put the pedal to the metal." Everyone laughed, and the Commandant just smiled over the whole idea.

"Everyone has checked in, and we hold the key to Europe! All objectives have been met." The lights that were red turned green on the big screen.

"The world has by now figured out what had happened to the o-called EEC. Not that it ha been wiped off the face of the earth, but we just gave it a different name."

"Our might and resolve will not be measured by what we have done here, but if we as a nation can stand the very ground that we have conquered here this day, then that will be the measure of our resolve. Unlike Napoleon and the men that marched against us three hundred years before, we will not fall back in despair. We will not run from the madness of decision. We shall stand as a country that has been asleep and has finally awoken to find itself anew."

The Commandant turned and smashed his fist down on top of the podium. "For which reason did we lose those that we have held? I am not talking of the Cold War, I am talking about the men and women that have fought for us so many times. Their feet under them, so many times, without the boots to help them move forward in the wars that they did not know why they fought. So the bellies of those in the USSR elite could be filled with the spoils given by the puppets that replaced the fallen? Never will the nation fall prey to a few self-thinking pigs, and not keep those that fight in the arms that hold them close. Never, never again!

BELGIUM

Bob called in for a breakfast that even made the chef down in the kitchen think.

"First," Bob said, "we will start with a Chateau neuf-du-Pape, Pinot Noir."

"What is that?" Stella asked?

"Well, I will tell you, my sweet. It is a full-flavored wine; full-flavored such as yourself. Then I will have a light crepes-suzette cooked with the pan lightly covered with olive oil. Then we will part our mouths with a kiss of the chefs sweet-battered Belgium waffles, in a sweet orange sauce. I told the cook to come up with the rest of the morning's menu."

Stella said, "Are you trying to seduce me?"

Bob stood in front of her and said, "You look far too delicious to be seduced."

They sat down to a beautiful breakfast, then they fell into an early morning of love making that very few people have found.

FRANCE

"Come on people, the light will soon be upon us. We must get this operational and the hell out of here before too long!" The truck pulled around and was throwing mud every where. They exited the vehicle, pulled the device out, and placed it on the ground.

"Ok, let's remove the holding container and get that back on the truck." They were moving like clockwork. Each member of Sergi's team had the job down pat.

"We are in place, Sir!"

"Very good." Sergi ordered them all to get in the truck. He kneeled down and entered the final codes into the main frame. The device came alive.

"All right, people the job is done!" he said, as he placed the cover back on. "Now we need to get a safe distance and wait." He then climbed into the back of the truck giving each one of his team a pat on the shoulder.

"We will find us someplace dry, then we can get ourselves some rest."

He sat by the rear and looked out over the field as the truck turned onto the road and sped up. A fine mist of rain blew in as the truck raced along.

"Sir?" Sergi turned and looked at his men.

"I know that we are to refer to this place as the map, but since we are here to stay, would I be out of order to ask where is 'here' that we must stay?"

A small smile came over his face as he sat and thought the question out.

"We're in France; Bordeaux, France." He then turned and took a long look back out of the truck as it sped into the early mist of morning.

The Rude Awakening

The Chief of Staff knocked on the door of the President as he was finishing up on a late dinner with his family.

"Sir, I am so sorry for this intrusion. But there is a very distinct possibility that Europe is being infiltrated!"

The President got up, grabbed a napkin, and wiped his mouth. "I'll be right out, Jim." he told his adviser.

"Yes, Sir, we will be in the Oval Office."

The President entered the office to see his entire staff assembled and charts scattered about.

"What do we have going on this evening?"

The Chairman of the Joint Chiefs stood and said, "Mr. President, we are in an auto-THREATCON two!"

"How in the hell did we get there?"

"Most systems were interrupted by a chain of events that placed us in auto-defense. We are just now receiving information on an attack that was staged on our three top sites in southern Europe to include the GBS systems at Sigonella. The attack seems to have taken place around 16:20

EST this afternoon. I also placed orders for all Air Forces Europe to stay where they are. We don't need them flying back to home air fields until we know exactly what in the hell is going on here."

"OK, what do we have and why was I not informed earlier?" The President took his seat at the head of the table.

The Secretary of State took the floor.

"Sir, I think it would be in the better interest of the nation that we head to the War Room." He looked across the entire room and they all hook their heads in agreement.

NAVAL AIR STATION, SIGONELLA

Rear Admiral Tracy Spencer looked out the window of his AH-54 and could not believe the damage.

"Set me down near the flight line, on the other side of the air terminal."

The massive helicopter sat down gracefully, and the doors opened and he jumped out. The NASSIG CO along with the Italian Base Commandant met him half way and started to brief him on what was new at SIG.

"Sir, reports are still coming in on the attack on Sigonella. We have word that the NCTAMS MED facility took a lot of damage, too. We are, as far as communications are concerned 'Out of Business'! They just stomped the shit right out of us!"

"Did we suffer any losses?"

"That was the good thing, if you can find anything good out of this. The base was relativity empty when the attack took place. NCTS was really the only active point on duty. But then again, that is where we were hit the hardest. We lost twelve people there, Sir. The place has been turned into dust. Most of our servers won't be up for weeks. Land-based communications, to include White House Communications, are out indefinitely."

"Shit, that is not the half of it, boys. Can we go to the Tactical Support Center?"

"Right this way, Sir." They climbed into a Hum-V and drove down the flight line to TSC.

THE MEETING OF MINDS

"Mr. President, we have lost much of our means to communicate with Europe by secure lines. Whoever hit us, Sir, knew exactly what to look for. This is not a Johnny-come-lately attack. This looks like years of planning, picking just the right places to hit!"

"But why?" the President asked. "In this kind of weather? You can't move as well, nor can you see the targets by air to insure precise target acquisition."

"Sir, it doesn't make sense at all. But the in-formation is coming in, small pieces at a time. It looks like a food fight at a Chinese restaurant, Sir. One fucking mess!"

MOSCOW

"The New Russian Order is what is on this morning's menu! I hope you all enjoyed the breakfast that was served to you this fine morning. Here is how the world goes according to us."

"All of Europe is under the umbrella of Russia. Most countries are so busy dealing with their own crisis that they have no idea what in the hell is going on with their neighbors. Each country's military are on full alert, and have most of the airports surrounded. Oh, how this plays into the hands of those that made these plans. You never bet the person that wagers the bet."

"By now, many countries are wondering, 'how in the hell did this get that far? Right under the nose of Mr. and Mrs. Make-a-buck. This greed led those who had any sense, to place aside the common sense of one's own security. We opened the door of opportunity, and they walked right in. We even moved their air forces for them. Now there is not enough cover from their own forces to have the ability to cover our airlift operations to reinforce their positions. The US is looking, this very moment, at one hell of a mess, and has no answers for the little countries that couldn't fight their way out of a paper bag."

"Just look at France! Where do you think they can point their once mighty ICBM's? They don't even know if they should put them on alert yet."

"There are only three things that can happen to dogshit: it can turn white and blow away in the wind; you can step in it and smear it all over; or it can be shoveled up and thrown away. So it is with the countries of Europe: they must be careful where the dog shits them."

SIGONELLA

Just as the Admiral and both CO's entered the briefing room at the TSC Center, there were those waiting with word on the night's attack.

"Sir, the Italian Carabinari have found the devices. of destruction across the street from COMSTA and the new billeting that had built just the year before. They used the Russian made 82mm mortar to do the job, and just left everything right there. It looked like they were there for at least half a day. It also looks like the two positions must have gotten help from inside the base."

"How in the hell can that be?" the Italian Commandant asked.

"Well, we found a mess along with the mortars. It looks like two Italian bodies were left, shot to shit. Plus, they found cell phones, all with the same phone number on them. The Carabinari are trying to track the number now. They will get back to us later, after they get more information."

"Well people, here it is in a nutshell." the Admiral said. "We don't need to get our civilian community in an uproar. Alert all the commands that they must get all personnel back here on base. I want armed guards at all housing areas tripled."

"Sir, we don't have the weapons to give. Many of our sailors don't know how to handle a firearm. They haven't handled anything since boot camp."

"Very well, I'll need to call over to my flagship and have some flown in here. I want this base closed up tighter then my x-wife's snatch. I mean nothing's getting in! When can we have the rest of that info about the attack? I need to get that out to chain of command."

"We are getting it for you, Sir."

THE WAR ROOM

"Mr. President, information is coming in on the situation over in Europe. We have this here on the screen." A large map of Europe was brought up. "It shows all International Airports throughout Europe that Russian troops have infiltrated. 106 out of more than 260 locations have troop involvement at present. We do not know what they have with them, the size of the troop force, nothing. Cloud cover is still a primary reason that we do not have more information on the situation."

"We also have more information coming in on our COMSAT at Sigonella. Stand by, Sir."

THE GREAT HALL

"Good luck has never been on the mind of Russia!" The Commandant said. "We make our own luck. In the early morning, we had all Europeans that are presently our guests rounded up. They will be confined to their hotels or lodges. The others, as of just a few hours ago, are stranded at Russian airports. They too will be rounded up and bussed to hotels throughout Russia, and they will be confined there. A final count has not made its way to my hand, but estimates are that we are holding more than 1,285,000 guests. That number is expected to climb as those in remote areas skiing are counted and confined. This is just one big card in our hand. Loved ones are always something of a gift. Over the years when one would hold others for reasons of their own, loved ones almost always were the centerpiece of the deal. A reporter stood up and said, "So Russia is now in the market of holding hostages? The world doesn't deal with terrorists."

The Commandant's face turned red with anger. "What in the hell do you know about the matter? Do you have someone that might not come back to you? It is so fitting the language others use to make a situation understandable. This is not an act of terrorism! This is an act of WAR! We are keeping within the guidelines of the Geneva Convention in that 'no foreign noncombatant peoples will be harmed in the matter of armed conflict'. But come up with one more stupid remark like that to me young man, and I'll have your immigration papers made up to make you a Russian citizen, then I'll kill you myself for being a traitor!"

The reporter sat down as fast as the comment from his mouth came out.

"It hasn't been twelve hours since we started the take over. No losses to any of our troops have been noted. Special Ops people are in place and are standing by with orders to act if an attempt to recapture the airfields is made. This is getting better as the time goes by."

The Commandant turned to the assembly. "Here is why we have made contact with countries we are now occupying: Years ago, when the world was tied up with the business of rebuilding Europe, we took steps to get back to the things we were quite good at, with the help of our German Specialists. We got underway with the production of a race of people that were pure of heart and mind. Thinkers in the strictest possible sense of the word. Fearless in conflict, and with the ability to remember everything presented to them. The best of everything, we've given to them. The time and money was spent to get them prepared for this moment."

"Two groups emerged from the masses. First are the troops that are now in place, and are in control of their objective. These are the Map Readers. They were taught to find the infrastructure of the city that was in the country of their training. The maps that they were taught were the cities and countries that they visited as 'tourists'. A society without those who run it is nothing but chaos. They searched for everyone that had something to do with the inner workings of the city, county, state, and that country's government. Where they lived, what work they did, what they looked like, the who, where, what, when, and why of every single person that makes life there tick. Everything about that person's life was observed. The information then was gathered and prepared for the next group of people."

"The second group was maybe the best of what we did in our search for the perfect being. These are the destroyer's of that system. The ones that, when the time is called for them, they have the mission to turn the lights out. We raised them to be self-reliant, the perfect chameleon. To blend into the very world that we most despised. We got them out in waves to Israel as Russian Jews that were exiled from this country. The world welcomed them with opened arms. So, into the wind they were blown."

"Now, as the countries find the bodies of their leaders, the aids and those who have very little experience in matters of foreign affairs have us to deal with. No longer will they feel left out, but now have been thrown into the pot of this fine salad of distrust, disarray, and complete and total disillusionment of the world. They will learn very fast what it will take, not to become one of their fallen leaders."

He shook his head, "And you, my friends, are in on the show. Some of you must think that I am mad. On the contrary, I am bringing dignity to what would otherwise be an all out brawl. Those poor little bastards that are now finding themselves in charge of their whole state wondering, 'what will we do?" There is really not much to do. We have them in the front lean and rest position. But I will not stop there. Because we, the big bad bear has these simple little countries under our foot. We must now invite our long sought after friends, The United States."

THE WAR ROOM

Just as the Chairman of the Joint Chiefs was about to start, some of his aids came in with the new developments.

"One moment, Sir" he said as he showed the Joint chiefs the new information.

"Sir, here is what we are now facing: The continent of Europe has been infiltrated by Russian Special Forces units!"

The President sat up and said, "What Special Forces?"

All the Joint Chiefs were on their phones getting information as the Chairman when on. The map of Europe was enlarged on the wall screen to show what has taken place.

"As you know, we have confirmed that 19 countries are now under Russian occupation. Some 106 Major airports and their surrounding cities are encapsulated by Russian forces."

The President asked, "How could this be?"

"Sir, it seems that they have used the new Inter-European Quest treaty and the commercial air industry to get troops and equipment into the regions. They are well armed and have fortified the areas."

"What is the estimated number of ground troops?" "Close to 900,000 troops on the ground and in the 106 locations."

"My God, 900,000 troops? OK, what else do you know?"

"Well, reports are coming in about some countries whose government officials have all been killed. Most of the larger countries have had their entire internal government wiped out. The place is in complete chaos. Mayors, Police Chiefs, doctors, etc. all those that make a city run."

The President sat back and said, "Have all our troops not in the area of influence to back off and keep their distance of the area. Those Commanders inside the occupied area are to stand fast for further word." The Generals got on the phone to their Commanders to pass the word.

"Sir, reports are coming in from Russia." the Secretary of Defense announced. "Russia has also detained some 1,3 million visitors in their country!"

"Jesus Christ, they have the whole ball of wax!" A great silence fell over the entire group.

"Sir, the bad weather is still cause of poor intelligence. We have no imagery that could have picked up any advanced warning or troop movement. Flight delays were posted all over the continent. There was just no reason to suspect that this was in the works. It is not an excuse that I am offering here, but as you know, Sir, the Europeans had entered into this one on their own. This was a long drawn out process to unite them. What a fucked up situation!"

"Are we in contact with Russia?"

"No, Sir, they have not made any attempt to contact us here or even the Ambassador to Russia."

"Could you try to get the President to Russia on the phone?"

"It seems that they are waiting for us to call first." the Army Chief of Staff said. "They did not even give a warning. Their damn troops are massed on the border in numbers we have not seen before."

"Have they moved any closer to Western Europe?" "No, Sir, they are just sitting there."

"Maybe that is for a defensive posture, General. The Secretary said.

"I don't care what you call it Mr. Secretary, we need to do some thing here before they not only have our pants down, but their dicks up our asses without even a kiss."

EMERGENCY SESSION OF THE UN

"Come to order!" Bang, bang, bang. "This place will come to order!"

"The President of the United Nations, his Honor from the country of India, Kimo Bishope!"

The assembly took a seat as the Security Council sat separated from their nation's Ambassador.

"We have awoken to the most disturbing event of our times. In a world that has seen great advances in democracy. We are now drawn into the plight of fear that at this time is spiraling out of control. Even as we assemble here this morning, not all of the information is in. For those of you who are late in the information age, I will bring everyone up to speed."

"This past Friday night and early Saturday morning, the country of Russia deliberately invaded nineteen countries of the European continent. Some 900,000 troops belonging to the Russian Special Forces have taken over at least 106 Major airports throughout Europe. They have also in turn, placed all European visitors in Russia under house arrest at hotels and lodges for the time being. No one has even been allowed to call family members, nor do we really know the true fate of these people. You will be interested that our Russian Delegates are not here this morning."

A member of the UPI asked, "How many people were there?"

"The estimate of those being held in Russia is about 1.3 million."

The entire UN assembly burst with outrage. The President of the assembly called the floor to order.

"We have yet to hear anything from Russia on why this action has taken place. We have reports of many deaths. We don't know everything about those who were killed. But we do have reports that many of the countries under occupation are involved."

The assembly broke out in a rage once more, as the President tried to keep order.

"We would ask that those of you whose country is occupied try to get more information and see what assistance, if any, that we can give to your country. At your best convenience please come and see me at my office here at the UN, thank you."

The US Ambassador to the UN made his way through the crowd. He got to his carport to find his driver.

"Please take me to the airport, I must get to Washington."

His driver said, "Right away, Sir."

The Commandant's Advisors

"Satellite reports are showing that US warships are moving away from ports to open international waters, Sir. No air forces have been detected, though we have learned that all NATO troops are on full alert. No movement outside of bases has been noted. All military training at Graffenwier, Germany Main Training Area has come to a halt, along with those at Hoënfelds, and Wildflicken. Air traffic throughout Europe is nonexistent. The airways are clear. The whole European continent has come to a stand-still." The Commandant stood in front of the tired assembly.

"Now we will find out if those who are at the hands of our forces want to deal with the cards we have given them, or wait for what is behind door number three. Any of you that wish to go back to your offices and work this out with your people, you may leave now. Those that wish to stay here to await for the answer from the United States, you may do so."

The international press looked at each other, and one raised his hand.

"Yes, what is it?"

"Do you mind if we stay to see the outcome?"

"The outcome is as you see it. What you may do is stay to watch how dumb some people are when it comes to how they play the cards that fate has dealt them."

A New Kind of Front

Sergi and his team sat just outside the Bordeaux Airport by the town of Pessac, France. The world was on hold for the people in the region from all the commotion that was happening in Paris and the other major cites. People stayed by the TV or radio for the latest news. Sergi had just returned to his team from the nearby village. He had with him bread, wine and cheese. One farmer even stopped him to see if he would like some smoked pork. It looked good so he brought it along.

"The time is passing without anything really going on." Sergi said. "Our troops are in charge of the airstrip. No flights in or out are taking place."

"I'm glad the rain has stopped." one of his men said. "It is fine that the rain stopped, but we need these clouds to go also."

"But clear skis mean dropping temperatures, Sir." "What, you can't be cold? The military doesn't pay you to be cold."

"Well, I'm cold-hearted, Sir, does that count?"

"Yes it does, and that is a fine character trait of yours, Sergeant. Here, you guys eat this up, try not to leave anything. Soon as we get word, we will get this job over with and then we will be heading back to the airport."

A EUROPE ENGULFED

The Chairman of the Joint Chiefs came back in with some charts to show just what it all means to have Europe down.

"Sir, as we speak, all of Europe has come to a relative stand-still. Air traffic does not exist. Railway traffic is down 91% all over the continent. We have had little help from Mother Nature with the storms that hit all over. It does show some clearing to the south, where a high pressure ridge is beginning to develop. But there is also another low pressure building, which means more rain for the entire area. This makes it hard for our satellites to get aerial shots of the airports to see what type of defense the Russians have built up. Questions are also arising about forces at Russia's borders."

The Air Force Chief of Staff began to talk.

"Since we cannot see from very high, we do have our two SR-71's at NASA we could be using for an over-the-horizon look at some countries. We can't say if Russia had transported any air defense that would put these planes at risk, but we need some kind of view of the land.

Two or three more days of this rain could make a workable solution unworkable. Time is not on our side."

"He is right, Sir, we can't be waiting much longer." the Chairman admitted.

"If we begin to lose face, if our ability to help defend Europe is in doubt, NATO could crumble as the smaller countries opt for a treaty with Russia."

"You know how that goes, Sir. France is barely anyone's friend, and their government could go one way or another." added the Secretary of State. "If that happens you can kiss Germany and the alliance 'good-bye'."

"The Army Chief of Staff mentioned that."

"The years of hate those two countries have for Germany could start a war all by itself. Germany doesn't have the bomb. France does and would use it on their own mother. The same goes with Russia. Germany leaves the worst of what one would call 'a bad taste' in one's mouth for the times Germany invaded both of them in the past."

"Sir, you could have Germany seeing the same thing happening that we do. She could do an all out invasion of France just to get her hands on France's ICBM to defend herself." the Chairman said.

"My God!" The President looked around the room. Everyone sat in silence.

"OK, let's go with the SR-71's, and get some pictures of that damn place. Do you know of anyone whose airspace you would like to cover first?"

"Well, France is a good start." the Air Force Chief of Staff said.

"She has by far has the biggest concentration of Russian troops of any nation. England is another. We need to see just what the outlying lands of England look like."

"Though it is estimated the Russians have two sites locked up, none of Scotland's airports are drawn down on. We could use some of the refuelers from there to keep the birds flying." remarked the Air Force Chief of Staff.

"We need to move those refuelers out to Keflavík, Iceland. The Black Birds will need to be refueled just before their runs. The SR-71's only need to make a fast and short run, in and out."

"Up and down would be the best course of action. Keeping it fresh and without any predicted flight patterns. That is my recommendation." the Chairman of the Joint Chiefs suggested.

"Is there some way to get the French Ambassador the news of our intent?" the President asked. "You know how much they hate Americans in their business."

KENNEDY SPACE CENTER

"Yes, Sir, I understand perfectly. You will have our full cooperation." The director of NASA's flight operations then hung up the phone.

"The shit is bad over there in Europe. The President has no imaging capability of Europe. The rain and cloud cover has hindered the ability of LandSat 6. All we have is our infrared earth imager. It doesn't show up well when everything is being cooled off by the rain. We don't have too much information coming out of there, either."

The flight director said, "We are going to need the two SR-71's. Get the crews ready along with the support crews. We are going to use Kaflavík, Iceland for their home base. The birds are going hunting with little or no rest. I want you to make sure that everyone that is over at DEA knows what is going on."

"Yes, Sir."

The director sat back in his chair, "This is one fucking mess."

The crews were alerted and they began preparations for the flight.

"First, we are going to coordinate flight schedules with the Air force to get the right fuel up there for you guys. Second, we're going to need at least four KC-135 refuelers to keep these boys topped off. Two will join us out of Iceland, and the Air Force will need another two from somewhere. We don't know the whole story, so you will be in-briefed on the plans of engagement while you are en route to the target area." The two flight crews sat as their teams helped with the pressurized suits and support gear.

"It is going to be a long flight. You are not going to have much time for sleep in the next few days, so we advise that you use the T-pac vapor-induced stimulants as you get ready for your long run. I don't know what more to tell you guys, but this is a mess. The weather over there is as bad as you will ever encounter. Be safe and we will see you all very soon. Good luck."

The two crews stood up and grabbed their support gear. They walked out of the hanger into the beautiful early Florida morning. The skies were as blue as you could ever want a sky to be.

The two SR-71's were sitting side by side as the ground crews were finishing up on the final preparations for flight. Two C-130's were being loaded with the support gear the ground crews were going to need in support of the Black Birds. Cameras and film were checked from front to the rear of these two monsters. Twenty-four cameras and a multitude of in-flight autochange lens were checked. They were ready and willing to go.

The SR-71's were on loan from the Air Force just after they were planned to be mothballed. NASA loved to use them for the high altitude long-range training flights for the astronaut program. They were also used for the DEA movement against those who would use open waters between South America and the islands of the Florida Keys.

WASHINGTON

"Sir, we were unable to reach the Russian President."

"Shit, that is not supposed to happen! Are you still trying?"

"Yes, Sir, as we speak. We did get a line into our Ambassador over there. He is waiting on the line for you, Sir."

"Put him on COM."

"Dave, how are you doing?"

"Not bad, Sir, things here are a little strange, but for the most part things are going along as normal." "Do you know what is going on?"

"Well, Sir, I do know that Russia had launched troops into many countries of Europe. Other than that, not much. It seems that we have had the rug pulled out from under us."

"Well, I guess we can throw that information treaty out the door."

"I was going to say the same thing, Sir." "Have you talked to any of your counterparts?" "Well, a short time ago I was invited to the Russian Ambassador's house for talks about all of this."

"We need to get word to the Russian President that we have been trying to reach him."

"Well, the President was taken by surprise by all of this."

"What do you mean?"

"It seems that the Prime Minister and one of the high ranking Commandants have thrown this into his lap."

"Do you know the name of the Commandant?"

"Sir, it is Gladimir Klakov, the new leader of the special forces throughout Russia, and as you know already, he is the CEO of 1 of Russia's largest Petro Company Rosneft.

"OK, wait one, Dave."

"I want everything there is to know about this man. I mean everything!" Some of the President's aids jumped up and said, "Right away, Sir!"

"Dave, you get as much information as possible. Then call me direct, we need to know more than we know now, which is absolutely nothing!" "Sir, I won't let you down! Good-bye."

BELGIUM

Bob was laying there in bed with Stella sleeping on his chest. He was watching the news that was going frantic over the killings of so many dignitaries throughout Belgium. He was thinking, "Just how many of those sorry bastards were killed? What makes you a dignitary? The people are just like you. But you sit in your big house, having parties and eating the finest food on earth. That is what you get for running for office." Bob wasn't aware that he spoke aloud.

Stella woke up and said, "What are you talking about? Are we going to have lunch brought up here? It has been forever since I have had anything brought to me in bed."

"Is that right? You know that it is already afternoon?"

"But I want to eat in bed."

"Well, my sweet, you shall have the finest lunch this place can offer. Stella sat up holding the pillow and smiling. She turned over and started to kiss Bob on the back as he was ordering the food.

"Are you glad that I came over?"

He looked at her, "You bet I am! You've made me forget I was an old man!"

"Well, you sure don't move like an old man."

"Well, I guess I was blessed with a gift."

"I'll say you have a gift!" she said. "What are we going to do today? The shops don't open all day on Saturday. Can't we just stay here in bed?"

Bob got up and said that he had to go and see some people.

"You know, I do have a job to do, here. But I will tell you something. Things haven't been so great for me at home. I was offered a job here, and I think I might take it."

Stella looked at him. "Well, I'm not here for work. My dad sent me here to get out of his hair."

"So, how long can you stay?"

"I don't know, I guess as long as I would like." "Well, if things work out, I'm going to look for a place to live. You can always stay with me, I mean, until you get tired or I get too old."

"Well, you can grow old." then she pulled him over to her.

WASHINGTON

The US Ambassador to the UN arrived at the White House. The Secretary of State met him at the door.

"We have a lot of work to do. I don't know how much time we have to get things in place."

"What do we know so far?" They both walked to the elevator and stepped in, and it took them down and stopped at the third level. As they got out both showed the security officer their passes, then walked over to the War Room.

"OK, people, what do you know about the Commandant?"

"Sir, he has belonged to a very secret military outfit for years. Not too much is known of him after the Great War. It seemed like he walked off the face of the earth some time ago and reappeared when he wanted to. He's attended Oxford University. Has a Ph.D. in Engineering and a Masters in Aviation. He has been the CEO of Rosneft 1 of Russia's largest Petro companies for the past six years. He speaks fluent English and seven other languages. He is a big man; doesn't smoke or drink. He loves a cup of tea. It was he who introduced the concept of 'One Europe'. He also made European Business Man of the Year this past summer. He is a very outspoken man of the former USSR and the old party, and he loves Mother Russia."

"What in the hell are we going to have to name this guy, Gladimir the Great?" the Army Chief of Staff's voice sounded as he entered the room.

"Let's keep focused on this, gentlemen. The birds are up and both are on their way to Iceland. They should be there in four or five hours. They have to slow down to refuel, but they will get there, Sir."

"We have the support crew airborn, but they won't get there for eight more hours."

"Can we go without them?"

"Well, Sir, we do like to go over every plane that flies overseas."

"That is not what I asked you! Can we go the distance and get some fly-over shots?"

"Yes, Sir, we can do it."

"Great! Now people, I don't want to seem like I've got a stick up my ass, but it feels like I do!"

"One moment, Sir" the Secretary of State took center stage. "Everyone throughout Europe has been told to stay home. Now this is going to break the bank. All industries are shut down for the time being. There has been no trade throughout Europe to bring in fresh vegetables, or even milk for more than a few days. To continue will have a devastating effect. Though the US has a GNP that towers over Europe as a whole, we will feel the shit in our boots, too. We still have a great trade deficit. It is going to play hell here at home tomorrow. Shit has never hit the fan like this before, and it will only get worse until things get back on track."

"What are we to do about this?"

"Sir!" one of the top advisors on the economy said. "We are going to have to put a freeze on some of parts of our own economy. It is really going to put a damper on the over-all growth of our own jobs and businesses. It is already going to drop everything out Tokyo's ass. This is not the way we need to start the new millenium. This is going to fuck up more shit than that Y2K scare of a decade ago, not to mention how the WTC disaster laid waste to the market in 2001. It would be to our better interest that we close our markets this Monday, and keep it closed until further notice."

Everyone agreed that it would be the best course of action at this juncture in time.

"Sir, he has planned this out to the "T". He knows that the economy of the world can not take this kind of pounding. He knows that countries that have very little defense will heed, or go hungry. NATO is in extreme danger at this time. The world is ticking like an old grandfather clock. When that bell strikes twelve, everyone turns into a pumpkin, and there is no 'Prince with a glass slipper' to come and make it all better."

Moscow

"Major, have you decided what you would like for dinner?"

"Sir, I was thinking about having a nice rabbit."

"Now that sounds good! Do you know of a place that can make us up one and have it delivered here?" "Sir, I will have us two here in thirty minutes. Would you like anything else with that?"

"Let's have some oven-baked potatoes with that."

"Now you are talking!" The Major got up and had one of his orderlies go out to retrieve them.

"Those of you that wish to stay, this is no longer the delivery house. Go get yourself something to eat, you are not going to miss anything." the Commandant said.

"Can we eat it here, Sir?"

"I said that you can cover the story, now don't be a pain in my ass!" he grumbled.

The Flight to Keflevíc

The Air Force had to coordinate with the flights of the SR-71's coming up from Florida. A series of in-flight refueling were needed to get the planes over to Iceland, and then onto the mission. Two KC-135 refueler were flying just outside the national waters of Newfoundland. An AWAC's jet was just on the outskirts of the SR-71's flight path, and on its way over for the hook up with their trip to Iceland. They monitored their flights to the refueler.

"This is Starlight, Star Bright, come in, Long-and-Tall."

"Hey guys, this is Long-and-Tall, you sure did get here in a hurry, do you know how much you would like to drink?"

"How much you got?"

"I've got all you can handle."

"Well, give it up. We are thirsty.

"Just head to 336. We will fix you right up."

"Starlight, Star Bright, this is Big Daddy, we are going to play a good game of charades. We will give you a picture and you tell us what it looks like."

"Sounds like great fun, Big Daddy, as soon as we get caught up with the Long-and-Tall one, we'll come out and play."

"OK, guys, see you in a little bit. Big Daddy out."

The SR-71's each took on their share and were fueled and ready to play in no time. They danced above the clouds that covered the horizon in the distance. With the sun setting behind them, they knew the cold of night will have to be made friends of, so they turned slowly eastward and began their descent.

"OK, Big Daddy, we are ready to go sonic."

"Drop your ceiling down to three hundred feet. You boys may feel like surfing, but please leave that up to those boys out there in Hawaii."

"Aren't you referring to hydro-planes? Those bad boys could throw up one hell of a rooster tail!" "Well, just don't go swimming with bowlegged women."

"That's a roger!"

WASHINGTON

The Air Force Chief of Staff informed the President and his committee on the Black Birds' present position.

"Sir, the SR-71's have been refueled and are heading for Iceland, for a little game of peek-a-boo. Then after that they will be on their way to France and the Brittany area as they swing out on a loop south to northern Spain. They will come back up the coast of France with a "bump-and-run' motion. We should get some good pictures."

"When is this all going to take place?" the President asked.

"They have another two hours before arriving at Iceland. That will make it around 14:00 EST, then six to ten hours after that for targeting and logistics. They should be hitting the northern coast of France some where around 18:30 EST. They can do a SATLINK and send us pictures as soon as they drop and pop them. We're looking around the area of 23:30 EST Saturday evening as they make their run back to Iceland."

"Sounds like the best thing to do. Keep in touch, General."

"Yes, Sir."

MOSCOW

"Though things are going quite smooth, we need to make a little noise. Has the President the time to call his counterpart in the US?"

The Major walked into the President's office.

"The Commandant wishes to have a word with you, Sir."

The President said, "Yes, of course, send him in." Major Kizir came out of the office and nodded his head.

Knock, knock, knock, "Sir, are you busy?"

"No Gladimir, please come in, and sit down." The Commandant turned and signaled to the Major. "Get the Prime Minister."

"Sir, I believe it is time to call the United States and set them straight on what has happened. All they are doing is watching the CNN network, and it is not telling everything we have done."

"Gladimir, though you hit me with this out of the blue, I want to say after looking over the pro's verses con's of this action you have done what no other had the mettle to do. This was a chance of a lifetime to get Russia, and her people the hold and place in this world we were longing for."

"Yes, Sir, we are on the top of the food chain. There is no need for us to be bottled fed from other countries. We have all our own resources and the manpower to build anything, as well as the will to see it through. Other countries are afraid to imagine their place in the world. We created an image for ourselves as one of the true superpowers. Now this statement stands as testimony to our greatness. We need not take second seat to anyone, anymore."

The President smiled, and nodded his approval. He reached over and picked up the international Presidential phone. The switch operator connected him to the United States.

WASHINGTON

The phone buzzed and all that were in the room turned to see.

Buzz, buzz!

"Mr. President, would you like me to get that?" "No, Mr. Secretary, that will not be necessary." Everyone looked as the President answered the phone.

"We have come to a juncture in the road to our self development, and found it necessary to set things straight over here, before some get the idea that there is some kind of 'New World order'. The only thing that is truly new is each day. Someone may invent something new today, but by tomorrow it will be obsolete."

"What are the intentions of this action?"

"There are no intentions at all. It is just the way it is. We control what is in the best interest of Russia. We will do as we feel necessary for our national security."

"What in the hell does this move have to do with national security?"

"Come now, Mr. President, what gives you the right to talk about things that have nothing to do with you? We are separated from each other by thousands of miles of water. I would understand your type of questioning if we were your neighbor, like Canada."

"There are treaties that bind you to the international law of the sovereignty of nations. They are not some puppets on a string that you pull whenever you want!"

"Now what is this for dialog? We need not go there, just because you have, in time, given back all the land that you have taken over the years. America wasn't displaying her greatness by leaving the Philippines, after Spain lost her to your Spanish-American war. It was just costing you too much money to keep that slum pit running! The same idiot made the plans for the turnover of your Panama Canal. What an asshole move, if I have ever seen one!"

"But you…"

But what? It is still fresh the smell of death from the disagreement between Russia and Ukraine. Many Russian soldiers died when your country and NATO sent Billions upon Billions of arms and money to help that so called country that you know was ours before the Great War.

But your country killed civilians by the thousands. Non combatants.

Oh so you are the so called policemen of the world. You were the route cause of those deaths. All your prior Government care about was the money for arms sales and kick backs to those who vote. Pay them voters first and pocket the rest.

That is not the same.

"Now, now, now, it is not polite to interrupt when I am talking."

The Russian President went on about all the world's problems that the US felt was in her best interest to stick her nose in.

"You Americans don't do anything without getting something in return."

"There are many ways the US helps out their friends replied the US President. The US has done many great things for the development of the world we all live in!" The US President went on to mention the help that was given to Russia since WW II, which has been condemned repeatedly.

Please Mr President, that was yesterday, a time long past. You got what you wanted out of that shit show.

The US President continued, "But let me get to this problem that we face at this moment. Is there some neutral place we could have a meeting to resolve this? Talking on the phone is no way for us to share each other's feelings on the matter."

"We should discuss this at a later time, a meeting anytime soon would not be in our better interest." The Russian President said his good byes, and hung up. "Shit, the bastard hung up!"

"What is the matter, Mr. President?"

"There will be talks later on the issues. Right now we must play a sitting game. We need to get a hold of every one of our NATO partners, and try to hold this alliance together at all costs. We are just going to have to grit our teeth and bear it."

"We still don't know everything there is to know."

The Secretary of State mentioned. The flyover should give us some kind of idea of the troops strength. If they do hold as many airports that are indicated and if they are ready to mobilize their total troop force massed on the border, well, do I need to say more?"

The President just looked over at the Secretary of Defense.

THE BLACK BIRDS

"The SR-71's should be almost finished with the Iceland training." the Air Force Chief of Staff opened. "We have also pulled a JSTAR from the Saudi forces. We don't want to get too much. Sources show that the main part of their ground troops is on hold, but we don't want them to match our air born forces. As long as they know that our aircraft are not flying in large numbers, then they may not feel the need to match them plane for plane. Because they have not committed their air power to this action, this may be a signal that there may be some way out of this."

The United Nations

Back at the UN, the assembly has re-adjourned for an update of the movement of Russian troops throughout Europe. The countries that have occupation troops in them have handed in the reports of the massacres that have taken place. On national TV the President of the UN spoke.

"We are all at a great loss for words over the many deaths that have taken place throughout Europe. Many of our friends have been taken from us, not to mention the families and loved ones. Some 101,040 law makers, delegates, doctors, police officers, and many of those whose lives were to make our society run have been killed by reasons known only to the forces that now control many large areas of nineteen countries of Europe."

The assembly gave a show of anger as the President tried to calm the fears of those who are in the countries of occupation.

"For well more then half a century, we have stood together on many fronts. We as the United Nations have had our share of troubles on the horizon. Time has come to heal these scars. Now as we stand on the threshold of one of man's greatest hardships, we must re-ignite the fire that shows those that are in peril, that we will be their light. We will never go dim in the midst of what may seem to be darkness. We must show that those that feel the need to throw their will upon another will never stand, as long as we, THE WORLD, stands as one. I have here, from the Security Council, the permission to assemble the UN international troop reserve. For the first time in history, we are calling upon the troops of the nations that support the UN, asking them to lend the world the men and machines of their countries. We are asking no less than the vast war reserve of the world. This show of force, in a united front, will be the backbone of our attempt to rid the world of tyranny."

WASHINGTON

"Well, that is one hell of a force. He didn't say which country will lead that international force, did he now?"

"There is still so much that is needed. We'll need to see those photo's as soon as they are available."

The President left the War Room to get coffee in the kitchen.

"Would you like for me to get that for you, Sir?"

"No, I need a change of scenery." The President left the room. Some of the members of the Joint Chiefs were still working on the situation, as the broadcast from the UN had ended and all the news about the deaths, along with troops being called, made the work that they were doing a little bit more stretched out.

"I sure hope that the Russians were listening to that. It just might get them thinking of something different."

"If anything, it may give us a little time to draw up some kind of contingency plan."

"We still have close to 450,000 troops in and around Europe. We just have the problem of having GBS (Global Broadcast System) being gown in that part of the world. Naval Air Station Sigonella, Sicily is out of commission. With Russian troops there in Catania, and Palermo, it is going to be hard to start up anything in that region. Diego Garcia is much too far east. The cuts that we have taken over the years in defense are just that, cuts."

"I'll say, along with a lot of bruises. We gave up so much for what the President feels is 'savings', yet no one wanted to come to the conclusion that something like this could happen."

"Well, as the saying goes in the military, 'we never get kissed before we get screwed'."

"The President's financial team had just finished the report on the short term impact that the closing of Europe will do to the US economy, and it don't look too good for us."

"Yea, we are going to take a beating on this. Japan closed last night with an almost 500 point loss. Now that is a killer, not to mention the European markets being closed for who knows how long. We must put a freeze on all overseas shipments of American goods traveling to Europe. This is going to be a real mess before too long."

THE SR-71'S ARRIVE

"Hey, Big Daddy, we are ready for that game of tag that you promised us." Starlight hailed to the AWACS that accompanied the mission.

"Do you guys need a time out before heading into a new game?" Big Daddy responded.

"No, this thing is red hot and ready to play. We will be fine, do you have anyone else that wants to join in a good game?"

"We sure do, one moment Starlight, Star Bright." Big Daddy cut comms to take a flash message.

"Star Bright, we are going to be playing for some time now. Mom said that you should have the second half of this game. She wants you to come home for now."

"Roger, Big Daddy, tell Mom that I'll be home for supper."

"That is an affirm. See you later Starlight, and good hunting."

"Thank you, Star Bright, we will set the playing field rules so you can come right in when you're ready. See ya soon."

Star Bright peeled off for the runway of Keflavík, Iceland with a flame of fire lighting up the sky. It would be an hour or so before she would land and await the ground crew that was still three hours off from arriving there themselves.

"With just one of you up here at any given time, we can cover things around the clock until we get the break in the cloud cover. We really need those views from the Landsat to show us the whole picture." Big Daddy added.

"Alright now, let's get going here. This is Big Daddy, we have you red hot and ready for that game, Starlight, so let's introduce you to the other members of the game. We will have you teamed up with Bloodhound on this round. They can tell you a bit of the rules as play goes along."

"Sounds like fun is just around the corner."

"Hey, Starlight, this is Bloodhound. Big Daddy has informed us that they might want to head under the three hundred foot ceiling for the first round. We don't know if they will track you or not. If they have control of all airports in the area, at that altitude they will barely know that you are there. So you are really going to have to burn up the sky in your run for the gold." the JSTAR advised.

"That is a roger, Big Daddy. Dropping now to three hundred feet."

"Alright here we go, this is Bloodhound we welcome you to the show."

"Outstanding, Bloodhound, glad you can play." The SR-71 dropped rapidly, then leveled off just below three hundred feet, "We are ready to burn."

"You are clear for the lighting ceremony, Starlight." The SR-71 kicked up on the throttle up and the afterburner was alive. Like a bright blue and yellow spear, the flame grew some two hundred feet long. She ran through a few right and left turns as she prepared to make her run. She slowed once more and leveled off.

"This is Big Daddy, Starlight, you are ready for throttle up. The show is all yours, Bloodhound. "That is a roger. Starlight, it is all on you, baby."

The JSTAR took over the mission from the AWACs.

"We copy that."

The pilot pushed forward on the controls and the after burners opened up wide. The blue and yellow flame came roaring out of the twin engines. It looked like it wanted to suck the horizon right in there with them. She dipped to the coast of France and started the run south.

"Starlight, we will have you heading south at heading 7745. If you keep the coast in your left window, follow it down and around, you may start filming any time you'd like. NASA had just installed a new filming concept called Transmetric time photography that the pilot can speed up the framework as the speed of the aircraft increases. This gives it the advantage of almost still, or slow motion shot. With the new lens and the whole works they will bring out an almost perfect 3D image of the entire area at any altitude."

"That is a roger, Bloodhound."

"Starlight, this is Big Daddy, you have no other aircraft in your vector."

"That sounds good; starting the picture show. We'll call this 'Vacationing the Bay of Biscay'."

They marked that the point of entry was 48 degrees latitude, 4 degrees longitude west of Greenwich. Just over the French city of Quimper, heading southeast along the coast.

"We just passed Lorient, and saw lights all along the coast."

Big Daddy was flying high and had everyone in view.

"Bloodhound, how is the game going so far?"

"Well, it looks like it is still our move, and we have no new players as of yet."

"That is a roger, Bloodhound."

"We are still burning and turning." answered Starlight.

"We see you, Starlight. You are on fire, keep to that heading. We have indications of heavy rainfall ESE in 21 minutes."

"Thank you, Big Daddy, wait until you see this!" said Starlight. "It'll all turn to steam once we hit it."

"We show that you are still clear of all traffic. Bloodhound, what do you see?"

"There is little if no surface movement. We have no return on radar tracking. No locks are present at this time."

"That is a roger."

"We are starting our move into the rain, Bloodhound."

"That is a roger, Starlight, we see your trail."

The SR-71 was in and out of the heavy rain in just seconds. The friction caused a large clap of thunder with lighting striking the ground below as she passed through. It left a twenty-four mile stretch of steam, like a tubular cloud behind her.

"Boy Starlight, that was a pretty sight on our screen, like a cold slap in the face."

"We didn't feel a thing, and we are as hot as ever."

"Ok Bloodhound, you can turn left out and return to heading 4144, Starlight is just about ready for your return run."

"That is a copy. We are going to need room for movement."

"That is a roger. You're going to be in need of refueling soon." said Big Daddy.

"Well, where can a nice guy like me find a good gal to have a tall one with?" Starlight began to move out over the open sea.

"Ok, Starlight. I have a tall drink standing by for you. Turn to heading 398 left. Slow and stay on that heading. You will find her to quench that thirst."

"Hey, there, Bloodhound, are you looking to get juiced up too?"

"Well, I can get some now, or wait until after the run and get it before Mom calls everyone home."

"Well, we might as well kill the time and get you full too. Head to 511, you should see the Long and Tall one there. I will inform her that you will need a good mixed drink."

"That is a roger, Big Daddy, see you in a bit." They headed off toward the C-135 refueler.

Brussels

Bob took his shaky-legged self to the shower as Stella answered the room service. She paid the waiter and ran to the shower and jumped in with Bob.

"Can you give me a ride to my hotel before you go to work?"

Bob said "Sure. Is the food here?"

"Yea, it is in the heating pans staying warm for us." They both finished with the shower and sat down for something to eat.

"Are you going to be gone for very long?"

Bob looked at her and said, "I don't know, maybe."

"What are you going to be doing? I'll change and do something. How can I reach you later, if you want to go do something?"

"Stella, right now I can't answer those things because I don't know what it is I must do."

"Well, that is not a very good way to work. I hope that you won't be doing this all the time."

"Maybe at first, but as I said the job is new. I don't know my schedule yet. Bob replied.

"Well, just leave a message at the desk for me. Stella said with a ho hum. I'll try to keep myself busy."

"Ok, are you just about ready?"

"Do we have time for… Bob turned and just smiled.

"Come on, Stella, you are like a machine!"

They grabbed their coats and entered the elevator.

Moscow

After dinner the Commandant and his aid, Major Kizir, went to bed. A small army of tacticians had been assembled to keep track of the progress and to inform the Commandant of any new events. It had been some time since either of them had a good night's sleep; they were out as soon as they hit the bed. All units were checking in with all airports being secured. The troops on the border were still on full alert and holding the ground that they paid for.

WASHINGTON

The President came back into the War Room, and asked if anything had changed.

"No, Sir, it would be late into the night in Russia, and their troops are still massed at the border. The fly-by of our SR-71's is still taking place at this very moment. The weather over much of the European continent is still rainy. There are some places where the rain has turned to snow. As we see the colder weather move in, there should be some break in the cloud cover. Imagery from space is still unclear. Only infrared pictures show up, and that is not much to go on."

"How long will it take us to get any kind of pictures from the SR-71's?"

"We should have them within the next few hours. We understand that one of the SR-71's is flying the routes near France, while the other has landed at Keflavík and is being readied to take the other's place as soon as her run is up."

"Do we have support people there in Iceland yet?"

"Sir, they should be arriving any moment now."

"Good, that sounds good to me."

STARLIGHT'S RUN

"Ok, boys, it looks like we are back in the race. Ready to kick a little ass up here in the sky?"

"You bet!" Bloodhound said.

"Hey, Big Daddy, we are red hot and ready."

"Sounds good, Starlight. OK, we need you to head around to latitude 42 degrees, and longitude 4 degrees west of Greenwich. That should take you just over the Northern tip of Spain, onward to the West Coast of France. Once you're on your way we need to have you fly an in-and-out pattern up the coastline. Now we don't think you should draw fire if there is any, but we need to get a better look at the outlying airports that might be captured. You all be careful."

"Roger, Big Daddy, do we still have Bloodhound to look out for us that far inland?"

"You sure do, and we will be there every step of the way."

"OK people, after this we can go get us a cold one. Let's hit it Starlight."

"Roger, we're making the move now. You ready, partner?"

The Pilot looked over to his Copilot as they started their run.

The SR-71 dropped down into the airspace of Spain and headed northeast back up the coast of France.

There they started their first turns that took them right over San Sebastain, Spain and into the French countryside. They passed over Bayonne and Dax that lay on the Adour River. Then they turned left and headed to Bordeaux.

"Flying so close to the ground at that speed should scare the hell out of any Russian down there!"

"That is a roger!" Big Daddy said.

"Your vector is still clear, Starlight. You should be coming up on Bordeaux."

"Yea, we see it in the distance, Bloodhound. Will make it in 36 seconds. Mark."

Sergi stood up as he heard the jet in the distance.

"That is no commercial flight, that is a military jet."

Roooooooooaaaaaaaarrrrr! It flew almost right over head.

"It has to be a recon jet. Damn, is that thing low. It will fly right over the airport."

"OK, Big Daddy we are heading back to the coast." Beep, beep, beep! The screen on Bloodhound's radar started to track an object.

"Turn left, Starlight, we have a missile fired from the airport. It is not locked on. Must be something track launched."

Starlight turned out fast and rolled.

"We have it marked, there!" said Big Daddy. Bloodhound pinpointed the location it was fired from.

"No worries, there, Starlight, that thing never made supersonic speed. Like a kid with a slingshot trying to knock down a 747."

The smoke cleared from around the BMP as some men came running up to see what had happened.

"What in the hell are you doing, you smart-ass? We don't have the ammo to replace those like we would at home."

"I just wanted to see it if I could make a lucky shot."

"That jet was here and gone before you had time to shit!"

"Hey, if I would have hit the damn thing you would have made me a war hero. Now I'm just an asshole."

"Well, no shit, where do you think that round landed, somewhere out there?!"

"Well, then they well see we mean business."

"They already see that we mean business! Don't fire any more rockets."

The gunner of the BMP just sat there talking to himself. "At least the round hit something."

"OK, Starlight, let's get back on course. We have the number of that dumb-ass! You were not even close to the action."

"Shit, there goes our Combat Service ribbon. Ok, Big Daddy, here we go again. Turning right and dropping to 290 ft."

"This next run should take you over the cities of La Rochelle and Niort. We need not get you too deep into France."

"That sounds good to me."

"So far there has been no triple-R flack from the target areas. All ground movement is minimal."

The plane just went on taking pictures as it flew over the area. They passed over Niort and took a big turn left to open water.

"Well, the Russians should know by now that we were in their panties. It is nice to have a little foreplay, now that we are introduced to each other."

"OK, boys, that looks good to me. Head up the coast then make one last cut over the countryside. We will send you over Lorient, then to Brest and over the English Channel and then home for soup."

"That will be a pleasure ride, boys. Big Daddy, I am starting the run and I am on fire!"

"You burn it up, boys, let them know that you are there!"

The SR-71 made the last run over the French countryside and then over the channel. She pointed west to the thin light of the sun on the horizon.

"All right, people, that is a wrap for the day. Good work, Bloodhound."

"Thank you, thank you, we will see you all at Mom's place. The time is close to 2349 EST. Mark."

"That is a big roger. Big Daddy has your backside, Starlight; you did a great job."

"Hey, we were just glad to get out of Florida. All that sunshine and women in thongs on the beach, shit it was killing us."

"Well, I hope you had someone pack you something for the cold, because that is where you are going."

"Well, when we get there we'll have the place on fire for you Big Daddy. See you soon!" and the SR-71 throttled up and in a mass off flame she was out of sight and burning it up.

"Sir, we have just been given word that the first flight of the SR-71 recon is over, and had only one little incident. Someone from the Bordeaux airport fired a small missile at the jet. It wasn't even close. We had a JSTAR help with the tracking, and it got the information on the type of rocket. A small wire-guided missile from a small track type vehicle, maybe a BMP. They probably shot it as the jet made its way over the position. The pictures should show everything. The rocket was just a fluke shot."

"But it is evidence that they do have some kind of fire power that could be antitank capable."

"That is true, Sir." the Army Chief of Staff concluded.

"Well, I hope these flights will give us a bit more info on the place. We still need to have better communications with their top people to see if we can resolve this."

MOSCOW

The Commandant was laying in his bed looking at the ceiling, thinking of the new Russian Order that now seems very much in control of the continent. Major Kizir was getting dressed, and asked if the Commandant needed to take a hot bath.

"No, I will just take a fast shower, but thank you, Major, for the thought. When we get the rest of this operation under way, you and I are going to a health spa for a week. But first we need to concentrate on dissolving NATO and the new alliance that will mark the true start of this millenium."

"I will have breakfast sent over for us, Sir."

"That sounds good, could you get me a cup of tea?" "Right away, Sir."

Major Kizir left the room and the Commandant got up and took a long hot shower.

As the Commandant came out from his quarters he walked over to the table that the Major had prepared for breakfast.

"I thought that a ham and cheese omelet with hash brown potatoes and pepper sauce would be right this morning."

"It looks good." The Commandant sat down.

The Major began reading the morning reports as the Commandant listened with interest. Many reports were coming in from all over Europe.

"The airports have been secured and were faced with very little problems other than some small groups of protesters. Most of the local police seem to have taken care of those problems for us. We have reached the second stage of our build up of supplies for a possible third wave movement. The troops on the border are ready, and the Commanders have received their posture orders in the event that they are needed to reinforce all areas throughout Europe."

The Commandant was pleased with the way things were moving forward. Many of the Commanders from the front were heading in for a meeting with the Commandant.

"We will be having our meeting in the President's office. It shouldn't be more than one or two hours. Please keep me informed on any developments."

He got up from the table and wiped his mouth. The Commandant then winked at the Major, then entered the room and his Commanders followed. Major Kizir sat at his console and helped take in the day's flash traffic.

KEFLAVÍK, ICELAND

"Hey, Mom, are you up?" Starlight radioed. "That's right, baby, we are looking forward to you getting your ass home. Is everything alright?"

"Yea, we are just in need of a cold one, that's all."

"Well, we have everything you need. The other kids are right behind me. They said that they will give you a call as soon as they can."

"Are the new kids ready to play?"

"Soon as you get home they'll be ready."

"That's a roger, this is Starlight, see you in a few." The lights of Keflavík were just over the horizon.

The dark water below passed so quickly that the reflection of the moon that could shine its way through the clouds gave the illusion that the earth was winking at them. It would be nice to get out of the cramped cockpit and walk around a bit. They were picking up the Keflavík weather forecast that was being sent out.

"Shit, it is cold, cold, cold, down there."

"Well, the next time that you think that the job we are doing in Florida sucks, you can always transfer to this place."

"No, thank you, brother!"

They turned to line up with the runway and started their decent to land.

MOSCOW

The meeting was soon over and the Commanders were coming out of the room, one at a time. The Commandant seemed to be pleased with the reports that he had received from his officers. He was ready to convey the next steps of the operations, when the Major walked over to him with a new development. Major Kizir handed him the report.

"Oh, the US wants to see what we Bad Russians have been doing?"

"Sir, it was the outer coast of France that had the fly over. They may have seen three or four airports in that run. We still don't know what type of plane it was. It was only off the deck some 300 to 400 hundred feet. Radar clocked it at more then 2400 mph. She was really burning up the sky."

"It sounds like a SR-71."

"I thought that the US put them out of service."

"Well, Major, just like us, not all that we say, we do."

"But, Sir, at that speed, that altitude, would it be possible to film?"

"I don't know, Major. If they got good shots, then good for them. We have the airfields, and the country to boot. They can play with all the pictures that they want. The only one true picture that will be in the history books will show the new boarders of Europe."

"We need to start our focus on negotiations. What do our neighbors want?"

"The US will want to be in on those new negotiations."

"That is just too bad! This is Europe! Fuck 'em! We are not here to see what will make our friends in the US happy. We are here to see what will make Russia happy. You will see that they do not dictate to us, we just tell them how it is going to be, and they do not have to like it. I am sick and tired of the outside always sticking their nose into the business of others. They do not live here! This is our land, and these are our people. Once they learn that the better off they will be."

WASHINGTON

"Mr. President, would you like to get some sleep before we start on the photos that are coming in from the first series of flights?

"Well, do we have another flight starting soon?"

"Yes, Sir, they are planning to get going in just a few."

"Well, let's take a fast look to see what we have here, then I will leave this up to your people to get a full assessment of the photos."

The Chairman of the Joint Chiefs said, "No problem."

"Let's see… so far, things are as they were. No advances are being made to have more troops reinforce the locations that are presently under the occupation?"

"No, Sir, there is little if no movement. We will be getting a break in the clouds, and that will give us a short time to look down on some parts of the playing field. But right now we are going to use the SR-71's at this point until we can get something better."

"Well, I will be at the White House if there are any new developments. You have the room, General. Keep me informed of the flight. I don't want them too far inland at that altitude. They are too valuable to be shot down. We don't need to lose one of these birds to those people."

"Yes, Sir."

"Well, good night to all of you. Keep up the good work."

BORDEAUX, FRANCE

Sergi and his team were waking up one by one. He had mentioned that if some of his guys would like to go into the small village to shower up that they could.

"But you go two at a time. Get what you have to get done without all the bullshit that goes along with it. We still have a lot to do, and I need you all right here when it is time."

"Would you like us to bring back anything?"

"Don't be making your presence known too much, do not be speaking Russian there to each other. Either you speak French or English. I would prefer you to say as little as possible, and get your asses back here."

"This may be your last opportunity to get away until we pack up for the airport."

They agreed, and took off, two at a time.

KEFLAVÍK, ICELAND

The NASA pilots were suited up and ready to go as soon as the returning aircrew had finished debriefing them. A new AWACS, code named "Peek-a-Boo" and another JSTARS, code named "Hollywood" were assigned to Star Bright's mission.

"You guys are going to have some fun. This sure as hell beats those little runs we do back home playing around for the DEA."

"But work is work, and we all have a duty to do."

"What in the hell are you talking about?" as they threw several handfuls of napkins at the head pilot.

"No, you guys be safe up there. It will be well into nighttime again as you start your last run. The cloud cover varies from place to place, but there are some breaks in the ceiling that you are going to be heading into. Good luck boys, burn it up!"

The crew left the briefing and headed out to the Black Bird. The ground crew stood ready as the men climbed into the SR-71 and went through the checklist. The engines came roaring to life. The crew saluted and gave the thumbs up as the aircraft tested its engines with a mighty burst, then they turned onto the runway.

"This is Star Bright, we are ready and red hot."

"Roger, Star Bright, you have been cleared to go. All other flights are standing by for your assistance."

The crew acknowledged the tower and pushed the throttle forward. The flames came blasting out from behind, and the sleek black plane raced down the runway and up into the sky.

"This is Star Bright, we are going supersonic in four mikes."

"That is a roger, Star Bright. Climb to an altitude of 47,000 feet and turn right to heading 4474 and meet up with Peek-a-Boo and Hollywood on your way. This is Keflavík, out."

"We will see you on the return, Mom."

The plane turned right and hit super sonic speed then it was gone from radar.

"Peek-a-Boo, this is Star Bright, are you out there?"

"We sure are, Star Bright. We have Hollywood coming up in just a short. Let's go through the game plan for today's run. Yesterday you were filled in on the previous flight. The cloud cover has given us a little bit more sky to work with. But then that makes what we do a little more visible. They might be waiting for us, but we don't think that they will bring fire to you. It still has to be done as if you are flying into the most hostile environment."

"We copy that, Peek-a-Boo. We have flares ready for deployment."

"Hey, where is the party? What's the game today. fellas?" radioed the new AWACS.

"Well, how are you doing there, Hollywood? Glad you could make it."

"Oh, I wouldn't miss this for all the money the Air Force is paying me."

"Well, shit, if it is that good, you can come to NASA and spend some of that on us."

"Shit, you guys get to ride in the Lamborghini of the Air Force. I've got this big duck-looking thing.". "Yea, but they don't allow eating in this car."

"I guess they don't like all the crumbs you guys at NASA leave."

"You've got that right."

"All right, fellas, we need to put in a few training rounds before we head off into the great wide unknown. We are going in just before 1100 EST, and the rain is still falling over most of the continent. With the daylight, we have an opportunity to get a different view, along with some good shots. We really need to keep our heads screwed on tight. They know that we were there once, and we might be coming back for some more. So we need to get some good training runs going, before moving towards the targets."

Everyone rogered up as the training program was set for the crews and listed for the day's flight.

Run after run, the SR-71 made its move. The job would be harder because of the daylight. The AWAC's plane was well over the clouds. No rain was in its forecast, just sunny skies above and rolling clouds below.

It wasn't really the same for the J-STARS, it had very high clouds that it had to negotiate, some spiked 50,000 feet or better.

Soon the runs were complete, and all felt comfortable with the day's business. AWAC's and J-STARS went southeast as the SR-71 headed up to the north just outside of Ireland.

"OK," Peek-a-Boo said. "Now that we all are in on this, say we get you fired up on the playing field. Star Bright, we need you to enter France after a fly over of England. You need to go straight for London then hit Calais. This will have you arcing right to Amiens and back over near Rouen and Le Havre, then out to the coast near Cherbourg. You can let the film roll from just before London while you are passing over Portsmouth and Brighton, then again as soon as you hit the French coast. You're going to start seeing some breaks in the clouds as you turn left back to the coast and over. We will pick you back up there for further flight plans."

"That is a roger, Peek-a-Boo, we are red hot and ready to burn and turn."

The SR-71 dropped down to just under 800 feet and made a beeline across Portsmouth and Brighton, England, then heading to London. The jet was burning up the sky across the country.

"We have a good look at ground traffic and things are holding for you, Star Bright."

Hollywood was at a standoff distance and Peek-a-Boo started her way down to just outside the coast of France.

"We are looking good and still red hot."

They turned right on their way west to the outer coast and Cherbourg.

"Boy, oh boy, was that a beautiful run. It wasn't as bad of weather as I thought it would be."

"OK, Star Bright, we need to have you begin your turn left then right as you enter France. St. Brieuc will be your first target, then on to Vannes. There you will need to get some altitude over the water and turn out to sea. That will give us and Hollywood, time to get down range a bit to cover your way back up the coast."

"That is a roger, will I have time to get a drink?"

"Yes, we will have a Long-and-Tall waiting for you at heading 334. They have just what you need."

"All right, Peek-a-Boo, we're going down and dirty. My ass is ablaze and they can kiss it!"

MOSCOW

"Sir," Major Kizir walked up to the Commandant. "The US is doing another fly over of the outer bank of France. It looks like they might be looking for a place to enter and seize some of their ICBM's to use as a trading chip."

The Commandant looked up at the screen and replied, "Well they really must be taught a lesson on how to make friends and not to piss them off. Get me the Special Ops people in here."

"Yes, Sir."

"It is time to get this page turned and the rest of the history book written."

OVER FRANCE

The SR-71 was over Vannes and then out to sea. "I will see you all on the return!" and she pulled up and got some altitude in a matter of just seconds.

"This is Star Bright, can you hear us, Long-and-Tall?"

"We hear you loud and clear, Star Bright, this is Long Tall Sally, we're four miles out and closing."

"We have a big thirst, sis, and a long job ahead. Can you fix us up?"

"That is an affirm. You stay put and we will do everything but wash the glass."

"Well, we like when it is dirty."

The long boom hung from the back of the KC-135. It slipped into the refill joint on top of the plane just behind the view of the Black Bird's crew."

"You guys were burning holes in the sky, I hear."

"Well, we are more like dotting the I's and crossing the T's."

"Well, you are just about finished here, Star Bright. We'll send your Mom the bill."

"Thank you much, Tall Sally. We are out of here." The Black Bird dropped down and made one hell of a turn left as the fire jumped out some 200 feet from its ass."

"We are red hot and ready to burn, Peek-a-Boo, are you out there? We are ready to play the game 'Show me the Money'."

"Ok, Star Bright, here is what is on the agenda for the last run of the day. We would like for you to make a run to the same location that Starlight took that small shot from at Bordeaux. There we need another picture before you turn left up to Le Rochelle. That area seems to have a great concentration of airfields that might have troops with ADA (Air Defense Artillery). Not that we feel that they will fire on you, but once again, go into this with your counter measures on. We don't need you popped, but if you are, at least you have the chance to get over water and be picked up by our guys."

"That is a roger, Peek-a-Boo, but I'm not going back home without my bird. The water here is much too cold for any swim, so let's forget about that kind of talk."

"You've got it, Star Bright, make your move and good luck."

BORDEAUX, FRANCE

Sergi's team was finishing up as he came running in to the farmhouse.

"You guys, it is a 'go' for show!" Sergi's team started to move in fast motion.

"We need everything closed and buried, and for us to take up defensive posture in seventeen mikes." Everyone knew what they had to do.

"Here is where the training is going to make all the difference. All troops at the airfield are getting prepared for the show. Command was tracking the same aircraft as earlier this morning. Another is on its way here. So just as it has cleared the airstrip, it is rock and roll!"

MOSCOW

"Sir, our teams are indicating a 'go' for the show!" The Commandant sat down and looked up at the screen.

"This will show that the resolve of some will be the plight of others. Now we shall see if the sleeping giant has a stomach for this!"

STAR BRIGHT'S RUN

"Peek-a-Boo, we are red hot and ready to turn and burn."

"That is a roger, Star Bright, you have a clear vector for your run. We show little if no movement." said Hollywood. "You look good for the picture show. The weather down there is light rain that will be moving into the area from the west. It shouldn't give you any problems on the run."

"Well, we thank you all for that weather report. My ass is on fire!" The SR-71 dove down from the sky on its run to Bordeaux and back up the coast.

The night was clear on the far horizon. Some of the streetlights were just beginning to show through the clouds as the Black Bird came screaming down from above.

WASHINGTON

"Mr. President, did you have yourself a good sleep?"

"No, but that is not your fault. I have never had a good sleep since I took office."

"Sorry to hear that, Sir. In the Army you have to get a good sleep, because that is the only good thing about being in the Army."

"Well, maybe one day you can give me some pointers."

The Chairman of the Joint Chiefs walked over to this big map of lower France.

"Sir, last night, as you know, we had one of our SR-71 Black Birds do a fly over of the area south of the opening of the Gironde estuary. We took these pictures of the airport at Bordeaux. It was upon entering the air space of that airfield that we took these pictures. It shows that the Russians have quite a build up of equipment located at strategic locations around the airfield. Other pictures of different airports that are under Russian control have the same build up; some more then others. In many, if not all cases, these airports were taken for their close proximity to major cities."

"Why do you think that was so, General?"

"It would look like the major cities have more to offer the tourists. That, Sir, is how I think the Russians were able to enter the countries in such large numbers. They used the agreement to allow those of European descent to travel and enter the country of their choice without a visa. The large travel industry made it possible for this to take place. The man that headed it all was the President of Aeroflot: Commandant Gladimir Klakov."

"He just walked right into a country, and they asked, 'How may we serve you?' They did it from the start of the opening. Not one moment went by without some Russian soldier entering somewhere in Europe. With the cover of the bad weather, no one thought of looking at the number of people traveling. The numbers just didn't add up, but all they could see was the money that was coming into the country. Their greed got them where they are today."

"Wow!" the President said. "Now Russia doesn't have to do a thing. She can sit on this until the little countries crumble, and its people are on the necks of the city officials, but there are none: they are all dead! So the aids are running the show with little or no experience in dealing with world issues. Russia will offer them places that will place them in charge of the country. How can this have happened?"

"Governments become too complacent as things get better, and the quality of life has everyone reaching for more. Sir, we show that here, in France, there are twelve major sites under the Russian umbrella. France is going to be the first to fall. Their government is mostly a communist state as it is. It will not be long until she turns belly up. Russia knew right where to hit!"

STAR BRIGHT'S RUN

"Hey there, Peek-a-Boo, we have Bordeaux in the front window. ETA two mikes, 48 seconds."

"That is affirmative, Star Bright, your vector is still clear. We show no movement outside the targeted area."

"That sounds good to me, and the film is rolling." The SR-71 was on fire and burning it up all over the night sky.

Sergi and his team were waiting for the jet to have its fly over, and he pulled out the detonator and held it fast in his hand. His crew was ready to move when the time was right.

"Command has given the 'go' for show. All right, boys, this is it, stand by!"

The old farmer finally made his way through the thick mud to the box that lay semi-buried in his field. He could see the remnants of truck tire prints in the mud, heading out to the road. The same way from which they came. He took a long drink from a goat's skin bag that he had tied around his neck. Then he pulled a piece of stale bread from a bag and began to chew on the end with a mouth that had all of three teeth. He walked slowly around the metallic box and wondered why it was left there in his field.

The rain had stopped and the old man took a seat on the box as he thought of a way to get it out of the middle of his winter wheat field. The sky to the west was showing a bit of clearing, and he thought that maybe the rain had stopped long enough to let him plant his seed tomorrow.

"Target in seventeen seconds. Film is running and we are on fire."

"That is affirmative, Star Bright, pass over the area and then turn left to the city of La Rochelle. You are looking great."

"Roger that, Peek-a-Boo."

Rooooaaaarrrrrrrr! The jet flew over the airport and in a dash she began to turn left.

"Your vector is clear, Star Bright."

Sergi looked up as the jet began its turn.

"Now!" He pushed down the small button on the hand device as he and the team dropped under their cover.

WASHINGTON

"Sir, cloud cover has lessened so we are able to get some long distance looks from LandSat 4."

"Great, can we get those pictures here on the screen?"

"Yes, Sir, we are ready to start broadcasting now.

THE FARMER'S FIELD

The farmer stood up as he took another bite of bread, his chin almost touching his nose in the effort to chew. His old eyes looked skyward as the sound of the jet passed just over his head. As he looked down at the box, he saw a light flash on and off. He gave the box a disgusted look as he took another bite of the bread, and then gave the box a kick.

VOOOOOOOMMMMMMMMM!!!!

FLAAAAAASHHHHHHHHHH!!!!!

THE WHOLE SKY LIT UP WHITE!!!!!!

BOOOOOMMMMMMMMMMMM!!!!!!!

The SR-71 was caught up in the flash of the massive explosion and it over took the aircraft in less than a second.

The darkening sky turned into day in an instant. The light radiated outward to all corners of the surrounding area.

"My God!!!" they screamed, "PULL UP, PULL UP!!!"

The SR-71 began to climb straight up. The pilot tried at first to pull down his visor but it did little good. His eyes were almost burned right out of their sockets. He knew that he had to climb, and climb up as fast has he could. They needed to get away from the shock wave that was sure to come.

Peek-a-Boo saw the blast and started screaming to take evasive action.

"Star Bright, GET THE HELL OUT OF THERE!!" Then, "May Day, May Day, this is Z22V1, eyes in the skies. We have a Class One Alfa emergency!! A nuclear blast has just occurred at quadrant 1323 near Bordeaux, France. Time: mark 2043. One SR-71 Black Bird Z22V2 recon has been hit by thermal radiation and is now flying blind. This is Z22V1, DO YOU READ?!!!!"

The AWAC's showed that the JSTAR was losing altitude fast and that it must have been hit by the EMP field.

"Hollywood has gone down, Z22V3 has no response! We believe she has gone down. We need SAR (Search and Rescue) here fast! Does anyone read this?!! This is Z22V1! Come in, anyone!!"

Star Bright was still in a drastic climb when the shock wave hit the SR-71. Peek a Boo could only watch as they just screamed into the radio. The plane felt like it was coming apart. The controls were rolling as the plane shook like a 9.0 earthquake.

"God help us, help us!!!"

"Keep climbing, Captain!"

Soon the SR-71 was out of the wave and in a matter of seconds she began to be more controllable. The Copilot took the controls saying, "I have her, Sir. I've got the bird Captain!"

The Copilot eased her back and he leveled her offat around 80,000 ft.

"This is Star Bright, can anyone hear us? We have climbed to 80k and have recovered the craft. Does anyone hear us?"

Meanwhile the pilot of the JSTAR was calling for the Copilot to try to restart the engines as the plane dropped like a rock from the sky.

"This is Hollywood! We are going down! EMP has knocked the shit out of us along with the blast. We have lost all power and are going down!"

The plane slammed into the water at 600 miles an hour. The exploding plane was silenced by the sucking of the ocean as it fell deep into the dark waters.

WASHINGTON

"Jesus! What in the hell was that?!!"

A small bright light showed up on the screen. The image from the LANDSTAT 4 satellite clearly showed a blast of some kind. The President jumped out of his seat.

"Oh, my God, Sir, it looks like a nuclear detonation!"

"Where has this taken place?"

"From the looks of things, in southern France. There was no launch vehicle spotted. It must have been a land-based device!"

The intercom from inside the War Room was echoing the reported blast as it was monitored.

"We repeat, this is US Space Command, there is no launch vehicle, detonation is from land-based device." "Sir, the US Space Command has just indicated that there was a nuclear detonation near Bordeaux, France at 2043 AET. There were no missiles fired."

"That was near our SR-71 fly-by. I want you to call an all out alert of armed forces worldwide! Get me the Russian President on that damn phone now!"

The President was in a rage.

"What in the hell do they think they're doing? Get NORRAD on the line, we need them to track the fallout!"

"Sir, we advise that you head for Air Force One. It is standing by!"

The Vice President came into the room.

"Sir, we must get you out of here, and gone!"

"I'm not leaving!"

"But, Sir, we feel that it is no longer safe for you to stay!"

A-Team came rushing in and grabbed the President as he tried to push them away. He screamed to be let go, then saw the urgency of the situation and left with them.

"I want full link-up on Air Force One, now!"

A helicopter was landing just as the President was rushed outside.

"Take care of my family!!!!"

Secret Service men wer e already sent to the White House and, once there, gathered up the President's family and drove them to get aboard Air Force 2 with the vice President.

BORDEAUX

The blast from the 1.7 kilo ton device was nothing less than devastating. Everything within a 6-kilometer radius was gone, vaporized. The blast itself reached out as far as 21 kilometers, with the flash being seen for more then 400 kilometers in the night sky. Sergi and his men were only 15 kilometers away and took a bad hit from the blast. The farmhouse nearby was completely gone. So were three of his men. He stood up to look around and made a head count. Of the survivors, all but the two men that had blood coming from their ears, were ok.

Sergi grabbed one man by the face, "Believe me, I am sorry!!" Then he said good bye. He pulled out his 9mm and shot both of the men.

"We have no time to bury the bodies! We have to get the hell out of here fast, people!"

The massive mushroom cloud was barely visible due to the overcast skies and the night that was on its way. But the fallout from the bomb was sure to cover a large area of the countryside. The down wind area was to cover some 62 kilometers. The width was about 21-28 kilometers in some areas. Tons of material was air born and raining down its contamination everywhere. Sergi and his men ran towards the airport. They had a lot of ground to cover as it became harder to see from the dust, dirt, and the night. Dead cows and pigs were everywhere. Cars with their paint burnt right off of them laid thrown about. Trees were uprooted, knocked down like bowling pins. Those that were left standing were burning from the heat of the blast. Some people were roaming around, calling out franticly for loved ones. The landscape was a total wasteland.

He could see some emergency vehicles that were coming down a large street toward Sergi and his men. Through the dust and darkness, the lights were coming towards them and they could see many people running to the light. Screams and cries were everywhere. Sergi watched a mother dragging what it looked like the remains of a child. The dust and dirt was now coming down and mixing with the fine rain that started to fall as well. Sergi told his men to push forward.

It was the pit of hell. "It's the end of the world!" people screamed. A dog with its fur burnt right off and its skin smoking was sitting in the middle of the road with his tail wagging as people would walk past. Thousands of small birds were flapping around in a massive pile as they were blown from their night roosting place. Everywhere Sergi looked, he saw the worst that he had ever seen before.

He came to a stop. He signaled for his men to come to him.

"Try to put something around your face, this will stop a lot of the dust that you breathe. The place is getting more and more contaminated. We can only take in so much radiation. We have to keep on moving and get out of this area."

MOSCOW

"Sir, the device has been detonated. We are waiting for reports from the area. It seems that the Special Ops people have done their job well."

"Yes, it would have seemed that way. I knew that officer." the Commandant said as he rose to his feet. "He is one of the finest men we have. He has a love for Russia like very few men do. He loves her with every breath he takes."

The Commandant's hand began to close into a fist. His knuckles were blue from the tightly closed fingers. "To love something so much to give your life for what you believe in! That Major is our first hero, and we will never forget him!"

The Commandant's eyes began to water as he mumbled, "For the love of Russia!"

WASHINGTON

Air Force One was airborne and the President's advisers were all seated at each of the consoles that were throughout the plane.

"Get high in the sky!" the pilot said. "Sir, we are hooked up with the world if you need it."

"Have there been any more detonations?"

"No, Sir, that has been the only one that has been reported."

"What about the aircrew that we had over there, are they all right?"

"Sir, we have yet to receive Intel on that."

"Well, get me the answers, man! I need to know about our people!"

Star Bright's Run

"Star Bright, this is Peek-a-Boo, do you read me?"

"Yes, Peek-a-Boo, we read you."

"Thank God! It sure is good to hear from you!"

"What do you know about Hollywood?"

"They went down from the EMP."

"My God, what a fine crew! How are you doing?"

"We were far enough away from the affects, but you guys! I thought that you were gone!"

"Well, we did get a beating. The Captain has lost his sight. I gave him some morphine for the pain. His eyes were burnt white!"

"Damn!! Are you Ok?"

"Yea, I was turned away from the blast. I'll be getting us home."

"I've got you heading west. You need to turn left to heading 178 and drop to 30,000 ft. We are going to get you into Loges Field in the Azores. There we can get some help fast for the Captain! I am going to help you get there. I'll be right behind you, all the way!" "That sounds good, Peek-a-Boo, thank you for all your help!"

"That's my job, Star Bright."

Fallout

Sergi's team was passed by a column of emergency trucks and ambulances. The airport had small fires burning here and there from the blast. Most of the police vehicles were gone down range to help with the masses. Sergi and his men slipped into the airport and caught up with the Commanding Officer who was counting the reports of the actions. Sergi walked up to the Colonel and said, "Reporting for duty, Sir!"

"Shit, how in the hell did you survive that?"

"Sir, my men and I need attention. We walked from the blast area. I have lost five men. Is there someone that can have a look at my men? They are hungry, cold, and have taken in a lot of RADS.

"Right away! Get the medics over here! They'll take you to our aid station. Good job, Major! You have done one hell of a good job."

"Hell, Sir? That is what is out there!" He turned and helped his men to the aid station.

The medical team looked over Sergi and his men. They were each given oxygen bottles to carry around with them. There was no true way to see just how much radiation they all absorbed. They had to take a "look and see approach". Sergi walked the lobby of the airport. Many of the soldiers were there, sleeping throughout the mall. He passed some sentries, and climbed up to the tower where command and control were busy cleaning up the glass from the windows that had been blown out from the blast. They had retrieved some of the civilian workers from the hanger where they were being held to help replace the glass. Sergi looked out to where the blast had taken place.

The rain had started up again, and he knew that it would have a good chance of knocking down the dirt and dust. The fallout area might be lessened with distance. He found a corner that was cleared and sat down. He thought back to when he was "only an instructor". The troops that he trained on the Maps were spread out all over the European continent. He knew that this was just the beginning of what was to be a very hard time.

"Russia was so far away," he thought, as he looked out the window of the air traffic control tower. He looked past the rain, and past the night. He could see the eyes of the Commandant looking at him. Looking at all that was now in their control. He knew that what was taking place was for Russia.

"The world knows now that it is Russia that is the true world power!"

Sergi fell asleep and dreamed about the time that he would be able to return to the land that he loved so much.

Many of the fires that had hit Bordeaux were under control. The damage from the blast did widespread destruction. Many lives were lost from buildings collapsing down on the sleeping city. People have been staying indoors since the take-over of the airport. Only the French police, and what national guards units that were in the area, were out on the streets during the blast. The sports stadium that was once filled with screaming spectators for the national soccer team was being used as a makeshift morgue to store the dead. The fallout from the blast stretched just south of the city limits and east to the city of Bergerac.

Word of the nuclear blast rang around the world. Many protests were taking place outside the Russian Consulates throughout the world. Police were called in to serve as protection, but many refused to do anything to protect the Russians from the crowd. The UN called for restraint from the violence worldwide.

"We cannot fall into the same path that Russia has chosen. If we do, then we are no better than those that chose the path of violence."

The Security Council could find little to do with the situation in Europe. Many of the members were themselves under the umbrella of the Russian occupation. The condemnations that were voted on meant nothing. Russia wasn't talking to anyone about the actions she took. Like the once great Iron Curtain, nothing was going in and nothing was coming out.

EDWARDS AIR FORCE BASE, CALIFORNIA

The President and his aids walked over to the elevator that took them down to the bombproof facilities that were twelve levels under ground.

The War Room there was in full operation and monitoring the situation in France.

The President looked around the room at his advisors, and asked them what they thought of the situation.

"You know, Sir, it is just a matter of time before they could detonate another nuclear device, anytime they wish to."

"Sir, as it looks like right now, we are helpless to do anything, and the Russian government knows it." "Sir, there cannot be…"

Just then, word was passed to the Secretary of State, that the Commandant of the Supreme Russian Special Forces wanted to have words with the President of the United States.

"Sir, we have a broadcast coming in for you from the Commandant."

"Yes. People, you need to listen to this!"

The eight-foot screen came on and the Seal of the Russian Special Forces appeared. The Commandant walked up with the seal behind him.

"Good day, Mr. President."

The President said, "Good day for you, maybe. Would you mind if my council stayed to listen to you?"

"No, no, not at all. I am coming to you from the Russian Hall of the People. It has been some time now that what has taken place needs to be discussed."

"Yes, it has." the President agreed.

"It had come to the attention of the Russian people that the time of being pushed around has to come to a halt. We have, on the other hand, been working very hard since the end of the Second World War that saw Russia lose more than 30,000,000 people. You can never fathom that number in one country's lifetime." Everyone just looked at the screen.

"We can no longer sit by and watch the rest of the world place their moralities on this great nation. The push for Russia to join the free world has taken a vast toll on our people. So much has been at the hands of our own government. The years of Communism had almost destroyed us. The selfishness of our leaders to have everything while, her people had not, was a travesty."

"What does that have to do with what has happened to the poor people of Europe?" the President asked. "Don't interrupt me again!" the Commandant snapped.

Everyone looked at each other.

"It is only from my morbid curiosity that I am even talking to you. You have nothing, nor do I have to tell you anything. This isn't a game. We don't intend to turn back the hands of time. You can't just turn this off!"

The Commandant became very angry. "We don't ask you "How high?' when you say 'jump!'

He gave a long pause and just looked at the monitor, then said, "When your arrogance as a country can take a second seat, then we will resume the talks!"

The screen went black.

"He's gone mad, Sir!" one of his advisors said.

The President just sat back in his chair and looked at the table.

"No, he is not mad. He knows exactly what he is doing. He knows what cards he's holding in his hand, and he is not ready to play them yet."

"So, Sir, what do we do?"

The President stood up and moved to the screen. He turned and said, "I would like to have just the Joint Chiefs here at this moment. Gentlemen, would you please?"

The aids got up and filed out of the room. The Chairman of the Joint Chiefs looked over at the President as he shut the door.

Lages Field, Azores

The SR-71 had just came to a rolling stop, with the AWAC's jet landing just behind her. Emergency crews were waiting to rush the Captain to the nearby aid station and help with any others in need of first aid.

The outer material of the Black Bird was a strange color of burnt blue and yellow, like that of an all-chrome exhaust pipe that got way too hot. The Captain was removed quickly as the decom team came in to check for radiation. The Copilot rode along with his Pilot to the aid station. With the AWAC's safely down, the nights ahead would never be the same. The crew jumped off the plane and hugged each other; they knew that they made it down and were in one piece.

MOSCOW

Many of the members of the Russian parliament came rushing into the Hall of the People.

"What on earth do you think you are doing?!"

More members became outraged that a nuclear weapon had been used.

"How can we answer to the people on this?"

"SIT YOUR ASSES DOWN AND SHUT YOUR MOUTHS! GUARDS!"

Troops began to run in with their weapons drawn. They filtered down, turned, and aimed into the crowd. Members were hitting the floor in anticipation of being shot."

"You worms of this world! We don't have to answer to anyone, and I will tell you why. Because they don't want this to happen again, and believe me, we will do it again. Your job is to meet with the people, to reassure them that life is grand, and that it will go on. My job is to make sure that you have a job. That is so they know that Russia means business. We are not going to fold up and go away. We are going to finish what we have started, and if any of you are not with me, then you are surely against me."

"Now leave me, all of you. Get your asses to work, and I will keep us strong. Now get out before I have all you cowards shot!"

The Commandant stood by his troops and the great room cleared in an instant.

"Sir, we have this request."

Major Kizir brought in a woman to see him. "People want to know how their loved ones were doing over here in Russia, so they asked the International Red Cross to see if Russia would allow them to visit the hostages."

The Commandant looked at the request and handed it back to be properly worded.

"We are not holding hostages. We are not a terrorist group. This is an act of war. So we will obey the laws that govern war. You may visit our guests, they are not hostages."

The Red Cross was allowed to bring in some 7,000 people that waited in nearby Poland to look into most of the 110,347 hotels, lodges and barracks where people were being detained until they can be returned to their homeland. Of those places that they were able to check, were found that all people were in great care, and that no one was mistreated in anyway.

The Commandant stopped the inspectors just as they finished up their reports on the treatment of foreign peoples.

"I will have for you soon, the list of names of all who are staying here in Russia. We don't wish harm on these people. We must live together and prosper. But the rules have changed on who will prosper and who has the second seat, and I will tell you this. It will not be Russia that is sitting!"

WASHINGTON

The US began work on expelling all Russian diplomats from the United States. It also had harsh words of criticism on Russia's occupations of Europe, and the unwillingness of the government to stop this unprovoked invasion of Europe. The Security Council had to be held without Russia and China. Each of those two countries hadthe right to veto the vote.

Many nations said you can say what you want, but don't go getting China pissed too. We have a very unstable world right now. A major war involving these countries would be the end of the world.

The President and his advisers made their way back to the War Room under the White House. The events that have hung over the heads of everyone weighed heavier than some could take, and their faces show that they have aged years in a matter of a week. The Christmas season not far away seemed light years down the road. The planned vacation of Congress was cancelled, and work on the laws of the time were put off for the up and coming weeks after New Years. No one had the answers to the problems that needed to be addressed. It was to be the worst of times.

MOSCOW

The Commandant awoke from a restless sleep. He got dressed and asked his driver to take him on a ride around the city of Moscow. A fine snow was falling gently to the ground, but did not stick. They drove around until he had his driver stop in Red Square.

There he got out and told his driver to wait there. He could see the snow falling in the lights that lined the square. Walking up to St. Basil's Cathedral, he pictured the countless years of the Czar's rule over this beautiful city. The street was shiny from the rain and snow that had been falling endlessly for weeks. Some of the building's reflections were distorted by the uneven cobblestones and gave off a strange light as their reflections shifted with the blowing wind.

He walked around for some time kicking a crushed can, then just stood under a streetlight. Oh, how old was the ground under his feet, under all the years of material upon material that now made up Red Square? His vision of a Russia was nothing short of those that ruled her in her infancy. From all that were the rulers before Ivan the Terrible, the first ruler to be given the title of "tzar", to the death of Nicholas II. Mother Russia was there, a vast land that covers an ungrateful earth.

"Well, soon," he thought, "those who think of us as the world's beggars will soon be on theirs knees to the most powerful nation on earth."

He made one more look around the square, then walked to his car and got in.

"The new day is awaiting us, let's get it on its way."

The car sped up and made its way back to the parliament building.

IT'S ALL ABOUT MONEY

The world's money markets have been on a tailspin for more than half a week. People were selling off, and cashing in their shares that had anything to do with the European or American markets. Frankfurt was closed and had been sitting idle since the invasion started. One by one, countries had started to negotiate with the Russian government as to allow normal trade with each other resume. No trade outside the European continent was allowed as of yet.

The new talks with Iran and Iraq soon followed with much anticipation. Having the two major countries that controlled much of the world's oil in partnership with Russia was a source of great pride. Iran itself shared a large border with Russia. Allowing the strong Islamic culture to flourish there could make for a more stable relationship. Russia was pushing all the right keys.

The US could do nothing but sit back and watch the world be eaten up piece by piece in just a short time. The Democratic party whose President, in the late 1990's helped to dismantle the great US military force over the years had given his later predecessors little to be the Commander in Chief of, and who was for the most part powerless to do anything. The call up of the Reserves and the National Guard could do little to match the forces that were already in place by the

Russians. All the years of money saving plans to cut here and save there had gone up in smoke. The Republican slogan, "Much too much; much too soon!" was now being cried in the Senate. "Where is your savings now, Mr. President?"

The White House could only send out signals that we must stay the course.

The world seemed to rotate around the Commandant. Slowly Europe began to blink, and see that what had happened could be lived with. Only England and Germany remained closed as Russia tried to talk with these two remaining governments.

England wanted all troops to be removed before she would start talking about anything. The cities of Portsmouth, near Southampton, and Brighton were in close proximity of each other. The English, seeing no reason that the Russians needed those two cities, hardened. So talks stalled, for the time being.

Germany knew that she had nothing to lose by staying closed. She had learned to save food in massive bunkers that could feed her own over a long period of time. Organization and conformity was something Germany was good at. Their people were themselves more on time than the trains that ran through their massive rail systems.

In just a week, the world's words were pointless. As pointless as trying to believe that this was all a bad dream. There was no waking up from it, it was just the way it was. The laughter was gone from the streets of Paris as the place of government there started to bury the dead of the once beautiful city of Bordeaux. France began to show her true color as a country. The same color that was displayed during the occupation that twice was by Germany. She was no longer the land that Napoleon lead on its conquest of Russia. Finding nothing at the end of his long fight, five months in Moscow proved to be long enough for him. Now France had no one to come to her rescue this time. Her isolationist attitude, her public disdain of the US over the years resulted in her ultimate lack of defense. Not even the nuclear arsenal that she once boasted could stop France from showing her true color. So, like so many times since Napoleon, the white flag rose up to take her rightful place above France.

The Commandant smiled a content, no-nonsense kind of smile, as he watched on his screen the great news broadcast from France. He knew that there were no plans to come to France's rescue. They lined up in the streets of Paris to watch the surrender to the Commander of Deployed Russian Troops Forward, at the Arc de Triomphe. A short display by the French color guards, and the handing over of the sword that once belonged to Napoleon himself marked the end of the ceremony.

The Commander remarked, "We are not here to be your masters, but your partners of the true beginning of a new Europe. We will work hard to keep all that is Europe, a true place among the leaders of the world."

One by one the smaller governments of Luxembourg, Norway, Poland, Lithuania, Macedonia, and the Netherlands began to have talks with Russia about forming a separate coalition of nations that was to be seated in Moscow. The newly United EuroNations was formed on the eve of the one-week anniversary of the occupation of Europe. Russia even had talks with Switzerland. The once neutral country still wanted that status. Russia insisted that she become a member, and then gave her two weeks the respond.

"Show good reason to stay neutral, and the rest of the UEN will vote on it."

NATO had suffered a great loss with the forming of the UEN. This meant that more were being pulled to join. Only the US, Canada, Iceland, Great Britain, Turkey, and Germany stood fast in their commitment to NATO, with Denmark, Italy, Spain, Portugal, Belgium, and Greece leaning to the left.

The first thing placed on the table was that of the withdrawal of all foreign armies, and for them to be removed from Europe.

"We do not wish to have the protection of the countries of the US and Canada here on our soil." It was so proposed to all of Europe and a final vote was soon at hand.

The President of the United States made a final plea with the Commandant of Russia, who had for the time being, taken charge of Russia by decree from the Russian President and their Parliament. The armed forces of Russia were also placed into the hands of Commandant

Gladimir Klakov. He stood proudly in front of the Parliament of the Russian people, and gave his first speech as the new leader of his country's Armed Forces.

"We had stated in the beginning, that all we wanted was what is rightfully ours. Europe is that which is rightfully ours. We do not wish to carry on with an armed occupation of our friends that wish to be our friends. We are there in a force protection capacity. We are there to help make the transition a smooth one from a Western government that was primarily set up by the US, to more of a European government that puts our needs above those who have placed their interests whereever they seemed fit. We don't need them. We have all we need right here at our fingertips. Natural resources are in abundance here. The European people have been here centuries before there was the existence of a North America. We will be, we must be, and will always be the leaders of this world. From now until forever."

The broadcast was seen worldwide. The US President and his staff watched the Parliament of Russia give the Commandant a standing ovation. News commentary began to give their assessment of the speech.

"Turn that shit off! I tell you, those bastards are ass-kissing motherfuckers!" The Army Chief of Staff proclaimed. "They jump on anyone's side that sells the most. It makes me want to boycott all the sponsors, fuckin' bastards!"

The Chairman of the Joints Chiefs looked over at the General.

"You do have a way with words. But we must keep a clear head on this and all upcoming events. NATO still has a great posture that can bring about the means to an end. We just have to wait for the right time, and fully understand the sacrifice that would be made, and to what ends are we prepared to go."

The President sat and reviewed all plans for the possible removal of troops from Europe. He looked at timelines and corridors to the sea that would allow them to transport the military out to neutral ground.

"We may be able to place most of the ground troops in the Middle East. This could be a very hot topic for Russia, what with the new alliance with Iraq and Iran. We must be sensitive to the matter at hand." one of the President's advisors told him.

"Sensitive? My ass is sensitive enough from all the fucking that sanctimonious prick has given us! What in the hell do you want to do, maybe give him the key to the Presidential yacht?"

"Mr. Chairman please, can you somehow control your General? This is a matter for the civilian government to handle!" the beady-eyed advisor said.

Just then the whole room exploded, with yelling back and forth. The President lost control of the moment and just sat there with his chin in his hand.

"All right, all right, that will be enough. All of you stow it, this is just what he wants us to do!" the Chairman of the Joint Chiefs said. "When you make your enemy angry, you win. We have real issues to look at here. We have many options that need to be looked at without everyone going off on their own little tangent!"

He then went to the screen and punched up the aerial pictures taken from the SR-71 fly-overs.

"As you can see here, most targets are relatively the same. On the outer boundaries of the airports are small ADA units with anti-armor set back from the front lines some two hundred feet. There are fortified emplacements here and here. The hangers have been used to house the hostages that were at the airports during their occupation. Talks are going on in the prospective governments for their release. The airport at Bordeaux is still operational. They have 106 locations, fortified and in their control. The thing about these places is that they cannot be moved, and they will be there for some time. That means that they are a fixed location." He went on with the shots of the airports and the possibility of constructing a communications station in Tunis, Tunisia.

FT. BRAGG

The troops were coming down from this morning's jump all over the training area. They moved out as quickly as they landed, and took up positions that were marked in the mock-up airfield. Helicopter gunships opened fire on the fixed bunkers, then moved out to pick up what troops were waiting near the LZ.

Training at Ft. Bragg was always going on. Night or day, you could find the airborne and air assault units doing what they do best, and Gen. Bill "JUMP" Chambers was right there with his men. The US Army's Airborne and Air Assault schools were a fixed position there at Bragg. They train for one thing: to fight and to win. The General wouldn't have it any other way.

"Sir!" the Captain came running up to the General just as his helicopter landed. "Sir, you have someone here to see you."

"Well, who in the hell is it, Captain?"

"Sir, it's the Assistant Army Chief of Staff!"

Jump looked over to a Hum-V and could see it waiting there for him.

"Captain, have my things brought to my office for me. I'll see you later."

"Yes, Sir, right away, Sir!"

The General walked to the Hum-V and shook the hand of his guest. They both climbed in, and they drove off in a cloud of dust.

"General, how may I be of service to you?"

"Well, Bill, I need you to come to Washington with me, we may have a job for you to do for us."

"What sort of job, General?"

"I will fill you in on the way to Washington. Right now we need to get there fast. Driver, get to the airfield just a little faster, please."

"What, I don't have time to shower?"

"Bill, by the time I am finished filling you in on this, you won't have enough time to shit."

The driver broke a small smile as the General asked if there was a kiss in the plans before all this fucking was about to take place.

"Bill, I don't kiss on the first date!" the General replied.

WASHINGTON

Admiral Spencer entered the room and took a seat at the table.

The Under Secretary of Defense stood and addressed the President and his staff, "Mr. President, we have some information on the bombing of the US Naval Air Station at Sigonella, Sicily. Admiral Spencer arrived last night with information that was gathered from the site. Admiral, would you please?"

"Thank you, Sir, Mr. President, and Chiefs. We have been working with the local authorities in Italy and down in Sicily and found that what had hit the Air Station at Sigonella Sicily, and that of NCTAMS on the island of Lago di Patria by Naples, came from just outside the bases."

"The individuals that were there to do the job left all the information that they themselves had gathered right at the spot from where they had fired on the bases. Troops belonging to the Russian Special Forces had somehow recruited Italian local nationals to help with the bombing."

He began to pass around pictures that were taken near Sigonella, then placed a copy on the Boxlight to be displayed on the screen.

"As you can see, the men used 82mm mortars to shell the COMSTA and the whole length of the airfield. The two positions that you see here on the aerial shot of the air station, one here," he pointed, "and the other here, were used to dump a lot of ordinance there at SIG. As you can also see by looking at the other photos, they shot and killed the help. We believe that they both worked on Sigonella prior to the recruitment. Papers showed that they were laid off from work some time ago at the Air Station."

"Well it looks like to me that they were pissed offat the Base and wanted a little revenge." the Army Chief of Staff commented. "But how did they get those rounds down range with such accuracy?"

"Well, Sir, we later found an Italian male who was using a cell phone to help with target acquisition. We traced a single number from both cell phones that were left at the scene next to the mortars.

Everything was just left right there: maps, photos, the mortars with unused rounds, everything."

The room sat, engrossed in the report.

"The bastards, it seems, were offered a lot of money to help get this done. Money was found at the residences of the two men during a search of their homes, and more found at the scene. The man that was arrested that next day was connected to the scene by having the same number that the cell phones left at the point of attack. He confirmed the payoff while under interrogation. But they were killed before they could spend the money."

"The motherfuckers had the plan and the help to boot." the Army Chief stated. "They are never happy for the time that they do get to work. What the fuck, we take it up the ass every time we have a base abroad. Give the local government jobs for their people, and if they don't steal you blind, they fuck you a different way. Then, when we close a base, we have to pay them unemployment. Why? Because it is the 'nice' thing to do. Just like we did in the Philippines."

"Are you just about finished, General?" the Chair-man asked.

"I'm sorry, Sir, it just pisses me off."

"Admiral, you can see that there is a lot of tension here. We are in a bad fix with this occupation."

"I understand, Sir. It is a lot to think about when we have our troops spread out throughout the area of operation. The Russians have the airports at Catania, Messina, and Palermo in Sicily, and they are occupied with troops strengths estimated to be around 4,000 to 5,000 at each location. That is more than we have at Sigonella on its busiest day. But even if we did have the manpower available there, they are not too much help."

"What do you mean, Admiral?" the Air Force Chief of Staff asked.

"Well, Sir, not too many of our forces there have the means to defend the base. We don't train Joe Smith sailor stationed at SIG to shoot a weapon nor do we train them to fight, other than their limited training in boot camp. The Naval Air Station is the Hub of the Med. They are technicians, mechanics, computer programmers, radiomen. They support the War Fighters: the naval surface ship, subs, and aircraft.

They are not army ground-pounders. We don't have individual weapons for every sailor on base to stand ready for this type of action. They only have a hand full, I hate to say, of poorly trained security officers that have never been involved in anything more deadly than a traffic accident. For 'emergencies', they add the ASF, or auxiliary security force, which consists of nothing more than ordinary sailors that can run in formation, know how to don protective gear, and who are taught to shoot a 22 cal pea-shooter. These two entities are more or less a figurehead. In addition, they have the Explosive Ordinance Disposal detachment, who are deployed 90% of the time to other parts of the world cleaning up the bull shit there. That doesn't add up to defense. We just haven't looked into the defense of that base."

"And why is that, may I ask?" said the President.

"The base falls under the Italian's control as part of NATO. They are responsible for its defense, but they were the ones who shit their pants once the bombs started dropping. We had to wait hours for the police to arrive with any kind of force. You see, Sir, it was a rainy, Friday night. Everyone was off or was not going to come in."

"What in the Lord's heaven are we doing to ourselves?!" the Chairman of the Armed Services Committee asked. "I have been sitting here for the last few days, just taking all this bull shit in. Where is the money going to, if not for the training of our forces; to give them the means to defend themselves? This is a total disgrace, and misuse of the American people's trust in us, the defender of the free world!"

"Sir, this is a NATO base, belonging to Italy!" Admiral Spencer interjected.

"Stop right there!" the Secretary snapped back.

"We maybe a partner at Sigonella with the Italians, but that should not render our people helpless and unable to fight! Are we just keeping our service members there to be captured? To become POWs? What in the hell is stopping the Russians from sending their troops to SIG? They could send a platoon size force over to Sigonella, and capture the base with more than 7,000 men and women unable to even throw a fuckin' rock. What about our families that are over there, too? Are we going to let them become hostages for their nation to plea bargain with? There is something terribly wrong with this picture."

The Chairman of the Joint Chiefs spoke up. "We did not consider it a possibility that while we were in a country belonging to the NATO alliance, that any extra force protection would be needed."

"General, force protection is one thing, but not having the means to defend your base is another. If we had to fight our way off the island of Sicily, would we be able to leave with everyone that is there? What are we going to do, storm the fuckin' Russians and hope that they run out of ammo before we run out of people to send? You all have gotten too complacent. We send our troops here and there to fight other nation's wars, yet we neglect to think of them in peace time, just in case some fuckin' group wants to over run our base. We might as well invite the girl scouts to have a go at it with the Russians to defend us. They are given more to work with than our own people!"

The Chairman of the Arms Services Committee got up and left the room. Everyone just sat there looking at the pictures of Sigonella. The President himself looked around the room. He stood up and started to walk around the table.

"Sir, I know that what the Chairman was saying sounds…"

"Stop right there!" the President said. "I have visited many military bases around the world, and you can bet that the Base Commander knew that it was important to show me that the base was ready and willing to do what it would take to get the job done. But were they really ready? I recall a time back in the late 70's, when I found out as a young soldier, the reason why we would tow our deadlined vehicles along with us towards the MDA, major deployment area near the Czech border in the town of Weiden, Germany. We were to tow these broken down trucks and tracks to the 'cold front' to show the USSR troops guarding the boarder that the 6th battalion, 14" field artillery was ready and standing by. I had asked my 1st Lieutenant who, at the time, was the battalion ammo officer, 'Why do we not tell the Battalion Commander that we are not combat ready?" His face was lit up with anxiety and wonder with the question. 'Sir,' I asked. 'If we were to tell the Commander that we needed parts, maybe we could come here really ready, not just a show of untrue force.' He answered that there was a fine line between truth and loyalty "You can't tell your Battalion Commander that you are not ready for war. You just don't throw that on his lap when he is depending on you!" I remember that time, and I will tell you, that is one time I said I would never let happen again when I made office. Yet I resumed the same ol' same ol' by letting it be done by my Commanders so that they would not be reported as not being 'Battle ready'."

"Now when I visit, many of the base members would show up with flags waving and the band playing, 'Hail to the Chief. What is this really for? So CNN can give me a high mark in public relations? I, myself, am guilty of this, so are my predecessors, as is the American public. But now, that is a little too late, and the Chairman is right. Do you all know that? The Chairman is right, and now we are deep into the actions against us and King David forgot his sling shot. Now Goliath is closing in. But we cannot turn back the hands of time. We need to stay focused, and clear-headed. We have to get ready to defend ourselves when the time comes. I need you to get messages to all Embassies in the occupied areas. We need to get word to the troops that are stationed there, and are wondering what the next move is."

Prepare the Troops

The jet took off with the two Generals in deep discussion over the plans that were drawn up and were to be presented to the President and the Joint Chiefs.

"It will take us just a little time to get ourselves together for the trip over there. Do we have any ships that are in the area?"

"Yes, but we don't want to move in any war ships that would alert the Russians of our intent. Therefore we have made provisions to have one of Exxon's fuel tankers that is in port at Hopedale, Newfoundland, standing ready to carry you all over to England. The ship is being cleaned inside and out. It has one hell of a storage compartment. It will take three days for you to get over to the island of Lewis, in the Outer Hebrides in Northern Scotland. There you will be flown in by helicopters of the Royal Air Forces to an area just outside your objective."

"This is going to be a joint effort, I see.

"It has to be. You see, the English are the least occupied of all the countries of Europe. They will not accept any Russian troops occupying their country before they have talks about the problems of Europe. The English alone are a force to be reckoned with, all by themselves, and Russia knows it. Even as small as she is, they are a nation of more than 50,000,000 all by themselves. That is not to include Scotland and the others. If they feel that they are going to have to fight… well, have you ever gone to one of their soccer games when they lose? They know how to kick some ass! That means man, woman, and child."

The jet was on its final approach into Washington, so they put all the plans up and sat back for the landing.

MOSCOW

"We have reassured the people of each country that they can start up some industries to help with the needs of food distribution. Our troops are still poised on the border, and spirits are high. COMMs have been set up at all locations that are in our influence."

The Commandant smiled and told the Major, "Thank you." He stood up and spoke aloud as he looked at the screen of Europe.

"Now, that was not too bad, was it? We understand that it will take some time for everyone to swallow the notion, but we will be a much stronger continent for it."

"Has the US come up with an answer about the withdrawal of the forces within Europe? They really have no choice in the matter, and should be very fortunate that we have even allowed them to have the opportunity to leave."

"We are prepared to start up re-supply flights to all locations in those countries that have joined the UEN. They are now under the command of occupying forces. They have drawn up governments that will be put in place as soon as the rest of the countries join in."

"Well, without the US involvement they will see that they have been standing on their own two feet all along. It has been far too long that Europe needed to kick the US's ass out. They need a true leader in the world. Russia is that new leader that will take them to new heights."

The storms throughout Europe have been letting up a little. Even though the rain and snow was still falling over much of the continent, bigger breaks in the fronts were occurring. The Spy-in-the-Sky was now able to get some photos of much of the European states; that is they were now being called. Snow had covered many of the mountains throughout the continent, and the colder air filtering down from the north made the air clear for some good pictures from above.

With the Christmas season just a few weeks away, life was reappearing throughout Europe. That was not the case for those still inside the occupied airport hangers. No plans were made to set free those from the air hangers, nor of those that were still in Russia. Many attempts were made to get some of the elderly released, along with the women and children. Talks for their release were, in the past, fruitless.

But the Commandant was feeling the spirit of the season. He suggested that those being held in Russia that are ill and the very young children with their mothers only can leave back to the country of their choice.

"This will give us opportunity to re-supply some of our troops with provisions, and maybe rotate some that need to get the experience of action. Our Commanders need to be with the troops, and some need to get the rewards that they deserve."

A meeting between the Commandant and the Ambassadors to the US and England had been approved. The two countries had been pressing for the easing of troop involvement throughout Europe in the past week, and the possible removal of US troops out of Germany. Without the removal of US troops, the cost of keeping them in Europe was a costly one. Though Germany was, at the time, the only country that could afford the removal of the troops, many of the smaller countries that depended on the work that the US gave them felt that the financial impact was unbearable. Russia was not prepared to pick up the slack of the troops' departure. The money factor was a big one. Many countries could now see just how badly they needed the US's money.

THE PLAN

The Assistant Joint Chief of the Army took the podium in front of the War Room as some aids passed around copies of the plans of operations to all members seated in the room. With him was General Bill "Jump" Chambers of the Elite Delta Force out of Ft. Bragg, South Carolina. US Navy Commander Jim Blankenship, the Officer in Charge of the US Seal Team Deep 1 Diver Group was also present. They had come to Washington with plans to present to the President and the Joint Chiefs on the operations that would gain control of England. The US and England were in talks over the possibility of doing a night operation to recapture the sites in southern England.

"We are here to demonstrate the use of power in a joint action on two sites; one just on the outskirts of Portsmouth, and the other at a small airfield in Brighton. Both targets are in Southern England and lie in close proximity to the waters of the English Channel. These two points have an advantage for the Russians, in that they can monitor shipping lanes throughout the Channel. We need to hit these places as hard and as fast as the Russians took over Europe!" The Assistant Army Chief of Staff introduced General Chambers.

"Good day, everyone. It was brought to my attention just a short time ago that an airborne and sea operation will be conducted on the two target areas with the support of the Royal Air Forces Air Assault Units out of Scotland. This operation is going to be a lightning fast knock down and reoccupation, using the US Army's Delta Force, the elite US Navy's Seal Team Deep 1 Diving Group, and elements of the

Royal Air Assault Teams from Great Britain. Plans have already been finalized for transportation to the spring point, then onto the LZ. This will involve units from the newly formed DQD units (Delta's Quick Division) of the 501" Air Assault Team out of Bragg. Upon arrival to the spring point, elements of the Navy's Seal Team 1 will accompany the DQD units in a HALO jump, Northwest of the targets. Four C-130's out of Keflavík, Iceland will meet us in the Outer Hebrides Islands of Scotland, where we will load up and from there fly to the jump site. I cannot tell you how proud I am, right now, to be an American, but I want you to know: many young men will die. But if we do nothing today, we will surely die under the hands of a country that has seen fit to force its will on countries that were free. We will not fail! Thank you!"

Commander Blankenship walked up to the front of the room, then looked around and began his introduction.

"Everyone, as described by my astute colleague, we are going to place two operations, here," the Commander turned to the large screen, and pointed to the map of Southern England, "on the small island of Wight, just across the water inlet to Portsmouth, and here at Brighton. Units from our Seal Team Deep 1 Diver will conduct a sea-to-shore infiltration of the target area from the Island. There we will wait until units of the Delta Force, Seal Team 1, and the Royal Air Force arrive to begin their assault, coming from the north side of the target. As the fight assumes, we then will attack the rear and left flank, forcing the enemy into a vice, where we will crush all resistance!"

"The same is to be done here at Brighton. Our Seal Team will wait offshore until the forces begin operations from the north. US Navy Seal Teams will be accompanied by US Airborne Special Forces Units from a HALO jump, just west of the targets. Both operations must be in close proximity to each other so not to give wind to the targets that an attack is taking place. US Air Forces out of Keflavík, Iceland will be assisting us with high speed, low altitude radio jamming throughout the Channel with their FB-111 Wild Weasels."

"Jumps will be made up of Special Forces and Seal Teams. About 800 men from four aircraft will descend onto each of the targets. The Royal Air Force's Radian Attack Helicopters will have stand-off precision munitions, and launch them at communications and field radar, then will join in with air assault troops numbering 500 for each base. We will have another JSTAR readied over the position prior to the operation. The Russians will not think that we could be in a position to strike. They would be thinking that, since the fly over of France, we would be hesitant to try anything like that again, if there were a possibility of a nuclear retaliation in it for us. We have to be prepared for anything that could happen, especially in the most likely areas of infiltration. This has to be quick and painless. If units of the Russian Nuclear Assault Teams exist there in the target area, we must be quick to find them, and disarm them! Units from our elite Nuclear Deterrence Team, also know as 'Squids' will be on the hunt for possible locations that the Russians would use to deploy such units."

The Commander gave his thanks for the time spent going over the plans.

"When can you leave?" the President asked.

"Sir, we can be ready to go in six hours!" General Chambers said. "Things have been in place for this since this morning. The time is a-wasting if we wait any longer. Transportation to the spring point is set. We need to fly into Newfoundland where we will be transported by tanker to Scotland. We will be ready to strike by this Friday."

"On the two week anniversary of the Russian's little trick. That sounds just about perfect. We are scheduled for a meeting with the Commandant himself in Russia. He said that he would welcome the Ambassadors of England and the US sometime this week. Let's set it up and kill two 'Bears' with one stone!"

"You got that right, Sir!" General Chambers said. "A stone cold kill."

The President shook the men's hands and they were all wished good luck as they prepared to leave. The Secretary of State was in contact with the English Ambassador to Canada about the move to rid the English of their Russian visitors.

"Plans are set, Sir. The tanker is in port for the troop's transport. As soon as they get up there we will give the Ambassadors the word to meet with the Commandant. This is going to be one hell of a show."

They left all together, and said that they will meet each other up in Newfoundland this evening.

The President seemed to be pleased to have everyone playing on the same sheet of music.

"We might have been caught with our pants down, but this is not going to be the way it looks in a few days. It is time to answer those who think that they can play this game all by themselves, without giving the other players their chance to move. It is far from over, people, and I need to know what we can do to put an end to someone's dreams. They might be sleepwalking right now, but we are going to slap the shit out of them until they wake up. I'll be at the White House to see my family." the President said. "Call me when our Ambassador to Russia checks in."

Everyone stood up as the President left the room. His aids were gathering up their things to return to their offices. It left the Secretary of Defense and all the Chiefs sitting there, looking over at the large screen.

The weather was still unstable with widespread rain and snow. Father south was a clearing with a high moving into Southern Portugal and Spain. Italy and Sicily here having low lying fog with afternoon thundershowers.

"This weather sucks!" said the Army Chief of Staff. "Christmas is coming up fast, and our boys are caught up in the middle of this shit, and we can't do anything to get out of it."

The Air Force Chief was looking at the numbers of aircraft in the area.

"Less than an eighth of our force is operational from inside the area of Germany. Italy is almost less than that. We cannot make an attempt of an air strike without alerting the whole Russian air force. From where they are perched, they would have the air covered just waiting for us to fly into a wall of fire. This is not our time to take up the issue of 'air supremacy'. It will take a shit-load of time to come up with a joint effort to get things a little more even in the air. Everything that we do coming from the US will be seen as a possible threat to the Russians, and who in the hell can tell what they will do because of it?"

The Army Chief of Staff was not so optimistic.

"Our ground forces are dotted throughout Germany and Northern Italy. There are some 400,000 plus, and that is a good number to have. Being far away from another base that supports our cause, our troops are isolated, and some units could be just 'sitting ducks' if they tried to move to join their sister unit. Like the great turkey shoot we had in Northern Kuwait, Russia would itself have a great opportunity to strike."

"See, you have ADA here, Armor there; no one has the ammo close to their base. They would have to try to re-supply from areas that I'm sure the Russians have already have targeted. Each base has very little to fight with. Some have enough to defend the base for two or three days against a moderate size force. But others have nothing. The plans to get support units closer to those who need them were too slow to take action."

"Why is that General?" the Chairman of the Armed Services Committee asked, as he walked in halfway through the briefing.

"Well, just like our Senators and Congressmen, we think of how what we do influences our constituents." The General looked over at the Chairman. "Germany wanted to have the newly occupied armies of France, England, Canada, and the US to be in areas that needed the most rebuilding after the 'Great War'. The financial impact of our military in that country alone was unimaginable. We were put where we were most needed, and that caused us to be spread out all over the land. We pumped in the money and the resources to rebuild Germany and Italy. The West was the 'good guys and if we helped these devastated countries, they would in turn let us keep a forward force stationed there."

"Yes, but why has it taken so long to get where we are today?"

"Well, as you will see, the US got caught up into something she always gets caught up in. With the war over in Europe and our troops now stationed there, we had to hire tens of thousands of German workers to help the US with the daily things that need to be done for its troops. Everything from cooking our meals back at the garrison to washing our clothes, we were putting a lot of money into the local economy. We ended up rebuilding the shit out of Germany as time went along. But just like time, it was our time to go. Some of the cities throughout Germany wanted us to leave. To make a point, just look at Erlangen in northern Bavaria. All the bases closing in that city alone would have prime real estate available for the growing Siemens Corporation. But other cities like the small town of Zirndorf, just north of Nürnberg, they depended on the US dollar there to sustain them. Three hundred homes plus were rented to the service members there alone. Add the bars and small markets depending on the US dollar, and you have an ʻeconomy. But as the order to withdraw was given, who was to move out first was the issue. It really left us spread out all over the place. We would have support units all the way up near Hannover, and its Head Quarters were down in Heidelburg. Things were moving at a snail's pace to get units closer to each other because mayors couldn't see their US dollars being moved to an other city. Sounds familiar?"

"But Germany wanted the US out, anyway. The plans may have been slow but it was inevitable." the Chairman said.

"Yes, Sir, that is true, but some cities were better off than others. They could use the bases for expansion by companies that were willing to build in their city. So the tax base would not have to leave."

"But with the smaller cities or villages that had very little industry, having the US soldiers there helped out the bars, clubs and small shops and markets. They still had a lot of money coming in for their tax base, and you had the Americans that lived off base; again my point comes up. Those people from the town were renting their houses to the soldiers at top dollar. Now you want them to have nothing coming in as income. It took a lot of ʻWe'll pay you this because we have to do that just to get were we are today." Sound familiar, Congressman?"

Well what about the forward troops in Poland? Bases are small. Mainly Air defense and heavy tanks. Finland, and the Sweds have few American soldiers there.

Makes you wonder "who is in charge of this shit show?

Everyone could hear the General's sarcasm, but no one added to the discussion.

"The Navy and Marines have their full force out at sea already." The Navy Chief of Staff jumped in. "But we are spread thin. It would take weeks to send what we would require as surface ships, such as our aircraft carrier battle group from the Pacific. Any way you look at it, the Russians have the means to monitor our movements. They can see everything we do."

"They know that time is not on our side, but we still have a great many people that will fight the Russians from inside the country of occupation. It is our obligation to help those that are willing to fight, to rid their country of oppression. We can win this, one base at a time. Pick away at the very means that make them want to take over the country in the first place." the Chairman of the Joint Chiefs added.

FT. BRAGG

The troops were loading up on the C-17's that sat back to back at the airfield at Bragg. The General was walking around with his aids talking to the troops, explaining to them why they were unable to call their loved ones before they would take off.

"We need to be as quiet about this movement as we have ever been quite about anything. To your family, we are just training late, and will be home soon. You must focus on what we need to do. No one, I mean no one can know what we are ready to do. Just as we watch CNN, the enemy does, too. No one has a bigger mouth than CNN. Why? Because they feel that it is their duty to inform everyone about the news. Well, that is fine. But we haven't made the news yet. Give us a week, and they can print all there is to know about the shit when it is burnt and the smell goes away."

The plane's massive rear ramp closed, and they started to taxi down to wait for final permission to leave.

The General looked back at his men. He could see those that have spent a lifetime doing the job of the soldier in love with his country. Then there were those that were just kids. Some were not even out of school a year or so, looking nervously at each other. The General knew his men would do the job. A job, he knew, not all would be coming back from. He began to remember how hard it was to write the parents of one of his brave men that was killed in action. It was never something that they teach you in some officer's classroom. The fine lines that are needed, to be said of a man's valor just before his lifeless body fell to the earth. Words were never enough to fill the loss that the family feels when they know they will never see or talk to that person again.

He looked back with a solemn stare, then turned around to take his seat as the plane began to take off.

Out in the shoals, the Seals were at it again, and getting ready for an operation was an everyday thing. The US had the best when it came to men that had a special talent for getting the job done. Every moment of every day there was something to go over, some training to do again. And this was just another day at the office.

The Seals did not like the idea of going in with others who were not Seals themselves, because they didn't knew what that motherfucker was taught to do when shit hit the fan. They hated the thought that they might have to baby sit someone. But if it is a job that needs to be done, they were sure as hell happy to be given the chance to get it done.

The Commander walked around his men. Most were quiet, thinking of the mission. No-one was married, or cared to be. He knew the men, each and every one of them. Any job, he could call upon them to do. It was something that they trained for everyday.

He called to them, and they turned around and sat immediately with their hands in front of them. They just sat looking straight at the Commander. With a quiet voice he filled in the points of interest.

"We are going in to fight a large number of Russian Special Forces. We do not have any information on what type of training they have been put through. So other than us, you figure them out to be the baddest sons of bitches we have had the opportunity fight. This will not be a cakewalk, we will be out numbered four to one, plus we have others to think about. I am sure that our Special Forces units will do the job that they were trained to do. Ours is a job that will crush the enemy's will to take this any further."

He looked over at his S & D Team.

"I will have a talk with you all just before we land in Scotland. So keep your minds clear and heads on tight."

The Lieutenant said, "Yes, Sir!"

The C-17's were ready to go on the tarmac, as they all stood in single file, waiting their turn to pass the open water tank to give their respect to the mascot of the Team.

A beautiful eleven-foot long bottle-nosed Dolphin swam slowly around in its tank. As each man came to the tank he would hold out his hand. The dolphin would raise up and spray a burst of water on the man, as if to bless him on his journey.

The Commander was always the last in line and would give him a nice blue crab for a treat. He would throw it into the air and the dolphin would catch it. It swam around smacking its tail on the surface of the water to wave good luck.

The engines roared from the C-17's as the Commander ran to get on just as the ramp began to close. He made his way up to the front, and sat next to the Command Master Chief, who was rubbing some oil on his new tattoo.

"That is beautiful." the Commander said as he turned his head back and forth to try to make out what it was.

"Come on, Sir, quit messing around! You know what this is."

The Commander sat back and put his finger to his head.

"That looks like a re-run of 'I love Lucy'."

The CMC looked at him and said, "I'll give you 'I Love Lucy'!" and gave the Commander an ugly look. "Come on, CMC, you need to stay away from that mother-of-pearl you smell all the time."

"Well, how can I tell if it is real if I don't smell it? You know you can spend a lot of money on something that looks the same, but it is not. My whole swimming pool is layered with mother of pearl!" he boasted.

"OK, now what about the tattoo? Why did you get this one? How many does that make, 47?"

"45, and I just like the gal that does the work. You don't find too many ladies smoking a big Cuban and cutting you at the same time. Now that is the perfect picture of the women of my dreams. Besides, she had a good collection of some mother of pearl that she let me smell, good quality."

"I'm not even going to go there."

The Commander looked around at his men, then looked at the CMC. He just looked up as their eyes made contact, and a small smile came over the CMC's face.

"It will be just fine, Sir. The poor bastards will never know what in the hell is hit them."

NEW YORK

The Chairman of the Fed put a stop to all the speculations of the rise in interest rates for the last quarter that would end just before the New Year. Wall Street Futures were down some 24% from the high that it enjoyed at the beginning of the unification of Europe. Now so much has happened to the market since the closing that it was hard to even move up 1 point.

The Presidential advisers were recommending that he put into action a law to be signed by Executive Order that for the month of December, no one has to pay federal income tax. With this Executive Order, they felt the public would see that we do not need Europe to keep America on top of the world's trade.

Many people would just have to buy "Made in America" products instead of European.

With French wine and Russian caviar at an all time high, other products took up the slack as the festive season took hold of the people. The troubles of the world were not going away anytime soon, but things do go on. In less than 120 years of the market, not even three generations of Americans had gone by. Trade would not put a stop to the US. We have the best of everything the rest of the world wished they had to offer. We just need to go through a different door to get it done.

A President's Saddest Moment

The President walked up to the podium at the Remembrance and the Resting of US Service Members ceremony for those that were killed over in Sicily and Naples. The Flag-draped coffins, all seventeen of them, sat out on the runway in Dover as a crowd of 100,000 plus gathered to pay their final respects to the sons and daughters of America.

The President was clearly shaken as he fought off the tears that seemed to over run his face.

"We look here today at a time that is so full of confusion, that it is some times wondered upon if it will ever go away. As if we fell into a hard sleep and don't hear the clock sound its bell to wake us up."

"It's crazy." he added. "We are a country only so big, one that is part of a continent, and nestled in a hemisphere on a planet that floats in an endless sky we call space. We have searched the heavens for answers to questions, yet we still wonder why."

"We have nowhere else to go, we can't just pack up our bags and take off to a distant world that is not as filled with the things that would make us want to leave in the first place."

"We can't conjure up a machine that will throw us back into time so we could do it all over again, maybe better than what we already thought of as a good job done."

"We just have to take the time that our God gave each and everyone of us and live it the best way we can. These young individuals that we see here, lying with our Country's flag that they can neither touch or see any more, gave their lives for that flag and country. These young service members would pass that flag blowing in the breeze everyday there at Naval Air Station Sigonella, Sicily, and in Naples. Our friend and partner of NATO, Italy, could see it too, flying along the side that of their own flag each and everyday."

"They would see our country's flag, the one that has meant so much to so many in the years that have passed like chances in one's life time. More people know that flag, more than any other on earth. And here we have 17 young members of our great Navy lying quiet under that flag."

"You may wonder at times of the reason that all of these young people wanted to stay and fight. We may call it a pride for one's nation, but they would add the love for one's nation."

"To the families, we give to you as a country, the gratitude of a Grateful Nation. We do not know the loss in your heart, we can only pray for it to be lessened with the pride of their patriotism. We will never forget the job they did in defense of this United States."

Then, a pass-over of the Navy's Blue Angels gave way to a lone bugler playing taps. Seventeen teams of horses with a wooden caisson being pulled behind each of them stopped along side each of the fallen. They were to be put on the wagon and then placed on a plane for their final ride home to which ever State that they had called home.

The President was clearly shaken from the ordeal as he took each of the flags that were folded so sadly in the shape of the Trinity, and he kissed each coffin as he received the flag, one at a time.

He then walked over to the loved ones, said "On behalf of a grateful nation" as he handed them each folded flag. His own tears fell from his eyes upon the flag.

"The sorrow was felt deeply by the entire nation." he told them. The pain sometimes so hard, the President had a hard time keeping his shoulders from drooping, his body so weak from shaking as each of the 17 service members' names were called out, followed by a lonely toll of the ship's bell.

He thought to himself, "To truly love the nation, it took all of this." He would never be the same again.

THE GATHERING

"Landing gear is down, Sir, and flaps are at 35 percent."

The words "You are cleared to Land" were relayed up to the planes from an Air Force advance control team down on the makeshift airfield. The C-17's appeared out of the cold clouds and touched down one right after another on the hard packed dirt surface. They came roaring past the support unit and reversed their engines as they came to a fast stop on the short runway in Hopedale, Newfoundland. The ground was hard and ice covered almost everything. Trucks were parked close to the runway, ready to carry the men and their gear to the port.

"Quickly, people, we need to get this from here to here in a short time. We need to be underway in one hour!"

They were jumping through their asses, then were on their way to the ship. The air was clear and very crisp. It seemed to almost snow when you would exhale. The moisture from your breath was very heavy.

The trucks pulled up to the giant supertanker as she sat there alongside a massive concrete loading plat-form. The rough waters around her seemed to move everything else that wasn't tied down. During the last two days, it had been scrubbed clean from top to the bottom, inside and out, and was ready for the troops to start loading up. The clouded skies were getting darker in the distance and what had seemed to be a cold wind was getting colder as night began to fall over the out-stretched Atlantic. Everything seemed to be gray in color. The water was choppy, and large waves splashed over the dock while layers of ice formed on everything close enough to be exposed to the mist and waves. The rails and ropes were covered with ice that looked like candle wax had been melted over them.

"People, we must finish up here and get inside!" the Commander said. Everyone started to climb the ramp and head indoor out of the weather. The Commander and the General were the last to come aboard, and the door on the great hull was closed.

The confines of the massive ta nker was like stepping into a football stadium. It was heated and very comfortable. The SF units headed towards the front as the Seals took up house in the back. Some of the crew came down to tell the officers that they can send 150 men at a time to the galley for dinner. They were given orders and provisions to feed the entire group for a week.

The General told the Commander to feed his men first, so he could have a talk with the guys about the up coming mission. Platoon sergeants were placing their men's sleeping bags in order of responsibility. There would be fire watches posted for the trip. Reveille was at 0500 and they were to PT for two hours. They were "Ready as a red head" the CSM (Command Sergeant Major) was heard to say.

The Exxon Cumberland pulled away from the port just as the last of the trucks drove off. The single tugboat pulled her past the jagged rock inlet and out into the open waters where she was released and headed into the darkening sky. The temperature outside was a bone chilling 23 below zero with a wind chill factor of 51 below. The crew plotted a coarse that placed them close to 58 degrees NE latitude. Scotland was a three-day sail away.

The food was plentiful and tasted great. That is one thing about working out at sea, the food is always good. You have to feed a hard working body, because out here at this time of year, work is hard.

The Captain of the Tanker said, "We have to sometimes stay out three or four hours just to keep the ice off the steel pump lines. The weather these past few weeks has been the worst I have seen in some twenty years."

"Don't you guys stay in port much?"

"Why would we? When you are in port, it means that you don't have anything to transport. What good is a transport ship if you are empty?"

The Commander sat and listened to the stories that the Captain told about weather out at sea.

"Sometimes it looked like you could never see the sky, the waves were so big. As large as this tanker may seem to be, we are but a dot in the middle of one massive motherfucker!"

Inside the hull of the tanker you could only feel a mild movement. It started to put many of the Special Forces men asleep, like rocking a baby.

"The men are tired, Sir. They just had an all unit night jump with more than 1700 men. Then this shit, you bet they are tired. But they will be ready for the job."

The Seals had finished with their dinner and were out bull-shitting around throughout the tanker. No one was allowed out topside due to high wind and rain. It was black as hell out there and if you were to get lost, well…

The General informed his officers that they may begin to send their troops to eat, and that he himself, the LTC and the Major were going to join the Captain and the Commander up on the bridge.

"Alright, Command Sergeant Major, we will be sending 150 troops at a time for dinner, you can have your NCO's stand fast until all others are fed." the 2LT called out, then turned away.

The CSM just stood there looking as the young LT walked farther away.

"LOOOTENENT!!!!" The words echoed like in a vast canyon and carried throughout the entire ship.

"You carry your young ass over here, soldier! Who in the hell ever told you that I was a part of your chain of command?"

The 2LT came shuffling back to where the CSM was standing, and who began to fill him in on life according to GOD.

"You dare even place your words in context with mine? Have you been smoking Crack? I am the COM-MAND SERGEANT MAJOR! Twenty-nine sucking parasites like yourself! We do not even breathe the same air! My NCO's are mine and your ass is theirs, for without them you are a lost sheep waiting for some lone herder to place your hind legs into his rubber boots and have his way with you!"

The young LT's jaw was open and frozen from fear.

"There is no need to even talk to my NCO's, and more so to me what needs to be done with the men that you see here this day. You may carry on, you little shit, I'll take care of my men!"

The LT walked away, and over to the other lower ranking officers that were the platoon leaders of the SF unit. It took them a minute even to look like they wanted to be associated with the young LT. But they eventually brought him into the group, constantly looking over at the CSM.

"You were really hard on the poor little bastard!" the First Sergeant said as he walked up. The CSM just looked at the First Sergeant.

"Top," he said. "do you know how many of those little shits I have sent home a-packing, because they don't have what we need in them? I don't have the time or the patience to give them to help them to survive."

"I know." Top said. "Just because they finished high school with a 3.5 plus, applied at the Academy, and got accepted because of their grades. With their snotty, arrogant, 'Holier-than-thou' attitude, they get placed out here in the mitts of the men that have eaten the shit that makes up our life, not to mention what we get paid. Well, you've gotta love 'em!"

"Well, I work for a livin'!" the CSM boasted. "I have done this on my own. But that is not even a concern. Most of the enlisted here have at least one degree, if not two. They have come from places like U of Michigan, Ohio, UCLA, FSU. They could have been officers, but you have to swallow the political bull-shit that comes with the position."

"No shit! And then what do you get for it? As an enlisted you get to mess with them about your re-enlistment. You can take them right to the edge then put it on the dotted line. Then they walk away looking all smug, like they had some kind of part in it."

The CSM started to laugh. "Yea, then when you have more'n twenty-five years, they begin to fear you. They think that you are a really old, rock-hard S.O.B.! Hey, remember that one time that I was talking to the men about this one jump? The officers were there in front and I was making sure that everyone had their cord attached?"

The First Sergeant began to hold his side laughing, while others were listening to the story.

"Well, I had cut my cord and I made believe that I tripped, and the cord broke and I fell out of the back of the plane, far away from the LZ."

The first Sergeant was on his knees. "Stop, stop. fucker! You are killing me!"

"Then, when you all came down, I was sitting there with my feet on the dash of that Hum-V?"

The First Sergeant was on his back. "Those guys were crying! I had to hold them back from jumping out and trying to save you. Ooh, that was a sight!"

"Yea, I kill myself! I walked around leaving my service folder open the next day in the CO's office. They shit when they learned that I had more then 4,000 jumps to my name. Twenty-eight years of falling from the sky. You've got to love this country!"

The General sat calmly eating a hoagie while both the LTC and the Major had some roast beef with mashed potatoes. The Captain and the Commander were telling stories about the ocean and how unforgiving the damn thing was. They sat there for a better part of the night taking turns telling about different places of the world and the adventures of the times. Each place was of some far-off land where wars were fought and little was said about them.

"The tales seemed endless," the General stood up and said, "but this night is not." He then said that that it was about time for them to head for the sack. They all agreed and cleaned up what mess they had made on the bridge. Then they all said, "thanks" and "good night" and headed for the holding area for what would be a good night's sleep.

The General and the Commander walked back to the hold of the tanker. Almost everyone was sleeping, all those but the CSM and those sitting around the CMC. They all got up as the General returned and the rest of his officers entered the room. The CSM walked up to the General and asked, "Everything alright, Sir?"

"Yes, it is. Everything OK here, CSM?"

"Yes, Sir, you can see that they are all sleeping soundly. How is the weather looking outside?"

"A little rough, but we will get there in time for the big show."

"The dinner was good, it made a big difference coming here, after staying up all night to boot."

"Well, let them sleep a few hours more tomorrow, they are going to need as much energy staying in here as they would need out on patrol."

The Commander agreed, and they said their good nights and all hit the sack. It was going to be a full day of "training" for everyone tomorrow.

A Word called 'Détente'

The world kind of took a step back on the harsh words that they had with Russia as time went on. They could see that Russia did not come flying over the border with more troops and having more people killed. The holiday season was moving in closer and good will was felt. The news that the people were to be released from the airports was a good sign that things may be calming down.

New agreements between countries on food goods had to be monitored. Much of the food that once left Europe to other countries outside of the continent had stopped.

"We must first learn to feed ourselves first." the Commandant told them. "There are far too many going hungry throughout Europe, much less the rest of the world."

Trainloads of foodstuff were heading to the far reaches of Russia as the new agreements of the UEN began to take effect. Some of the NATO countries that were still members, protested the favoritism shown to Russia, although she was paying for it. Those that did not yet sign the agreement found it hard to trade for much of anything. An open market with a touch of the "Mob Rule" was the setting throughout the New Europe.

Back home the US was monitoring the flights that started up throughout Russia and the rest of Europe. Commercial fights were still grounded, but flights to resupply the Russian troops were being permitted. Congress debated back and forth on the issue of Russia's resupply of the positions, and the mixed message was a waste of time for those who were looking for the strong support that the US once boasted.

"We can't support talks between the US and Russia in the upcoming days if they feel that there is a 'So what, let them have Europe' attitude in this country. We have to send a strong message that they will be getting nothing from us whatsoever!" the Speaker of the House proclaimed.

"We can not show any indifference to those that will divide us."

"They already have the airports, and they don't seem to be moving to populate the rest of Europe with troops, let them resupply. It is not like we can stop them in the first place."

"Russia has even allowed the US to have food and what it needs to keep the troops there healthy while discussions were taking place for the removal of all foreign troops from Europe. What more needs to be done at this time?"

Italy was being flooded with people trying to leave the north. It was one of mans most trying times with the mountain passes through Austria being closed due to snow. There were people freezing in their cars trying to get out of Germany. They were frightened about the feelings that Russia had with the Germans after the Great War. Many felt that there was no other way but try to get out as soon as possible.

Armadas of small boats were found by some of the navies that patrolled the Med. They were trying to get to Africa and to freedom. Many had sunk due to the bad weather of the season. Though the increasing numbers leaving seemed to show a dislike of those of the new Europe, it was still a far cry less than the numbers that ran during the German occupation of Europe just a little more than a half a century earlier.

"People," the President said, "we must go out and tell the people of the United States that we will be in this for the long haul. We can only do so much before the world goes crazy on its own. We will be there for our friends in England, as they face this holiday season. We have to take this one step at a time, and we must be strong. Together we will pull through."

The lights on the Presidential tree were finally turned on. Snow was falling lightly throughout the capital, and stores were putting up decorations in the windows. It was a little late to be finishing up on the Christmas speech to the nation, but the President didn't have too much to say, "these times are the best of times. But being the country that we are, it is the best of times."

"No, that doesn't sound right. You guys are going to have to get this thing right before I go on TV in three days. Make it about the country sure, but include the countries that are having the hard times that we... ah, you know what I mean. Here go finish it!"

"Right away, Sir!" The speechwriters took it back and left the room.

"I don't need to be writing a speech, I need to be talking to the Russian President. We haven't spoken a word since the start of all this. There has been no open forum on talks."

The Secretary of State interrupted by saying, "No one is talking. The Ambassador, the new heads of state, no one. And if you look at it, Sir, that might be a blessing in disguise. We can have a clearer head by knowing nothing, than if it is filled with possible lies and disinformation from the Russians. We really don't know if what the Russians are saying is true or not. They have lied to us in the past. I say 'good!' Just stay tuned."

The Secretary sat back and took a drink of his coffee.

"Damn, you running for office, or just too much coffee?"

"I'm sorry, Sir, but…"

"No, that is quite all right, you always seem to bring a smile to my face. I mean that you are right, but we all have pulled out enough hair over this. The country is still strong, our people are well, and we have a need to help others that want our help. So if you look at this right now, of all the countries that are under some kind of occupation, only one is asking for our help."

"England."

"That's right, England. And we are right now, at this very moment, on our way to render that help. Maybe there are other countries that need our help, but we have done nothing to show them that we are able to help. I don't want to see this go on. I don't want to do anything that could jeopardize our troops' safety in those countries."

"We have people in our think tanks coming up with different scenarios, and the outcome of those scenarios should they be put into play. The ultimate question is; Can we survive?"

Moscow

The Commandant was finishing up with his meeting with the President, and the newly appointed representatives of the UEN. The Head Quarters will be in St. Petersburg and will have 1300 seats of the different governments.

"We are well on our way to bring about real change to this continent. Changes that were needed well after the last war that tore us apart as a people."

The President agreed. "We can be strong as a country, but we can be stronger as a continent. Everything that it takes is right here within the boundaries of Europe."

"Our vast oil fields, once tapped, will supply the continent with a more affordable resource. It will be a great source of revenue for Russia. Billions upon billions of dollars that we once only pondered.

It has been a SOB waiting to out live the restrictions the world placed on our oil and natural gas. We lost billions over the Ukraine invasion thinking they wanted to be Russian again. Freedom had taken over. We lost too many people and should have backed off once we learned they were not going to change.

A new birth for our great country. Our new relationships with Iran and Iraq can prove to be a plus to us as their oil can be sold here instead of being boycotted by the west. Let them hurt themselves, we shall prevail." Not even China knows what is the hell is going to be hitting. Fuck China he added. They are nothing without our oil.

The Commandant said, "You are absolutely right, Sir, and as time goes on, we will have what their money and military could only dream of. They have not fought a war in some time. The BS threats over Tiawan, do it or shut the hell up.

When things settle down, we must, we will be able to take better care of our troops with pay that will help out their families. This will insure that not only the Special Forces are well and are in good health, but are our young men and women who serve our great nation are taken care of, too. We have for too many years not taken care of our own as well as we should have. And that, Sir, is going to change." I was sick to the bone to hear of our over all loses. This is not longer going to be done to the army. I didn't care for the use of those who were jailed, but I had to at the time look for the positive.

The Major knocked on the door. "Sir, are you busy?"

"Major, I am never too busy to hear what you have to say."

"Sir, we have the Ambassadors to the US and England on the phone. They are requesting a private meeting for 2 weeks from this Friday with you and the President." "Are they waiting for an answer?"

"Yes, Sir, would you like to take the call in here?" "No, Major, I will come out there and talk to them, but first we must call a meeting with the press to show them that we are willing to come to some kind of agreement with the US and England."

"Yes, Sir."

The Major turned around and left to convey the answer to the Ambassadors.

The Commandant looked at the President. "Sir, I shall talk with you later."

He walked out of the office and the reporters were all ready gathered up front of the great hall to take pictures, and ask questions about the future meeting between the three countries.

The Major was standing by with the Ambassadors on the other end of the phones waiting for his response.

"Members of the press!" he started as he moved the microphone closer to his mouth. "I want to make a statement.

2 weeks from this Friday, I, along with the President, will entertain the Ambassadors to the US and that of England. We need to resolve differences between us and those two nations. I am optimistic that, with us finally coming together for talks, we can put down in words what it is that Russia sees as the future of Europe. Right now I will talk with them on the phone to invite them here for these talks. We wish for at complete understanding between our great nations. Thank you."

The Commandant walked away from the podium and over to the phones. He stood there as the reporters took photos of him in conversation with the two Ambassadors. His smiles were caught on film as he discussed the time frame of the meeting. Then he hung up the phone andreturnedto the reporters' questioning.

As he reached the podium, he turned around and asked for a drink of water. He placed the glass down and asked if anyone had a question on what was to be a meeting of the three nations.

"Sir, can you tell us if it is a 'go' for the meetings and if so, where they will be taking place?"

The Commandant opened up with a small statement.

"We have seen the light at the end of a long tunnel, and now the light is getting brighter. The meeting is set for 2 weeks from this Friday at 21:00. We will be entertaining the Ambassador of the United States and that of England at the residence of the Prime Minister. As you know, that is the former State's House of our great statesman Nicholas II, tzar of Russia."

"Can you tell us what the discussions will be about?"

"You have come here to learn about a story that is breaking here in Russia. It is a meeting of the Powers of Europe and those of the self-proclaimed Free world. Many things must be worked out in order for our nations to come together in a mutual understanding. How can I say what they want, if they have yet to tell me? We all must just take the time to learn about each other. This is a new chapter in the world, and the story that you all seek is not yet written. So now you have the date, the place, and with whom down. Now let us and our guests talk to each other about the things that give us the need to talk, thank you."

The Commandant turned away as the reporters yelled out more questions. He just smiled to them and walked into the office of the President. They all then turned and ran like hell outside to call in the story to their press editors.

"You know, Sir," the Commandant said. The President just looked up and smiled. "These people that find a need for a long, drawn out questions sometimes hurt my head." He plopped down into the chair in front of the President's desk. "I mean it, Sir, there are times I wish that I could not hear. It would make my life so much easier."

They just looked at each other and laughed. "Would you like a cup of tea, Gladimir?"

"Yes, Sir, I sure would!"

He called the Major and asked if he would have some tea sent in, and for the Major to take a break and join them.

WASHINGTON

"Sir, yes, that is fine. OK. Well, good luck, and I will convey that to the President." The Secretary of State hung up the phone.

"We are in." he said as he entered the War Room from the adjacent office.

"I was just on the phone with our Ambassador to Russia and the Commandant agreed to have the meeting 2 weeks from this Friday at 2100 hours Moscow time. That is the perfect dinner time, to eat while your plans are fostering into a wonderful display of the resolve."

"Mr. President!" the secretary turned when he walked into the room. "I was just telling the Chairman, here, that our Ambassador just called about the meeting this Friday."

"Really? Is everything a "go"?"

"Yes, Sir, 2100 Moscow time they should be starting to talk. It will be a good start, being the last week before the New Year.

"Well, it is for the most part a very hard sell. We must take precautions that what we give as a present isn't returned for exchange. I want everyone hot-to-trot this Friday night. I want all Air Force squadrons to be ready for anything. I want word sent over secure lines to all units one hour before the actions are to take place. It won't be pretty, but it will sure as hell be effective."

ABOARD THE TANKER

The morning sky was overcast with a light rain falling, as the giant tanker sailed northeast towards Scotland. The ocean was a little more forgiving than it was last night. The General and his officers, along with the Commander joined the Captain on the bridge for coffee.

Ice was being knocked off the fuel lines that had gathered on them overnight. The crew would then pick up the great sheets of ice and throw them over board.

"Even though we are not carrying any fuel, lines still need to be cleared for two reasons." the Captain explained to his guests.

"First, so they don't bend under all that weight. Second, Russia flies patrols over these waters and it must look like we are carrying fuel. That is also the reason we are throwing sand on the deck where we need to walk. The ice on the deck would normally have been cleared too, but it will give us the appearance of having a heavy load, and it makes us sit deeper in the water. Normally oil is quite heavy, but I just have you all to transport, a big difference in weight. The sand disguises the thickness of the ice. We don't need to give those bastards any help at all in finding out who we are and why were we sailing northeast."

"The good thing is that we are alone." the Captain went on. "They see many tankers on the open seas with loads bound for Iceland, Greenland, places that have to pump the oil in from other countries. We will be OK. But make sure that your men stay indoors, they photograph everything. They know how many men are on a tanker, and if they count more than there should be, well they will stay right on top of us the whole trip."

Everyone agreed and said their thanks for the info. They finished up their coffee and filed down to the troops.

The echoing of the men working out was getting louder and louder as they got closer to the holding tank.

The Commander opened the door and the sound hit them like a brick wall being tossed by a tornado.

"My God!" the General said as they all entered the vast compartment. They all just stood there as they watched the Special Forces on one end and the Navy Seals on the other try to drown out the other with their cadence.

"1, 2, 3, 4... 5, 6, GIVES US SOME MORE!" The general smiled to see his troops so fired up. "They are sure working up an appetite. They will eat the week's rations in about two days."

The Commander watched his Seal Team kicking out fifty four-count pushups. Every man in sync with the other, it looked like one massive machine.

"Got to be proud that we are Americans." the General said. "You couldn't ask God for better men to get the job done for the country."

Everyone shook their heads as they walked down to the platoon sergeants and squad leaders.

The platoon leader turned and saw the officers coming down to talk to them.

"1,2,3,4," then his voice got really loud to indicate that this was the last cadence. "1, 2, 3, halt! Stand… at… EASE!"

The platoon leader turned around and saluted the General as he walked up the troops.

"You all look great. I just wanted to mention that I am so damned proud of you guys, I hardly have the words to say it."

The General turned to the platoon leader and saluted. "You keep up the good work, son."

"Yes, Sir!" he shouted back. He dropped his salute then turned back to his men.

The Commander had his men go up to take a shower and file in for breakfast. This gave the SF units time to run on the inside of the containment tank.

"Give me six fast laps in three columns!"

"Fall in!" and they lined up right behind the platoon leader. "Double time, March!" They all gave out a yell, and took off on the outside wall of the hold.

"Up in the morning too soon!"

"Don't want to rise until high noon!"

The General waited until the last man passed him, then he joined in the run. His officers followed suit as a long line of men made the turn around the tankers inner hull. The songs were sung from many years of the US Army training the soldiers that fought our country's wars. And like before, they trained to be thrown into the pit of a fight, and the outcome was only known to God.

The six fast laps were over in 30 minutes, and they too broke to the showering rooms, then off to eat.

The Commander had himself a can of silver spray paint and began to draw a picture of the United Kingdom. He stood on a ladder and started with Scotland and the Outer Hebrides Islands. Then made his way down and round mapping out Wales, and southern England. Back up to finish the country of Scotland. He made the border of Ireland and the shore of the French Normandy coast. The map was some 40 feet in height.

The young 2LT got chairs for all the officers who stood on the side observing.

The Commander instructed his men to take a seat down here in front and as the Special Forces men finished breakfast to have a seat behind them. Within 30 minutes the Commander had everyone in attendance.

He walked up to the front of the men and introduced himself and his men to those of the SF.

"Good morning." He looked over to the General

"Sir, it is an honor. My name, for those of you that do not know, is Commander Blankenship. I am the OIC of the US Navy Seal teams that are here with you on this very important and dangerous mission."

"Some of you know some parts of the mission, but I am here, along with LTC Mayers of the Special Forces, to update you and fill you all in on the mission."

"As you see here behind me, I have drawn a map of the United Kingdom. This is where we are heading, to help our friends, the English."

"We are going there to start a fight, with a very competent aggressor, the Russians. They do not know that we are coming. No one knows that we are coming that can put up a fight to stop us. We must keep inside this massive tanker at all times. Do not go out on the topside of the ship. I will say that only once. And I will not tell you, and my men know, what I will do if you are caught out topside."

"Now, with that being said, may I present to you LTC Mayers." The Commander turned and exited the front and LTC Mayers came up to the map.

"Good morning. We will be arriving here," the LTC pointed, "in less than two weeks in the Outer Hebrides Islands of Scotland. We will exit this fine ship and will stand fast for pick up by four US Air Force C-130s. We will all board the planes at that time and they will fly us down to the Island of Man, just west of England in the Irish Sea. There we will team up with the Royal Air Force Air Assault Units."

"Units of our 501 Air Assault Teams, a platoon size force from US Navy Seal Team 1, and the Royal Air Forces Air Assault Team, will come together as one unit."

"You will then board the Radian Air Assault helicopters and make a Bee line to the target areas."

"Those of the 501 Special Forces Airborne Units will stay on your C-130 and will proceed to the Drop Zone Pawn, and Drop Zone Bishop. Before entering the DZ the aircraft will then climb for your HALO jump."

"Navy Seal Teams DID and elements of the Seal Team 1 will be flown to their objective via two US Marine V-22 Osprey aircraft. Seal Team 1 will take up positions here on the Island of Wight with your Fast Act craft, after a sea drop 12 miles off the shore of the island. DID will have to wait in open waters after their twelve mile drop offshore."

"This is all going to be under the cover of darkness. The time of force action will be approx. 1800 GPM. You all will be going through your own individual training prior to the leaving the Spring Point."

"This must go off as a unit, not one thing, then another. As the Airborne is hitting the ground, Air Assault should be knocking down the door. Then the Seals should hammer them into the anvil."

"We have the support of your President, and after this is done, I'm sure the love of the English people. I don't need to tell you all that this is one of the most important operations that your country will ever call upon you to do for her. And I don't have to tell you that we are not facing a force from out in the sands. These are well trained, highly motivated and dedicated men who believe in what they are doing. What we need for you all to do is also believe in what you are doing, and kick some Russian ass and get this job done."

The whole group demonstrated their intent by giving out yells and screams to show that they were fired up, grabbing and giving each other the "high-5". It was a great sight to see.

Commander Blankenship then walked up to the front. Everyone turned quiet again.

"It does a warrior good to see others like him ready to do battle. When your focus is that of tunnel vision, all you see is the end of the fight, and you are victorious. But there are things you must put yourself through before victory can be tasted."

"When you enter a fight and you are out-numbered, the first thing you do is go after the fucker with the biggest mouth and silence his ass for good. Then you look for those who want to fight and give it to them fast, and furious. Then you will see those that are hesitant. Kill them. Don't waste your time. Last, you well see the ones unable to fight. That is when the body count starts, and you include them."

"Not one, and I mean not one man should be standing. He should be dead, or minutes away from that state."

"If you have wounded, you do not leave them. If you have dead, under no circumstances leave them. Don't you ever give them the means to persecute your dead. To humiliate your dead. If you can't carry your dead, then you make sure that there is nothing left of your dead."

The Commander walked around to his men. He looked down, and pulled one of them up and looked at him face to face.

"Do you understand me?"

"Yes, Sir!" Then another, then another.

He chewed and spat the words to all about him. "The importance of being an American. We don't do that to our men."

"Team up with your units and go over the plans of your attack. I will be making rounds to see you and answer all questions about the action.

RUSSIA

The flights to and from Russia began to pick up as their guests began to fly home to their countries. The airports throughout Europe were reinforcing the troops strength to some 6,000 men and women. Units of the regular army were being flown to areas that needed to be reinforced, and for rotation.

Families were so happy to see their loved ones. No one complained of poor treatment, it was more of an inconvenience than anything. They were not charged for the room or meals, even though they could order food and have rooms cleaned with maid service.

The Commandant was a little cautious about flights into England with very important talks to begin in just weeks, so the guests were flown to the French and English Channel Tunnel and were provides with the means of transportation for them to return home. Agreements were made to supply Russian troops there in England with food and water, as the Russians were doing the same for English troops stationed throughout Germany.

Most of the people that were held at the airports were also released as their respective countries entered into the agreement with the UEN. Slowly, very slowly, Europe was coming back to life. Many people were still frightened of the troops' presence throughout the country. But they could see that they were not forcing their will outside the airports. They were a staying power in the event that compliance was not the order of the day.

Christmas Markets all over Europe were opening late, but opening just the same. Many countries were sending packages to Bordeaux, France for the victims of the blast. Candles were lit every night to show sorrow over the tragedy. No lights were placed on the Christmas tree there in what was the remains of the City Hall in honor of the lights that made up the lives of those that had died and could never shine again.

Things somehow do go on no matter what the outcome is. As those that spend their whole life through waiting for the end of the earth to come, just to find out that they passed away before they could see it.

"Major, is it a possibility that you and I can get our asses out of this place and have us a real dinner? Everything is fine, we have good people here to keep things the way we left them."

"Will it just be us, Sir?"

"Yes, the President has gone to spend time with his son and his wife. So it will be just the two of us." "That sounds great, Sir, do you know Moscow very well?"

"Well, Major, I damn-near built the place."

They both laughed and headed out the door to the car.

"Driver take us to…"

A LONG HARD WAIT

"They will be arriving at the spring point about 1400 hours their time, 0900 here, Sir. They have been out of contact with us since they left Newfoundland. Things seem to be on schedule. Eagle-Eye has the ship heading NE towards Scotland. The weather from there is shitty. A large front that moved out from here is now heading to the coast of England, and they don't know it. Unless the ship's radar picks up the storm on Doppler, they won't know of the bad weather until they land in Scotland." Anything can change in the coming time.

"We can not send any word to them about anything. They have orders and they will make the final judgement just before it's time."

"They have my complete confidence, Sir." the Chairman of the Joint Chiefs said. "General 'Jump' Chambers will do his country proud."

The President's advisors laid out the different scenarios for the Chiefs to review.

"We have the one that is in play now, or these. The men can be called off up to one hour Zulu of mark. Then they will be too far into it to do anything else but strike."

With everyone in on the scheme of things, there was not much more to do but wait.

The President said that he was going out with his family and that everyone should take a break before tomorrow afternoon has them stuck in there and they will never be able to see their families.

The Air Force Chief said that he still had some planning to do with his people to insure that support aircraft are ready.

"I will keep track of the comp time you all owe me."

The President smiled, "I will see you all soon. Enjoy your evening."

The Air Force Chief of Staff called to the Chief of USAFE Space Command; he needed a little help with some aerial views that called for their expertise.

"We need you to be over the southeastern part of England no later than 1300 EST this coming up 2 weeks from this Friday, for the Eye from the Sky look down. Now I already know about the weather, but if we get some kind of break during the night's cooling, then we will be there."

The General quickly placed another call.

"Yes, I need to talk to General Grooms. I need a plane, a couple of planes. Thank you, I'll hold."

"Hey, Josh, this is Raymond. Do you think you could get your ass over here to the War Room? I know it is late but you have 15 minutes to get here. I'll see you then, "bye."

The Chairman sat at the end of the table as the Chief of flight operations walked in.

"Josh!" the Air Force Chief walked up and held out his hand. "How are you doing?"

"I was looking to go see the 'Nut Cracker Suite'."

"Well, that's all nice and all, but we have something for you to take care of first." the Chairman of the Joint Chiefs said.

"Not a problem, Sir, I am at your disposal."

"Josh, we have been in this office forever it seems, and we have a mission for your people to help us with."

Josh just sat back into the chair.

"We are going to need some air support from you, and it is going to involve several planes to pull this job off."

"You have already made requests for planes."

He shuffled through some papers. "Here, four C- 130's that are waiting in Iceland and will be flying to destinations unknown."

"That is right, they belong to this mission. But I need you to get going here on these aircraft. After I will tell you what they are, I will fill you in on the mission." He handed Josh the list:

6 C-130s	Request Approved
1 F-111 Wild Weasel	Request Approved
4 V-22 Ospreys	Request Approved
2 FAST Deploy Helos	Request Approved

"These aircraft are needed for a top secret mission into England, orders are from the President and flight plans will accompany pilots just before flight times. We cannot broadcast this until the last possible moment. You have full power to pull the four Ospreys from the Marines, and the Chief of Naval Operations will call ahead with that request."

"We have JSTAR's and AWAC's ready for the flight. Your additional aircraft must be ready to fly before tomorrow, 12:00 hours."

Josh sat with his jaw open, and then closed it with a tight smile.

"I am sorry to spring this on you at the last minute, BUT WE NEED THE PLANES, UNDERSTAND?" The Chairman looked over at him.

"Why, yes, Sir, I understand perfectly. I'll get on this right now."

"Thank you, Josh, talk to you in a little bit."

He left the room quickly clenching his briefcase tightly.

The Chairman looked a little disturbed about all of that.

"Sir, I know he might look fragile, but he is the best at what he does. He holds four masters degrees in engineering, and computer programming. And I sure would hate to lose a man like that to the outside world."

"We are a military of diversities."

"Yes, Sir, we are."

MOSCOW

"Sir, what are you going to have for dinner?"

"Well, the wild boar here is great; they oven bake it with carrots and wild potatoes. It has a strong pork taste and I love food that has some flavor to it."

"I think I will try the pheasant, with sweet potatoes and corn. Sure wish I could have gone hunting this year. I know a great place for pheasant hunting."

"Well, Major, after all of this settles down a bit, you and I will do a little hunting. Get away from all this and free the spirit."

"That sounds great, Sir." and they sat down for the first time in months to eat like humans, out of view of the reporters and out of earshot of the phone calls. It was well deserved.

After dinner they both took a ride through the Red Square. The snow from the past few days was shoveled up throughout the square. Kids were having snow ball fights and threw one at the car as it drove by. The cold and almost peaceful night called them home for a fitful sleep.

UNDERWAY

The training inside the great tanker was filled everyday with movement techniques, and area sweeps. The hull was large enough to make half of the mock up area of the LZ. The Captain was able to pull up charts of the shoreline of Portsmouth and Brighton, along with aerial views. These charts were for navigation of ships in those areas. Some almost better than were afforded some military units. They were clear and copies were passed around to all teams to study.

The Captain was sitting in the bridge when the General and the Commander came up.

"Permission to come on the bridge, Sir?"

The Captain said, "Permission granted." and had his First Mate retrieve some coffee.

"Radar is showing the coastlines of the Outer Hebrides, we just can't see them yet because there is a lot of rain moving through there. It looks like you guys will be wetter than a duck in all of this."

The General said, "That's great with me. My men work harder when they are the most miserable. Plus, no one would think to launch in such weather."

The Commander agreed, saying, "Weather is a great equalizer. Everyone is effected by it. We just have the advantage of knowing the time that we have to deal with it. They have to deal with it every time. You fall into a lulling rhythm like that. And that is when sounds and shapes no longer register. It really dulls the senses."

"Well, we should be coming up on land fall within a matter of just a few hours. I would say that you all need to get ready to get wet."

The Captain of the ship called all hands to prepare for docking. "We do not have the luxury of a tug boat, but we don't have all that weight to worry about, nor the worry of the oil. This water is deep, and we don't see the possibility of running aground."

They made their way down to the hold. The teams were in training and they looked good. Everyone was in high spirits and ready to get on with the mission.

"All right, everyone!" the Commander said aloud. "We need to pack up here and you all have to get ready for this in your head. This is not going to be easy, and it is not a cakewalk. The weather is rainy and cold, but you will still be in an airplane for some time before the fighting starts. They have to be out in this all day and night. So use that to your advantage."

The General stood and said, "We will need to forget all that is around us. We have what it takes to be an American. We are the best fighting machine in the world! You can leave much of your pack here; we will not need the sleeping bags for we will be staying in a hotel after this job is over!"

The troops gave out a mighty yell.

"We are going to kick the shit out of these bastards, and send their boys home in a bread box!"

The troops were all pumped up, and began final preparations for the assault. The officers were told of their mission and objectives. The sergeants knew what it was going to take to get the job done. Everyone knew there was only one road in front of them, and victory was the only exit on the road to battle.

The US Commander called for his Squid Team. This was a small but maneuverable group of men that operated inside the Seal Team with one purpose in mind: to search out any element of the Russian Nuclear Team, if any, and destroy them. They had learned the tactics of nuclear warfare and how to maximize effectiveness. Who, when is best, and to what extent do you get the most damage for your money. This would have to be done by studying the contours and natural shape of the landscapes, weather conditions, social considerations, everything. In other words, when and where would be the best place to detonate the baby. They knew the difference between an airburst, and one that is on the ground, took into consideration the time of day to produce the most casualties for each detonation. They could track the fall out and how it would travel in the weather and wind. The very best art of killing was more than just "flash to bang time". As they say, "Nuke's kill economically, you get more bang for your buck."

These guys were on the edge of what was real and what was the end. They knew that the Russians would be expecting them in any attack. That they were targeted from the very start, and life was no longer a thing they talked about. They would live from day to day, recklessly and on the edge. But you would never see a group of men more hungry for the chance to go in on a mission, and so out of their minds when they came back.

The days turned to night and with all that was happening the time did take its time. Plans are moving forward. Men and women on both sides tried to keep their minds on the here and now. The season brought heart break to all as the plans that were in the works march to the beat of the silent war drums.

Then some people thought of the Twin Towers in New York City that were knocked down so many years ago. How it marked the some what beginning of the change in the world. The wars that all nations had fought between themselves and a few with others.

America after some small punches thrown in small fight here and there were right in the mix of it all. Iraq and the Afgan wars ran some 20 yrs. Way longer then the 13 war in which many of the older soldiers of the time called "The Nam". Where we lost more than 58,000 American lives. Compared to the few thousands lost in Iraq and "The Stan". The cost for that war which was placed on the people of America was heavy. Yet they bore the cost and in time forgot about the loses.

The wind of change blew as new governments took offices Throughout the world. Europe became the European Union. Kind of a joke were the so called Leaders there let millions of non Europeans invade and changed the whole damn place. Too much to add about that shit show.

America with all there ups and downs of you're a racist or this a – fobe or that a- fobe. Gave a Black man the job of president. The 1ˢᵗ Black man. Real important to have a skin color as a qualifying factor. I will not call anyone anything different then you're an American.

America too through another change in leaders got invaded by the world without firing a shot. Millions upon millions crossed their border free to have what Americans paid and worked for. All given away. Funny how that is when it is not your money. America is good about doing that.

The world fought an invisible squerge call Covid-19. Killed millions world wide. Seems like it changed itself out over time. Proved to be a man made thing as a test to see if it could be a population control effort. Everyone wearing a mask that "Did Not Work". Drove people more crazy than ever. Killed a lot of the wrong people.

The mess of the Ukraine War. The money and war machines of other nations that fought that war with other people was the King of all shit shows. A sad time indeed. Boys sent off to war to fight an other man dream of being some kind of King. But only died with his name too being removed from all places and would never be mentioned again throughout history.

History was rewritten. New news was not reported.

MOSCOW

The Commandant's morning was filled with the reports showing the airlift to be right on time. Places were almost doubled in supply points and he could see the ease of the continent's worries about it all. Things were running smooth, as a knock on the door was heard.

The Commandant turned around and saw a man with a face that was lined with fear and eyes that were tired. He stood in the doorway of the Commandant's office at attention and a salute that couldn't be broken. A tear immediately hit the eyes of the Commandant. He said, "Enter." and the man walked to the desk and saluted once more.

"You may stand at ease, Major." and the Commandant came from around the desk and hugged Sergi. He had tears in his eyes as he backed up and looked at his man. He placed his hands on Sergi's shoulders and stood there a moment without words.

"You have done it, Sergi! You have made our country the land she was meant to be: strong and confident. The world is now on its knees and we say what is best for Russia."

Sergi stood there for one moment and then said a faint, "Thank you."

The Commandant called for something to be brought in for him to drink.

"We shall sit and have tea, and you will tell me about your mission."

Both men sat and talked for some time. It was plainly visible that Sergi was not in the best of health, and the Commandant wanted him to see the doctor that was on call there at the Great Hall of the people.

"You and your men are invited to the residence of the Prime Minister at 2100 hours. We are going to be entertaining the Ambassadors to the US and that of England. We have a great gesture to hand to them. And you and your men will be decorated with our nation's highest honor!"

Sergi smiled and said that it would be an honor to come.

"You and your men will never have to work again, your country will take care of you for the rest of your lives."

The Commandant hugged Sergi once more as he was lead out to see the doctor.

"This is a great day for Russia! We have our greatest hero back with us and we will demonstrate to the world that Russia can give as well, show our intent not to control those with an iron fist, but as the continent's true leader." You're dismissed.

The Commandant returned to the reports of the re-supply of his men, then started to write a speech that would honor his men. Afterwards, he began to prepare for the meeting, which would be nothing less than a show of cooperation with the once allied partners of the last Great War. But this time it wasn't just England and the US that would rule the world, as General Patton once said. But Russia will stand great and the others will ask of her greatness.

WASHINGTON

"Sir, the ship has arrived at the port, and the men are moving off and standing by to board the C-130s. The weather has been the same since last night, with rain forecast to fall into the late hours of the night throughout all of England. We do not expect that the run down to the south will be called off. It is a 'go'. from this time on."

We do not need to make a traffic jam of this movement. We are hitting the ground running. Let there be nothing to stop the coming of this fight. We are moving like the rain storm that me must become. It is our cover, it is nasty and it will be a GO!

The President just looked at the force that was put together. Many a man was in one fight or many over the years. We will not rethink everything now. Once seen we can not un-see it. The President called for the Ambassadors to be contacted, to relay the message that "the pie is done and who wants a piece?"

The message was relayed to all of those that had a need to know, and everyone began to monitor the events of all forces outside the US.

"The planes were refueled and air born hours ago, Sir. They should be only 34 minutes out of their objective. The C-130s are in Scotland with the others to join them on the Island of Man just before their arrival. They have their orders and it looks good from here."

"That sound great, Captain. You keep in touch with me on an hourly basis. I will convey the message to the President."

"Very good, Sir, I will call in an hour, out."

The Chief of Staff for the Air Force said that the four V-22 Ospreys were well on their way to the Island of Man. The orders were clear and they will be filled in on the mission when they arrive.

"We are looking at the first of the flights that are needed to get this in full swing. AWACs is already air borne as well as the JSTAR. We have several KC-135s up and heading for refueling of the birds as needed."

"What is the word on the F-111 Wild Weasel?"

. "Sir, we have that bird ready for launch in about one hour and it will be making its run through the English Channel just as troops are landing in the DZ."Are those old bastards ready to do the job? Sir yes sir. They might be an old platform, but they have the right signature and can fly like a bat out of hell.

What do you think LTC? Sir they are Good very good. They like any flying machine, have their own SIG. Because over time the newer air platforms being used today are very identifiable. The F111's do look like anything, nor do they fly like anything. No one uses swing wings. They (The Russians) will have no Idea what to think. Could be a decoy.

In any case we have not made a move in these past weeks for them to think differently. Plus the weather will really mess things up. Perfect.

"Everyone had been given their orders on the upcoming action. The weather might be a bitch to deal with, but things are going to go off as planned." the Chairman proclaimed.

"Remember, I don't want any one else to be notified until a least one hour before action. The less the Russians know about this, the better." the President said.

"That's right!" the Army Chief of Staff replied. "Our troops over there in Germany, Poland and everywhere else, are being watched by the Russians and they are monitoring them every minute. If they get wind that something is happening, they will have their bases closed up tighter than the pockets of the people in charge of military spending."

Everyone looked over at the General as he looked back.

"Just a little humor in the middle of all the pressure. I'm getting myself ready for the reports that will be coming out later this month."

"You are one-of-a-kind, General, but I am glad that you are on our side, because we do know what you mean."

THE RESIDENCE OF THE PRIME MINISTER

The Commandant's car was waiting for him and the Major to finish up things at the office. The snow was lightly falling and the steam from the sewers was filling the street with slow-moving clouds of moisture that sometimes gave the impression of a dancer moving to some strange music. They would go away with the passing of a car as it drove through them.

They came outside and both grabbed a hand full of snow that had piled up on the rails of the walkway. Making them into make shift snow balls they began to throw them at their driver who's window was down and had been sitting there smoking.

"You are losing heat and stinking up my car!" the Commandant said.

The driver jumped out and flicked his cigarette and said that he was sorry. A snowball hit him in the chest as he stood there with the back door open.

"Never get out of a car when you see men wheeling snowballs. It could be very dangerous for you." "Yes, Sir, I'll remember that for next time."

"Take me to my quarters, and do the same for the Major. I want you to then return to pick me up in one hour. Please do not be late or I will send you to the Russian front."

The driver made a face that was part, "What did you say?" and part, "Oh God, help me!"

The Major was laughing hard as the Commandant bullshitted with his driver. The car sped off into the mist and steam, and out of sight.

Joint Operations

"This is Zombie, we are ready to get this ride under way."

"Roger, Zombie, you have been cleared to burn up the tarmac here. Good hunting, boys. This is Keflavík tower, out."

"That's a roger, we are gone."

The engines slowly began to roar, as the pilot pushed on the throttle. The plane stood there on the runway a moment, then let out one hell of a rumble, all at once. Flames shot out five times the length of the jet as it raced down the runway, and then up into the darkening sky.

"We are heading out to play some music for our guys abroad."

A loud boom sounded as they went sonic.

"That should get someone's attention!" The ground disappeared below and they climbed up into the clouds.

"Busy-Body, this is Zombie, are you out there?"

"We sure are, Zombie. You need to change your heading to 1449'er and stay at your present altitude. We have you fixed up with a new friend out here on a blind date."

"Well, I can't say that it will be love at first sight, but if she kisses on the first date, we'll be in Vegas by week's end, tying the knot."

"You sure do work fast and talk sweet! I bet you feel that way with all the planes."

"Just the big and fat ones! I love me a gal with meat on her bones!"

"Well, we have just the right stuff that you are looking for. Stay tuned, Zombie, we will be right back."

"That is a roger, Busy-Body."

NORTHERN SCOTLAND

The General said his good-byes to the Captain and thanked him for his hospitality, then walked down the ramp that took him just behind one of the C-130s. He stood there looking inside at his men and they whooped and hollered back as the massive ramp closed.

The LTC said, "Good luck!"

The General embraced the LTC before he climbed aboard the C-130, saying, "Luck has nothing to do with it. It is in the hand of God now!" He saluted as the ramp came up and then closed behind the LTC.

The remaining aircraft were loaded up and ready to leave. The General made his way up to the cockpit and said, "Let's get this show on the road!"

The ramps closed and the six C-130s raced one right behind the other down the rocky strip and off into the cloudy sky. The rain and clouds moved across the window of the C-130 as it banked right to a course that would take them flying toward the west coast of England, over the Irish Sea to the Island of Man.

The General once more got up to look at the fine group of men that he had the privilege to command. He took a seat between some of his men and shot the shit with them awhile. He really did love his boys. And that is what made the difference to his men. It was like he was one of them. He wouldn't let a single one of his soldiers do something he himself wouldn't do.

The planes banked once more right, and then left as they came up and over the clouds into the beautiful open sky. The night was just off in the distance and the stars began to shine as the six planes, one right behind the other, began their slow descent to the Island of Man.

Moscow

The US Ambassador pulled up in front of the old English-style house of his friend. He got out and rang the bell. The butler opened the door widely.

"Sir, please come in."

The Ambassador turned to his driver and signaled to him to wait for them. He entered the house and the butler took his coat as he closed the door.

The house was brightly lit inside, with all the flavors of an English home at Christmas season filling the air. The tree was beautifully decorated with a still having a few gifts under it. Candy canes and bowls filled with different nuts were placed on almost every table in the room. A big wreath with some mistletoe was at the entrance of the dining room, where candles were lit and burning brightly.

The English Ambassador came walking down the stairs to greet his friend.

"Dave, welcome to my home." He then reached and gave him a candy cane and told him, "Place this on your tree."

Dave took it and said, "Thank you, I will. Hopefully I won't need to regester it as a gift. Then he laughed. Well, Richard, are we ready to get on with this?"

The Ambassador turned around slowly and looked into the eyes of his counterpart and said, "Dave, we are going to have to be strong tonight. Stronger than we have ever been. A lot will change from this night forward, and it falls on our shoulders."

They walked into the living room. "Drink?"

"Why, yes, thank you."

Richard poured them a tall glass of scotch.

"Life has changed as we know it. The passive state in which we have, in the past, enacted our authority is no longer that rule of thumb. We have calmly left the door of deception unguarded, and now we have fallen into a world that our old friend, Alice, would gladly purchase a ticket the hell out of here, if she could."

Dave downed his drink and returned it empty to Richard. "You ready to go?"

Richard finished and placed both glasses on the table in the dining room. He grabbed his and Dave's coats and called upstairs to his wife that he was leaving. She said that she loved him and he returned the gesture.

"I shan't be too late!"

He turned and said under his breath, "I hope!"

They both walked outside and down to the car.

The snow was falling harder and it had accumulated on the top of the car. They looked at each other and got in. The car sped off into the early night as the snow swirled from the roof and down behind them.

THE ISLAND OF MAN

"Sir, we are coming in for landing." the pilot said, "Would you take your seat, Sir?"

The small strip of land came into view as they descended down through the clouds and the rain beat itself on the windows of the aircraft. The field was lit with small lights that were put in place by the

Air Force's First Response Team. They were responsible for getting the planes in and out as soon as possible.

The planes' landing gears were lowered as lights came on from the wingtips. Corkscrew trails of clouded mist, "slinky-ed" behind each plane as they landed. They roared and then turn to line up as they came in. As the C-130s came to a stop, the ramps were let down and those that were to join up with the Air Assault Team were marched off.

The Commander of the Royal Air Assault Team was standing by the aircraft that would be taking the General and his troops to the fight.

"Sir, I am Commander Billings, and you will be with me. My ground support team is responsible for plotting the fight from the air."

The General said, "Good to meet you, and thanks for the support. We are going to make a great difference. I'll be back in a minute." and the General walked over to speak to his troops.

His men then filed to the helicopters as the blades began to rotate and the aircraft came to life.

The General said, "You boys keep a good head on about all of this, I will be right there with you on this!"

He gave a thumbs up to all that sat on the helicopter, and moved over to talk to the others waiting to get underway.

Far off to the left of the airfield stood the four V-22 Ospreys, ready to take the Navy Seals to their drop points in the English Channel. The Commander was giving his men their last talking to, and they all knew what the Commander expected from each of his men.

"Remember, no one left standing!" and he stood back as the ramp closed up and the planes began to move in to position on the runway.

He then walked over to the Squid teams. The rain was being blown onto his face by the blades.

"You need to get close to each other on this. You must find those units. I don't care how you get it done but I want all of this to be over fast. Don't let them do to you what they want to do. Understand?"

They all said, "Yes, Sir!"

He shook his head and said, "Good luck!" The Commander walked back to stand by the General and the word was given for the V-22s to be underway.

The first of the Ospreys went screaming down the rain-filled strip and up and off into the dark of the rainy skies. The second was right behind. The Commander could see a face looking out one of the small windows with a thumbs up, and what was made out to be a smile.

The C-130s were in waiting for the thirty minute delay the V-22s needed to dump their loads and for the Seals to get into position. Those that had to relieve themselves were lining the airfield, side by side. Some were horsing around and pissing on their friend's leg, saying, "the wind!" or, "It wasn't me!"

The General laughed as he watched them push each other down and were playful. One man was still holding on to his penis as he fell backwards and he shot his stream up into the air.

The men were full of life. Most of them were young, with a wife and maybe a child or two. They grew up with play stations that for some helped them sharpen their shooting skills. But the General's smiles turned to a blind stare as he visualized the faces of those who names were going to pass his eyes tomorrow, with KIA, or MIA attached to them. It was something that he always tried to keep out of his mind, but he could not run from the worries of war.

There will be the mothers and fathers that always call to find out if the number that CNN reported had the name of their son on one of them. Or see them come to Washington to talk to him, to find some final feeling that their son may have said about his father, because of the fight they just had the week before. But there were no words that helped, and the father or mother would fall to the floor saying how sorry he or she was

"Son, I love you so much!" they would inevitably cry.

The General pondered the question: "How many nights will I spend walking around the monuments that covered the grounds of Washington in honor of the fallen?"

He remembered tracing the names of his friends at the wall of the Viet Nam Memorial, over and over again. Thinking of the last words that they had said before they had died.

He turned to wipe the tears from his eyes and the rain from his face. He knew that he did not have the power to stop what was about to happen, nor did even God have the means to cause what man has created to show his might here on earth to be placed in a box or be thrown to the wind.

The Air Assault teams were ready, and with a salute they pulled up and off into the night.

The C-130's engines roared and then raced down to the sea and up toward the stars that lay above the rain filled skies.

The General and the Commander entered their helicopter, and it too pulled up and was off to the fight that was surely to be in full force in a matter of just a few hours, and many would never know the real outcome at its end.

THE DINNER ENGAGEMENT

The Commandant and the Major arrived at the residence of the Prime Minister, and entered the beautiful estate. The double winding staircase that filled the entire foyer was beautiful in its own right. And the massive chandelier sparkled and illuminated the room with sharp specks of light from its hand cut crystals.

The men turned and took one last look outside. They stood for a moment looking off in the distance wondering. Could this be. The rain was beginning to mix with the snow. They both knew that if you didn't like the weather wait 5 minutes. Then turn again and entered the massive home.

The butler took their coats and they were lead to the smoking room, where the Prime Minister was waiting for them. The President and some of the members of Parliament were reviewing many of the articles from Nicholas II.

"Gladimir!" the Prime Minister called as he entered the room. "So glad you could bear the weather and make it this evening."

"Yes, the snow is really coming down outside, and it looks as if we may get a bit more of it."

The Major gave his greetings and asked the Commandant if he would like some tea to get them started.

"Yes, Major, that will be fine. Are the 'Guests of Honor' not here yet?" he asked with sarcasm.

"No, Sir, maybe the snow/rain/snow/rain was more than they could handle, you know how the Americans drive, they are probably in a ditch somewhere."

Just then the butler called, "The Ambassadors to the US and England are here!"

The Prime Minister moved over to the entrance of the room to welcome them.

"David, Richard, it is an honor to have you here at my home this evening." He took both of their hands and then led them into the room.

"You both know the Commandant?"

"Why, yes, how are you doing this evening? The weather is beautiful this time of year. I love the Christmas season and the up and coming new year, it reminds me of home." said the Ambassador to the US.

"And where is that?" the Commandant asked. "Minnesota. Leech Lake, to be more precise."

"Yes, I have fished there for walleye. Best tasting fresh water fish I have ever eaten."

"Is that right?"

"I have a very good friend that lives in a very small town called Boy River. Years ago, and I do mean years ago, I was up there visiting and a friend of mine who had just shot this 365-pound Black Bear, and they prepared in on the grill. Wonderful, I might add."

"So, have you ever visited any of the other States?" "Oh, God, yes, I have seen a lot that America has to offer, but unfortunately it is over there and I could not bring it with me. But I still have time."

He looked at the US Ambassador and gave him a smile, then took a sip of his tea.

"Gentlemen," the butler announced. "Dinner is served."

They all slowly headed to the dining room and what would seem an endless evening of talks on the topic of Force Reduction.

THE NAVY SEALS

The V-22s weaved in and out of the clouds as some lights from houses down below could be seen shining and undisturbed. The aircraft then made a hard bank to the right as it dove and headed out to open waters. It swung out past the coast and the lights of Plymouth. The black waters raced just feet below the Ospreys as they headed toward the water just outside their drop zones.

The Seal Teams checked and rechecked their equipment and ammo that they were going to need for this action. They all sat just all in a daze, exploring the attitude of what was going to be needed, and how it was going to get done.

AWAC's picked them up on the screen and logged in with them.

"This is Busy-Body, how you all doing down there, boys?"

"We are doing just fine, Busy-Body. This is Surf-Leader, and Wanna-Be. We're in a little bit of foul weather at this time, but are staying on course."

"You both are looking good with your approach. Keep to your heading, I see you entering your DZ in 12 mikes."

"That's a roger, Busy-Body, we read you loud and clear."

The AWAC's closed out for a moment while it picked up the C-130s and the helicopters as they made their approach from the northwest.

Busy-Body had the C-130s begin their climb to 48,000 feet as it approached the target drop zone.

"You all hold on course, then turn right to heading 439'er and meet up with a Long-and-Tall to get rejuiced."

They confirmed and started to level offat 48,000 ft. area.

"All right, men, we have been given word that it is a 'go' for drop. We have just twenty minutes before we are on the floor and out the door. I need you all to recheck each other and do not load weapons until you are in sight of your objective. Now let's start the count down and be ready in the head!"

The LTC had his men ready for the drop into DZ Bishop, all checked and ready.

"The weather down there is a pisser!" he said. "And you may feel like a ton when you hit the ground. Bend your knees! Unass your shit and head for cover in the outlying building as seen from the aerial maps that we went over. We are going to crush the enemy north as we meet up with the Air Assault Teams. Those that are behind us will be pushed towards us as forces of the Navy's Seal Team come ashore. Hammer and anvil, we will reshape their asses, but fast!"

They went through the drill as the other officers on the remaining C-130's heading to DZ Pawn did the same.

The HALO jumps were most effective because their high altitude made all the noise from the plane's engines under normal circumstances, minimal. The planes would drop the load at a very high altitude and just turn out to sea and out of the way.

WASHINGTON

The President and his advisers were hooked on the large screen and following the communications of the AWAC's with the rest of the planes. The Joint Chiefs had their people on line to pass the word to bases throughout the world and those over in Europe to stand fast, and do not make any movement while this action was underway.

"We are going to blow the pants right off this guy, and we will have him in the front lean and rest, massaging his prostate for a change!" the Army chief said. "This is just what the doctor ordered."

The President just looked over at him with a blank stare.

"You never took classes on the English language, did you, General?" the President asked.

"No, Sir, but I am willing to try anything once."

"The mission is just a short time from hitting the mark; there is no turning back, men." the Chairman said. "We are committed to the battle."

They all looked at each other, and the White House Chaplain opened a prayer for the safety and well-being of our troops.

"We need you, our Father, our only Savior, te watch over these men this great moment. We ask that you keep the shield of love strong and true. We are your children and you are the one and only true God. May your eyes pass over your children and keep them safe. In the name of your most blessed son, Jesus Christ, amen."

Many kept their heads down longer, adding a word or two of their own. The room was quiet and everyone was concerned about the men heading into harm's way.

SOMEWHERE OVER THE ENGLISH CHANNEL

The wail of the plane's engines and the shaking of the frame signaled that their V-22 was slowing down, positioning herself to hover and settle just above the water. The water seemed to be separating like Moses and the Red Sea as the tremendous wind blew down from its blades. The ramp opened and it was just hitting the water as the men took off out the back.

The long and sleek Fast Attack inflatable crafts were thrown into the water as they started to inflate. The Seal Team 1 jumped into the black waters and hurtled the sides of the crafts. The engines were attached and were started. Everyone grabbed the ropes on the sides, and they were on their way. The lights from the Island of Wight shined in the distance but were faded and obscured by the mist and rain that seemed to be falling like a thousand buckets at a time. It seemed that the rain was getting them wetter than the waters of the English Channel.

The V-22s slowly pulled up and the ramps were closed. The rotary bladed wings were tilted forward and it moved out and back from where it came from.

The second Seal Team DID was dropped off from their aircraft and they too were heading inland to their holding spot just outside DZ Bishop. There they were to wait in the cold waters until it was time to strike. They trained for months on end to withstand the cold water. Submerged with nothing more than some scuba gear, they conditioned their bodies for water colder than that of the English Channel. Now with that training behind them, they waited for the fire works to signal the Team to hit and hit fast.

The C-130s were flying high and on target. A yellow light signaled the preparation for the jump was to commence. They all stood up and turned towards the back of the plane as the ramp was lowered and locked into position. The stars could be seen shining in the distance on the horizon. The clouds below were thick and covered the entire earth, it seemed, from where they stood.

AWAC's called to them as they came into the DZ. "You are two minutes out and are looking good. Your vector is clear and no returns by radar are visible. Good luck to you all!" they said, as they picked up the signal from the JSTARS and the F-111 coming into view.

The screen had the helicopters on course and some 15 mikes out from target acquisition. The V-22s were observed as they had all ready dropped their load and were heading out of the attack flight pattern. They were called to keep turning right and keep low altitude until the area past Plymouth, then to climb to 38,000 feet and to heading 223 to meet up with the Long-and-Tall one for a drink.

The JSTARS was flying the southern coast and already had one target area in view, and moving into the outer area of Brighton.

"We have a fix on the playing field, and are ready for target knock down."

"That is affirm, we need to match you up with Zombie, Wolf-Pac, they are going to bring in the music. You have to let them know when you need them to start playing."

"We copy that, Busy-Body. Welcome aboard, Zombie. How do you have him coming in here, Busy-Body?"

"Zombie will be flying into your vector from the south, cutting his way east north east through the Channel at a very low altitude and subsonic speed. It should be able to cover the range for the first few minutes of the fight. Then he will turn right and restart the run to the west. That should be more than enough time for the communications to be out of business. Anyone on the receiving end of their transmission will blame it on the bad weather."

"A roger, roger, Busy-Body, you can have him up and singing in three mikes. Over."

"Affirm, Zombie, can you drop your ceiling down to 300 feet and be prepared to start the music?" "Roger, there, Busy-body. I'll be right down."

The F-111 Wild Weasel fired his after burners and dove down to the 300 foot altitude that was requested in just a mater of seconds. He kicked back on the flames and slowed to 650 mph and subsonic speed, ready for the radar and communications jamming to commence.

JSTARS could see his approach and signaled for Zombie to be ready to start the music.

THE TRUE GUEST OF HONOR

The doorbell rang just as the men were about ready to start on the main course. The butler was there to open the door and in walked in the "Man of the Hour".

Sergi and his men each gave up their coats and walked into the dining room. Everyone turned as the Commandant called for the men to come in.

"Sergi, my God, I thought that you were lost, or did you forget about this evening?"

"No, Sir, I was just sleeping in a bit. I forgot what it felt like to be able to just sleep without having the one eye opened, just in case."

The Commandant took Sergi and his men by the arm and led them to the chairs at the end of the table. They were seated and the

Commandant returned to his chair, and grabbed his water glass and fork and rang the side of the glass.

Ding, ding, ding!

"I would like to make a toast!"

Everyone grabbed their drinks in their hands.

"We are blessed this evening to have with us four great Russian heroes that have just returned from their perils in the country of France!"

Sergi and his men tried to bring smiles to their faces, but for them it wasn't truly a happy moment.

"These brave men risked their own lives to set the example for all others to follow. I will not get into the inner workings of their mission, but I am so proud of these men!" He took his glass and tilted it towards Sergi and his men.

"And after dinner we will recognize these men for their bravery and selflessness on the battlefield by receiving the Russian Government's highest award."

The whole table applauded but the smiles were not there for Sergi and his men. They just shook their heads and said thank you as they placed the glass of wine to their lips.

THEY CAME FROM ABOVE

The green light started to flash, and the Jump Master yelled, "GO, GO, GO!!"

Like a football team rushing onto the field, they piled out the back of the C-130s. Down into the clouds they fell. The whistling sound that rang through their helmets made them forget about the numbing cold of the wind.

The Crew Chief watched them fall away from the planes. Their silhouettes were picturesque against the clouds below. Like little beads falling from the vast sky, they danced around on the current of air. Slowly, they started to fall into the clouds and out of sight.

The C-130s then banked hard left and headed north to Scotland. The jumpers had all disappeared into the clouds as the ramps were closed and the Crew Chief moved back up to the front of the plane.

AWAC's had them moving out of the target area. The C-130s had cleared the attack lanes and only the Helicopters were then visible, moving in on the targets.

The troops fell through the clouds and seemed to pick up a thin film of ice all over their jumpsuits. The numbing cold was being felt even more now as they entered the rain and were pelted by the high speed rain drops that seemed to be coming up from below as they passed through the downpour.

The lights on their altimeters were showing the time until they needed to deploy the 'chutes, and their silent fall would be slowed down so the rain that stung like a thousand little bee's would be falling downward again.

"Sir, AWAC's have confirmed that the Air Borne have dropped their sticks to the wind. And they are on target. We look at this all kicking off in about 10 mikes."

The President got up from his chair and walked up to the screen. He placed his finger on the two areas that will, in just a few moments, become hell right here on earth. He put his hand to his chin, and stepped back and just looked at the sites.

"Everyone has been informed about the action. Higher command have been told not to alert their men unless some kind of action against them is imminent."

"Sir, it is show time." the Army Joint Chief said. "Very well." the President acknowledged. "May God help us with this one!"

THE PLEASANTRIES

For dinner they had a very large side of pork, with sweet potatoes and carrots. Cheeses and fruit dishes were abundant. The smell of hot coffee filled the air. Rice pudding was for dessert, and they all sat there as the talks of troops were hot and heavy.

"We will not go further with the plans to hold onto all of Europe. We don't need to. You can see that we have made no advances into other parts of their countries. That is because we don't have a need to!" the Commandant expressed.

"Then why are you still in England? We will never join the UEN and take part in your creation. We hold ourselves to be a free and independent country. We will never follow the rule of Russia, as much as we follow the rule of the US!" the Ambassador to England announced.

"Oh, yes, the US, and the money belt. Are you prepared to finance the likes of England if she could not take care of herself?"

Dave stood up, "We will help anyone that is in need of our help, be it for a week or a life time. This just isn't a poll to find out what America is willing to do or not do. These are issues of Free and Sovereign countries being held against their will for your own good."

The Commandant looked over at Dave.

"One's own good.' It is funny to hear that coming from a land in which everything is for its own good. Your national interest here, national interest there. Your influence has touched every corner of this big planet. Like you, we have nowhere else to go. But you are worried about things that you are powerless to do anything about."

"This is what I will do for you, Mr. Ambassador of England, and for you to Mr. Ambassador of the US. It is the season of giving, and one's heart can only be filled with the thoughts of giving."

ASSAULT FROM ABOVE

"All right, we have the tower and all communications locked and are ready to fire."

"That is affirm, Red Dog, hold your pattern. We show no movements as of yet on the ground. Troops should be coming into view momentarily."

'Hey, there, Busy-Body, we have Red Dog ready and standing by. Get Zombie to play a love tune so everyone can get up and dance."

"Roger that, Wolf Pac, here we go."

"Zombie, you may play your music. Make it clear as a bell so that other stations don't cut into the broad-cast."

"That is a roger, Busy-Body. Here you go, this one's for you."

The F-111 started its run through the Channel and put everything he had into the air.

"That should make those little bastards confused as hell."

The 'chutes opened up as the troops were just making out the land mass below. They could see the perimeter of the airfield and began to get ready for a heavy hit. The rain had them weighing at least 20-50 pounds more.

The LTC's 'chute opened as he began to search the area for ground troops. Just then, several yells were heard as troops fought to get out of their tangled, wet 'chutes, falling helplessly to earth.

They watched in horror as some of them couldn't make it and careened into the runway in a mass of body parts. Others heard screams as men too heavy hit hard and bones shot through their pants; legs were smashed as they hit almost full force.

"This is Red Dog, we have target acquisition and are firing. Missiles away, missiles away!"

It seemed like the Fourth of July.

"Shit, this is Wolf Pac! Hold your fire, hold your fire!"

The whole world was on fire by then. The troops were down and heading for cover as a machine gun opened up, sawing them down like grass. More were down and firing into the bunkers that had been placed at the entrance of the taxiway.

The helicopters were coming in and firing their rockets as they laid on the 40 mike-mike.

"The Russians were caught this time with their pants down!" the LTC said as he gathered his men and over ran three positions near the hanger.

The Russian BMD's and ASU-85's came racing around the back of the hanger and the ASU fired into the troops that were scattering from its view.

Boom!

The round ripped through the side of the hanger just as some made their way there for cover. The blast from the SD-44, 85mm gun was devastating, causing the whole side of the hanger to fall in a mass of fire and steel.

A Radian Attack helicopter fired its 40mm cannon at the ASU and it was turned into a melted lump within seconds. The fight was everywhere. The sky was filled with tracer rounds and the sound was deafening. The 501" SF grouped and started to push up to the main concentration of Russian troops. The resistance was heavy and the first wave was knocked down when rockets from the BMP slammed into the center of the forces that had begun to make a swing run over to the right of the tower.

The Royal Air Assault helicopters were searching and knocking out the BMP's as soon as they found them.

"This is Wolf Pac, you have several tracked vehicles still in the outer perimeters."

"We see them in a stationary position. Red Dog three, move around to the rear but not to close. Red Dog five, cut right across them and burn their asses!"

The helicopter opened up as it came right over the top and then the one from the rear fed fuel to the fire.

The General and the Commander wanted someone to call the police and the damn fire department to get into the fight.

"We damn opened the road! Get your asses in there with some fire power people!" he screamed over the microphone as they passed over head of the emergency vehicles. "Get your asses into the fight! Let's kick those piece's of shit Russians out of here!"

WASHINGTON

"Sir, it has started!"

The whole War Room stood up, and looked over to the screen. The Chairman of the Joint Chiefs walked over to the screen as map images were shown of the airfield in Portsmouth and the compound in Brighton.

"As you can see here from these images that are coming in from our JSTARS, the fight is in progress. These are not images that you are used to seeing, but I will point out to you the areas of interest so you can see what they see and how it is interpreted."

The lines you see here would be the perimeter of the airfield. They have hit targets here, here, here, and here. Those were to be Russian BMP's. They are more or less troop carriers that are very effective in their movement and have good armament. Here is the hanger, it looks to be destroyed."

"Reports are coming in from both targets that we have suffered heavy casualties, along with the Russians. The weather is very rainy/snowy mix, and that caused some troops to be weighed down. Some 'chutes were saturated and they fell from the sky like rocks from heaven."

The President sat there in silence as the Chairman went on with the reports.

"As we speak, our wounded are being flown out to hospitals throughout the greater London area. We should be having problems soon in keeping the word from spreading to this country."

Then the discussion went back to Russia.

MOSCOW

"Shall we all go to the smoking room to continue our discussion on giving?"

The Commandant stood up and they all started in to the other room.

"Please be seated, we will soon be decorating our men here as soon as we get on with the business of 'détente'. That was a word widely used by the US in explaining small talks to a country that was having troubles in its own government."

The Commandant explained why the US was picking away at what they thought was the cold war. As he was talking to both of the Ambassador's they were looking at their watches and knowing what actions have been well under way, yet it seems that word of it has yet to be received here. They just sat back as he went on with his diatribe.

THE ENSUING ATTACK

"Get your asses moving front!" the LTC was screaming to the troops that seem to be bogged down across the parkway.

"Here, you need to get the fire going into that position so those guys can move forward!"

The Seals had made their way to the edge of the fence and just lay there as they looked for positions near them that needed to be neutralized. All along the outer perimeter north you can see the fighting going on. There were fires everywhere with Russian tracks stopped and on fire. The flames made for an eerie scene, with bodies laying all over the place.

"Shit, they must have been catching hell inside!" "That is where we need to be and push what elements that are here in the rear, forward to the fight over there!"

They cut through the fence and began to push what troops that were guarding the flank, out. The helicopters were making quite the difference to the fight. They had positions locked up on and blazing. Many were landing and the troops were getting into the fight as more troops ran to the heaviest concentration of Russians in the terminal.

Glass was flying everywhere when one of the Radian flew side ways, firing its 40mm cannons into the terminal, and the building was consumed in one massive explosion.

Outside the complex in Brighton, the Squid team crept quietly towards its objective. They had located one of the Russian Nuclear Warfare units that had been in place on the outskirts of Brighton in an old farming area.

The Squids sat there for the better part of 30 minutes, and could see the fires in the distance.

The Russians were aware that attempts on the bases were going on. They had their positions guarded with soldiers on the perimeter and fields of fire laid out. They did not know that the Squids were there, watching them.

"We still need to find the device and learn its capability. Things need to move along. We don't know if they have orders to use it or not!"

They all agreed that a move had to happen soon.

First they had to encircle the area; find out how many are guarding the device. Do they have radios and who would be most likely to be the button pusher? They split up, one at a time moving around the outside of the Russian position, as slow as a snail on the wet grass. The falling rain covered much of the sound that you would normally encounter. The breaking of dry twigs and crunching of dead grass was no longer a factor. The team was worried that the Russians would be given a call, or be in position to move it closer to population.

The fighting inside the airfield was furious, and the dead and dying were everywhere on both sides. The Seal Teams were working their way through that complex and had the Russians pulling back. A mighty push was put down when the Russians tried to flank the Seals, but they were ambushed by the SF hit team.

The police were having small fire-fights as they moved in to reclaim part of the runway. The General's helicopter cruised overhead, directing the fight.

The AWAC's was getting word to Zombie about the fight and it was being picked up by Wolf Pac.

"Zombie, you need to make your run closer towards the west and not too far east. Wolf-Pac said that he is pretty clear that all communications are out from the Russians. We don't need you being seen from off-shore patrols and relayed to their commands."

"That is a Roger, you have me in your arms, there, big guy."

The F-111 burnt a little flame as he turned sharply back closer to the fight with his music still being played.

To No Surprise

The President was watching the screen when… "The fighting is going on as we speak. You can see here…"

What in the hell is that?

Sir, I believe it is CNBC on location outside the airport in Portsmouth.

Mother-fucking, son of a bitch! Here we go!" the Army Chief said.

Moscow

"I would like to get on the US's ass more, but this is a great night with friends and heroes that need to be up here right now. Come on, Sergi, I will make this as informal as I can."

The Commandant stood proudly, with the Major holding the boxes that contained the medals for his men of honor.

Sergi and his men walked up to the front of the room and came to attention. The Commandant placed the Merit of Valor around each of the men's necks, and kissed them on both sides of their cheeks. The room of men applauded as they returned to their seats and their drinks.

Gladimir stood there with his glass of water and tried to settle the room down as he went on about the reason for talks this evening.

"As you know, Christmas is season that many countries observe. This is a time that we can set aside for the renewal of trade and better relations between the countries of the newly formed UEN."

He walked around to get a better view of the Ambassador, and he said, "Let us start here, this day to heal the bad taste of occupation. I pledge right now that Russia will have her troops removed from the country of England, starting tomorrow."

The English Ambassador dropped his glass of wine as he stood up and looked over at his US counterpart. "But, this cannot be!"

"What cannot be?" the Commandant asked.

Just then, one of his orderlies came running in and said, "Sir!"

The Commandant turned around.

"You have an important phone call."

The Major and the Commandant looked at each other as they both left the room.

The Ambassadors sat quietly on the sofa. Sergi looked over at the two, then his eyes opened wide when he heard the Commandant yell in the other room.

"WHAT HAVE YOU DONE? WHAT IN THE NAME OF GOD HAVE YOU ALL DONE?!!"

He came running back into the room screaming those words, over and over again.

He stopped in front of the two men.

"DO YOU KNOW WHAT YOU HAVE DONE?"

He turned to the President and the Prime Minister and they went to the study. The Major was looking at the Ambassadors when he was called into the office. Everyone just sat there with looks of fear and bewilderment.

The Major came out and asked the Ambassadors to join the Commandant in the office, and then he asked all but Sergi and his men to please go home.

They walked into the office as the three men were all on phones and trying to find out what was happening. The Commandant slammed his phone down and walked up to the Ambassadors.

"Is it true?"

They just looked at him.

"WELL, IS IT TRUE? ARE YOU ATTACKING MY TROOPS IN ENGLAND AT THIS MOMENT?"

He had gone nuts, and was kicking and throwing things off the desk. He came back to the men and said, "Is… it… true? Because I had to hear it from those who watch CNBC. Now tell me what I want or so help me…"

The English Ambassador pulled down on his jacket and said, "Yes, we are kicking your ass out of my country."

The Commandant came across the jaw of the Ambassador, sending him flying into the wall.

"Gladimir!" Dave jumped in front, "You can't do this! You already know that there is an action against your troops in England."

"Yes, go on."

He just sat on the edge of the table with his hands in a tight fist.

"Well, troops from the US and England were assembled last week to repel your troops from the English mainland by force."

Gladimir just stood there. "Do you know what you have done? These are not just troops that fight a nation's war, but are made to fight 'The War'. You will have to kill all of them to get them to go."

He put his head down and shook it side to side. "Though you come here to eat my dinner, and you knew this all along as the pleasantries were said all around, you still don't know what you have done."

He walked to the phone, and started to get things underway.

"I am sorry for my display, but I have other things to do right now, so if you will excuse me. We need to get over to the Hall of the People, and we need to get this action stopped before all is lost."

He had everyone's coats handed out and then he told them to follow him over to the Hall of the People.

THE UNVEILING

"I see him, Sir, he is right there just left of the third tree!"

The LT looked through the night vision goggles and could almost make out the device.

"It is about 53 meters from this position, and has two positions that are guarding it to the front. We have to come up with a diversion to the left and rear to have any kind of move on the device."

The fighting was still raging on the complex some 19 kilometers from the point of the Russian Nuclear Unit. They radioed in to the Commander on the helicopter, along with the General.

"They have found one of the devices along with the unit. They're getting in position to spring and disable the unit's ability to move or detonate."

"How about the second unit? Have your men found that yet?"

"No, they are still checking location suitable for that team."

"Well, we need to get this fighting contained and dropped."

The helicopter made its rounds as word was passed to AWAC's, and then back to Washington.

WASHINGTON

"Sir!" an aid came walking in with an updated report of the fighting.

The Chairman walked back up to the board.

"You can see that things," he pointed to the screen, "have not changed very much. Other than the fact that we have a very large area reclaimed, the fighting is just as hard as it ever was. We have had, at this moment, 47 of our troops KIA. 17 others were killed when their 'chutes became so saturated with the rain that they fell to their deaths."

Everyone just talked back and forth to each other.

"You know that the world knows about the fighting and we have scheduled a press conference for later this evening to set the press straight. We don't know how much longer it is going to take for us to stand down from all of this. No actions have been made against our troops stationed over in the occupied areas. But we do know that they know what is going on. They have the same reliable CNBC as we do to get them the story first."

"No information can be sent out of that area because their capabilities are down. No air movement has been dispatched to rescue the Russians. It seems that they got a taste of their own medicine."

The President looked up as the secure phone rang. He looked at everyone as he got up and answered it. The Russian President sounded a bit edgy, and was very rushed.

"We need to have all of this ended right now. You all have placed yourselves way out on a limb."

"This is something that had to be done. The US has…"

"Don't give me this US bull-shit! You made no efforts to talk to us, and that is the fault of your government. But this is not the time to place the blame on anyone. You must call off this action right now!!"

BRIGHTON

"We need to get this fight contained, Sir! They are really giving it all that they have. We are trying to find out if there are some kind of under ground inlets to enter through."

"Captain!" the General said, "Get your ass going on this. You have the means to hit them, so hit them! I don't care if you have to call Scotty to beam you into the place, just get this damn thing over with, out."

The Captain hung up his phone and tried to get the thing rolling along like the General said. "Let's see what the Royal Air Force can do."

"Yea, that sounds like the ticket, we can come a rollin' on it, one at a time, mate. Stand by and hold onto your asses. You leave it up to me. I know just what you need."

The Commander of the Royal Air Forces called for all helicopters to make a drag and shoot at the air terminal.

"Make it quick, the boys are bogged down and they need an opening to rush the place."

They all swung out wide of the main terminal then made a mad dash damn near flying in the front door. Kawoooshh!!

BLAMMMMMMMM, BLAMMMMMMM!!!

They unleashed everything that they had. The place exploded into a massive inferno that could be seen for miles away.

The Squid team was moving in just as one of the soldiers came running up and grabbed the one guy that was sitting next to the device. The LT was watching every one of the Russian soldiers drawing back as to form a defensive fighting circle.

Just then:

ZOOOOOOOOOOOOOOOOOOOOOOOM!!

This blinding flash of light came from the airport at Portsmouth. The Squid team covered their eyes then waited for the BOOOOOOOOOM! The blast sounded with a crack and the shock wave blew the hell out of the place and had all the grass that they were laying in knocked down as a faint mushroom cloud could be seen climbing high into the distant sky.

The LT and his men along with the Russian soldiers stood up as they watched the cloud moved upward and outward. They knew that it was only a matter of time until the blast would have its effect on them. They turned to see the Russians looking over at the men that were spread out in an almost circle around them. They grabbed their guns as the LT ran towards them pulling out a white tee shirt from under his uniform and waving it at the Russians. It seemed forever as he ran shouting in Russian, "Don't do it!" his hands over his head with the white flag in clear view.

"Don't do it, don't do it!" he screamed as the heart beat inside his chest almost exploded out. He just kept running towards the soldiers.

THE GREAT HALL

The Commandant's car stopped outside the Hall of the People, and he ran up the stairs to the large screen. People were standing in shock as they looked at the map of England. Gladimir moved closer and closer as he stared at this massive color of red flashing in the area of Portsmouth. His aids were all screaming to him at once as he got closer to the screen. Things were jumbled as he tried to think, and he turned around and everyone was confused and calling on the phone.

He turned back to the screen and was watching the area flash off and on, this large patch of red. His voice seemed to come out slow and words were garbled.

"W H A T I S H A P P E N I N G H E R E!" came out as one long scream.

He looked once more at the screen, and his eyes opened up wide. ZOOOOOOOOOOOOOOOOOOOOOOOM!!

Another flash of red lit up on the screen. He just stood there looking at these two red lights flashing off and on. He shook his head and gave out a yell.

"NOOOOoooooooooooooooooooooo!!!"

It carried through the hall and out into the air of Red Square. Everything was gone; Portsmouth, Brighton, both were wiped off the face of the earth. He just dropped to his knees and stared up at the screen. All he could think of was that his men were now gone, and somehow it was all for nothing.

THE WAR ROOM

"As you can tell by the pictures being sent in by the JSTARS on the battle field…"

The screen went blank and everyone asked, "What happened?"

The phones were ringing all at once as the aids answered.

Alarms went off throughout the War Room as A-Team came rushing in to secure the President.

"Sir, they detonated a bomb!"

Everyone stood there for an instance as the A-Team surrounded the President.

"We have Air Force One ready for you, Sir."

Just then a view came on the screen from the AWAC's aircraft with audio.

"This is NM23D1 we confirm a detonation near Portsmouth at 16:40 EST. Please stand by."

Just then a call from The US Space Command was broadcast in the War Room.

"This is US Space Command. At 1640 and 1642, we show indications of at least two Nuclear Detonations on location of the southern mainland of the country of England. There were no launch vehicles."

The message was repeated over and over again, and the President just stood there looking at his men. He grabbed his chair and plopped down into it. The Chairman was on the phone as well as everyone else. The reports seemed to be pouring in from everywhere.

All the Generals were on the phones talking to their respective commanders on the positions of troops throughout Europe and to insure that they are ready for any attacks.

"Sir!" The President just looked up at the Chairman of the Joints Chiefs. "A message is being transmitted from the Russian Hall of the People. We have this coming in right now and it is on the screen ready for you."

The President stood up and walked up to the screen just as the Commandant's face appeared. He was clearly shaken and tried to stand tall and fit for the broadcast.

The Commandant opened up with, "So I can see that we are brought together by one common disaster. Do you see what you have done?"

"What we have done?!!" the President yelled back. "You bastard, you have killed many people with this reckless action against the continent of Europe! You will not get away with this, I can assure you."

The President went on. Just then, the Commandant interrupted:

"You cowards of the free world. You stand in judgement of me? I stand in contempt of you. Do you see the clear and winding road that we both stand on at this moment? You haven't the foggiest idea what is going on here. Nor are you in any position to dictate to me on the matter."

The Commandant came closer to the screen.

"You, as always, couldn't keep your nose out of things that have nothing to do with you. You, the United States of America. The self-proclaimed world's police. The judge of what is right or wrong. You and you alone are the solely responsible for this terrible tragedy. The world will see that clearly now." He wiped his face and went on.

"Russians have gone through things that would have meant the end for many countries on this earth. But we prevailed and became stronger for it. You all have spent a lifetime fighting over the strategies of what was 'Russia's paranoid delusions'. Thinking that we were on the brink of the unprovoked nervous breakdown from being continually surrounded by hostile countries. Always first to tell the world about the strategies and thinking of the Russian Government. You, the so-called keeper of the free world's history, the history the way you write it. You could no more write it as it did not involve you."

"Your years of sitting back as Europe fought her wars, and then you came in well after each side was exhausted from the fight and put and end to something that was on the brink of an end. Then you returned home to the fanfare of victory as we cleaned up the vast devastation and mourned for the fathers and brothers that would no longer be coming home."

"You sit there so high and mighty as if some divine being placed the US in dominion over the planet. Yet more people are killed on your streets and roadways there than wars that have consumed the earth."

He stared hard at the screen.

"Come on, do you have it in you, Mr. President? Do you have the stomach to get this over with, once and for all? We have been at this bull-shit game of 'who's who' for more than a half a century now.'

Take a good look at the country you call "The United States of America". United? United? How can that place even hold that title?

Just look at what you have done to the once most powerful country on earth. You took what God had given you and could not have fucked it up any worse then it is right now. United?

The President answered back, "I'm not sure what you're getting at, but you are getting off the subject of this action!

Commandant Klakov, you have come to your end of this occupation and the world will not stand for it any longer!"

Don't know what I'm getting at. You already did to America the things that no other country could do. You have down right destroyed her. You couldn't lose a war from the outside, so you retarded no goods did it from the inside.

The rest of the world laughed as you and your party turn men into women, boys into girls. Labeled everyone who did agree with you the far this the far that. You took a nation over the years and brainwashed your children in schools. Pussafide your men. Everyone's feelings matter. Black Lives Matter? Your nation as a whole matters. You divided the states, killed you babies "BY THE MILLIONS"!!!!!!!!!!!!!!!

You killed you elderly with the release of the Covid 19, took grand parents and placed them in homes to get infected. Killed them and took their SS Checks that the dead no longer needs and gave the money to those who invaded your borders. Your "VETS" killed themselves by the thousands. You Bastards who think you are the top of the food chain. United???? I think not! So who are you and your party going to blame this on? The Russians?

"DID STUPID FUCK THE RETARD OUT OF YOU?

How dare you speak that BS to me and the free world!!!! Proclaimed the President of the US.

"You meaningless little bastard. We have endured the loss of more than 30,000,000 people in just this last world war alone. You have plotted the use and the meaning of an exchange that you called 'mutual self-destruction' for years, and have boasted that you alone were the victor's of a cold war that we alone were the adversaries. We have our country intact."

"Come on, you little piece of shit, get on the phone, call your major TV stations. Talk to CNN, MSNBC, CBS, ABC, all the news papers that back your ass up on everything. You can use the paper to wipe your dumb ass with. That is all it is good for. See if it will take the time to run a poll of US viewers to vote for an all-out Nuclear exchange for the price of Europe."

The Chairman turned to the President as he stared blankly into the screen. "Sir, don't.."

"What is the problem, Mr. President?" the Commandant needled. "Come and see the peoples' response from Washington, New York, Detroit, Chicago, LA or Dallas! Sure, we would love to die for France!""

"France and the Eiffel tower is calling your name. Germany? They are right here if you want them so badly. What, you want that armpit that is Italy? Are your people going to miss Gucci or Armanni?"

The Commandant started yelling.

"COME ON, LET'S TAKE THAT FUCKING VOTE. COME ON YOU PIECE OF SHIT. CALL FOR THAT STRIKE THAT WILL INSURE YOU THE NEXT ELECTION. YOU CAN BE RIGHT THERE IN THAT BIG CRATER, TELLING EVERYONE THAT WHILE YOU WERE FLYING HIGH IN AIR FORCE ONE, YOU COULD SEE YOUR FELLOW AMERICANS EVAPORATING RIGHT BEFORE YOUR VERY EYES. BECAUSE IF YOU ARE READY TO DO THIS FOR EUROPE, THEN PUSH THE FUCKING BUTTON, BUDDY.

COME ON, PUSH THE FUCKING BUTTON. SEE IF YOUR FELLOW AMERICANS FEEL THE SAME WAY."

The Commandant turned and ordered his troops to get the country ready for total nuclear exchange. Then he turned back to the screen, and gave the President a hard, cold stare.

The screen went blank.

The President stood there as the whole room exploded with calls to stand by for possible attack. The Chairman called for A-Team to get the President out and up into Air Force One. They grabbed the President, and he looked bewildered about the actions that were happening right before his very eyes. They carried him from the room as all looked on for the Commandant of Russian Forces' next move.